T0312430

AUTUMN CHILLS

ALSO BY AGATHA CHRISTIE

Mysteries
The Man in the Brown Suit
The Secret of Chimneys
The Seven Dials Mystery
The Mysterious Mr Quin
The Sittaford Mystery
The Hound of Death
The Listerdale Mystery
Why Didn't They Ask Evans?
Parker Pyne Investigates
Murder Is Easy
And Then There Were None
Towards Zero
Death Comes as the End
Sparkling Cyanide
Crooked House
They Came to Baghdad
Destination Unknown
Spider's Web *
The Unexpected Guest *
Ordeal by Innocence
The Pale Horse
Endless Night
Passenger To Frankfurt
Problem at Pollensa Bay
While the Light Lasts

Poirot
The Mysterious Affair at Styles
The Murder on the Links
Poirot Investigates
The Murder of Roger Ackroyd
The Big Four
The Mystery of the Blue Train
Black Coffee *
Peril at End House
Lord Edgware Dies
Murder on the Orient Express
Three Act Tragedy
Death in the Clouds
The ABC Murders
Murder in Mesopotamia
Cards on the Table
Murder in the Mews
Dumb Witness
Death on the Nile
Appointment with Death
Hercule Poirot's Christmas
Sad Cypress
One, Two, Buckle My Shoe
Evil Under the Sun
Five Little Pigs
The Hollow
The Labours of Hercules
Taken at the Flood
Mrs McGinty's Dead
After the Funeral
Hickory Dickory Dock
Dead Man's Folly
Cat Among the Pigeons
The Adventure of the Christmas Pudding
The Clocks
Third Girl
Hallowe'en Party
Elephants Can Remember
Poirot's Early Cases
Curtain: Poirot's Last Case

Marple
The Murder at the Vicarage
The Thirteen Problems
The Body in the Library
The Moving Finger
A Murder Is Announced
They Do It with Mirrors
A Pocket Full of Rye
4.50 from Paddington
The Mirror Crack'd from Side to Side
A Caribbean Mystery
At Bertram's Hotel
Nemesis
Sleeping Murder
Miss Marple's Final Cases

Tommy & Tuppence
The Secret Adversary
Partners in Crime
N or M?
By the Pricking of My Thumbs
Postern of Fate

Published as Mary Westmacott
Giant's Bread
Unfinished Portrait
Absent in the Spring
The Rose and the Yew Tree
A Daughter's a Daughter
The Burden

Memoirs
An Autobiography
Come, Tell Me How You Live
The Grand Tour

Plays and Stories
Akhnaton
The Floating Admiral (contributor)
Hercule Poirot and the Greenshore Folly
Star Over Bethlehem

* novelized by Charles Osborne

AGATHA CHRISTIE

AUTUMN CHILLS

TALES OF INTRIGUE
FROM THE QUEEN OF CRIME

HarperCollins*Publishers*

HarperCollins*Publishers*
1 London Bridge Street,
London SE1 9GF
www.harpercollins.co.uk

HarperCollins*Publishers*
Macken House,
39/40 Mayor Street Upper,
Dublin 1
D01 C9W8, Ireland

Published by HarperCollins*Publishers* 2023

6

Cover and endpaper design by
Holly Macdonald/HarperCollins*Publishers* Ltd
Illustrations: Shutterstock.com

A catalogue record for this book is
available from the British Library.

ISBN 978-0-00-847097-5

Printed and bound in the UK using 100% renewable
electricity at CPI Group (UK) Ltd

This book is produced from independently certified FSC™ paper
to ensure responsible forest management.

For more information visit: www.harpercollins.co.uk/green

CONTENTS

Introduction: Down in the Wood vii

Murder in the Mews 1
The Case of the Rich Woman 64
While the Light Lasts 81
Triangle at Rhodes 92
Death by Drowning 123
The Bird with the Broken Wing 146
The Lemesurier Inheritance 170
The House of Lurking Death 185
Tape-Measure Murder 206
The Voice in the Dark 223
Four-and-Twenty Blackbirds 244
The Witness for the Prosecution 263

Bibliography 289

INTRODUCTION

Down in the Wood

There was a girls' school in Torquay kept by someone called Miss Guyer, and my mother made an arrangement that I should go there two days a week and study certain subjects. I think one was arithmetic, and there was also grammar and composition. I enjoyed arithmetic, as always, and may even have begun algebra there. Grammar I could not understand in the least: I could not see *why* certain things were called prepositions or what verbs were supposed to *do*, and the whole thing was a foreign language to me. I used to plunge happily into composition, but not with real success. The criticism was always the same: my compositions were too fanciful. I was severely criticised for not keeping to the subject. I remember - 'Autumn' - in particular. I started off well, with golden and brown leaves, but suddenly, somehow or other, a *pig* got into it - I think it was possibly rooting up acorns in the forest. Anyway, I got interested in the pig, forgot all about autumn, and the composition ended with the riotous adventures of Curlytail the Pig and a terrific Beechnut Party he gave his friends.

I wrote quite a lot of poems from time to time. A sudden excitement would come over me and I would rush off to write down what I felt gurgling round in my mind. I had no lofty ambitions. An occasional prize in *The*

Poetry Review was all I asked. One poem of mine that I re-read lately I think is not bad; at least it has in it something of what I wanted to express. I reproduce it here for that reason:

Down in the Wood

Bare brown branches against a blue sky
(And Silence within the wood),
Leaves that, listless, lie under your feet,
Bold brown boles that are biding their time
(And Silence within the wood).
Spring has been fair in the fashion of youth,
Summer with languorous largesse of love,
Autumn with passion that passes to pain,
Leaf, flower, and flame - they have fallen and failed

And Beauty - bare Beauty is left in the wood!

Bare brown branches against a mad moon
(And Something that stirs in the wood),
Leaves that rustle and rise from the dead,
Branches that beckon and leer in the light
(And Something that walks in the wood).
Skirling and whirling, the leaves are alive!
Driven by Death in a devilish dance!
Shrieking and swaying of terrified trees!
A wind that goes sobbing and shivering by. . .

And Fear - naked Fear passes out of the wood!

Agatha Christie

AUTUMN CHILLS

Murder in the Mews

'Penny for the guy, sir?'

A small boy with a grimy face grinned ingratiatingly.

'Certainly not!' said Chief Inspector Japp. 'And, look here, my lad—'

A short homily followed. The dismayed urchin beat a precipitate retreat, remarking briefly and succinctly to his youthful friends:

'Blimey, if it ain't a cop all togged up!'

The band took to its heels, chanting the incantation:

Remember, remember
The fifth of November
Gunpowder treason and plot.
We see no reason
Why gunpowder treason
Should ever be forgot.

The chief inspector's companion, a small, elderly man with an egg-shaped head and large, military-looking moustache, was smiling to himself.

'*Très bien*, Japp,' he observed. 'You preach the sermon very well! I congratulate you!'

'Rank excuse for begging, that's what Guy Fawkes' Day is!' said Japp.

'An interesting survival,' mused Hercule Poirot. 'The fireworks go up—crack—crack—long after the man they commemorate and his deeds are forgotten.'

The Scotland Yard man agreed.

'Don't suppose many of those kids really know who Guy Fawkes was.'

'And soon, doubtless, there will be confusion of thought. Is it in honour or in execration that on the fifth of November the *feu d'artifice* are sent up? To blow up an English Parliament, was it a sin or a noble deed?'

Japp chuckled.

'Some people would say undoubtedly the latter.'

Turning off the main road, the two men passed into the comparative quiet of a mews. They had been dining together and were now taking a short cut to Hercule Poirot's flat.

As they walked along the sound of squibs was still heard periodically. An occasional shower of golden rain illuminated the sky.

'Good night for a murder,' remarked Japp with professional interest. 'Nobody would hear a shot, for instance, on a night like this.'

'It has always seemed odd to me that more criminals do not take advantage of the fact,' said Hercule Poirot.

'Do you know, Poirot, I almost wish sometimes that *you* would commit a murder.'

'*Mon cher!*'

'Yes, I'd like to see just how you'd set about it.'

'My dear Japp, *if* I committed a murder you would not have the least chance of seeing how I set about it! You would not even be aware, probably, that a murder had been committed.'

Japp laughed good-humouredly and affectionately.

'Cocky little devil, aren't you?' he said indulgently.

* * *

At half-past eleven the following morning, Hercule Poirot's telephone rang.

''Allo? 'Allo?'

'Hallo, that you, Poirot?'

'*Oui, c'est moi.*'

'Japp speaking here. Remember we came home last night through Bardsley Gardens Mews?'

'Yes?'

'And that we talked about how easy it would be to shoot a person with all those squibs and crackers and the rest of it going off?'

'Certainly.'

'Well, there was a suicide in that mews. No. 14. A young widow—Mrs Allen. I'm going round there now. Like to come?'

'Excuse me, but does someone of your eminence, my dear friend, usually get sent to a case of suicide?'

'Sharp fellow. No—he doesn't. As a matter of fact our doctor seems to think there's something funny about this. Will you come? I kind of feel you ought to be in on it.'

'Certainly I will come. No. 14, you say?'

'That's right.'

Poirot arrived at No. 14 Bardsley Gardens Mews almost at the same moment as a car drew up containing Japp and three other men.

No. 14 was clearly marked out as the centre of interest. A big circle of people, chauffeurs, their wives, errand boys, loafers, well-dressed passers-by and innumerable children were drawn up all staring at No. 14 with open mouths and a fascinated stare.

A police constable in uniform stood on the step and did his best to keep back the curious. Alert-looking young men with cameras were busy and surged forward as Japp alighted.

'Nothing for you now,' said Japp, brushing them aside. He nodded to Poirot. 'So here you are. Let's get inside.'

They passed in quickly, the door shut behind them and they found themselves squeezed together at the foot of a ladder-like flight of stairs.

A man came to the top of the staircase, recognized Japp and said:

'Up here, sir.'

Japp and Poirot mounted the stairs.

The man at the stairhead opened a door on the left and they found themselves in a small bedroom.

'Thought you'd like me to run over the chief points, sir.'

'Quite right, Jameson,' said Japp. 'What about it?'

Divisional Inspector Jameson took up the tale.

'Deceased's a Mrs Allen, sir. Lived here with a friend—a Miss Plenderleith. Miss Plenderleith was away staying in the country and returned this morning. She let herself in with her key, was surprised to find no one about. A woman usually comes in at nine o'clock to do for them. She went upstairs first into her own room (that's this room) then across the landing to her friend's room. Door was locked on the inside. She rattled the handle, knocked and called, but couldn't get any answer. In the end getting alarmed she rang up the police station. That was at ten forty-five. We came along at once and forced the door open. Mrs Allen was lying in a heap on the ground shot through the head. There was an automatic in her hand—a Webley .25—and it looked a clear case of suicide.'

'Where is Miss Plenderleith now?'

'She's downstairs in the sitting-room, sir. A very cool, efficient young lady, I should say. Got a head on her.'

'I'll talk to her presently. I'd better see Brett now.'

Accompanied by Poirot he crossed the landing and entered the opposite room. A tall, elderly man looked up and nodded.

'Hallo, Japp, glad you've got here. Funny business, this.'

Japp advanced towards him. Hercule Poirot sent a quick searching glance round the room.

It was much larger than the room they had just quitted. It had a built-out bay window, and whereas the other room had been a bedroom pure and simple, this was emphatically a bedroom disguised as a sitting-room.

The walls were silver and the ceiling emerald green. There were curtains of a modernistic pattern in silver and green. There was a divan covered with a shimmering emerald green silk quilt and numbers of gold and silver cushions. There was a tall antique walnut bureau, a walnut tallboy, and several modern chairs of gleaming chromium. On a low glass table there was a big ashtray full of cigarette stubs.

Delicately Hercule Poirot sniffed the air. Then he joined Japp where the latter stood looking down at the body.

In a heap on the floor, lying as if she had fallen from one of the chromium chairs, was the body of a young woman of perhaps twenty-seven. She had fair hair and delicate features. There was very little make-up on the face. It was a pretty, wistful, perhaps slightly stupid face. On the left side of the head was a mass of congealed blood. The fingers of the right hand were clasped round a small pistol. The woman was dressed in a simple frock of dark green high to the neck.

'Well, Brett, what's the trouble?'

Japp was looking down also at the huddled figure.

'Position's all right,' said the doctor. 'If she shot herself she'd probably have slipped from the chair into just that position. The door was locked and the window was fastened on the inside.'

'That's all right, you say. Then what's wrong?'

'Take a look at the pistol. I haven't handled it—waiting for the fingerprint men. But you can see quite well what I mean.'

Together Poirot and Japp knelt down and examined the pistol closely.

'I see what you mean,' said Japp rising. 'It's in the curve of her hand. It *looks* as though she's holding it—but as a matter of fact she *isn't* holding it. Anything else?'

'Plenty. She's got the pistol in her *right* hand. Now take a look at the wound. The pistol was held close to the head just above the left ear—the *left* ear, mark you.'

'H'm,' said Japp. 'That does seem to settle it. She couldn't hold a pistol and fire it in that position with her right hand?'

'Plumb impossible, I should say. You might get your arm round but I doubt if you could fire the shot.'

'That seems pretty obvious then. Someone else shot her and tried to make it look like suicide. What about the locked door and window, though?'

Inspector Jameson answered this.

'Window was closed and bolted, sir, but although the door was locked *we haven't been able to find the key*.'

Japp nodded.

'Yes, that was a bad break. Whoever did it locked the door when he left and hoped the absence of the key wouldn't be noticed.'

Poirot murmured:

'C'est bête, ça!'

'Oh, come now, Poirot, old man, you mustn't judge everybody else by the light of your shining intellect! As a matter of fact that's the sort of little detail that's quite apt to be overlooked. Door's locked. People break in. Woman found dead—pistol in her hand—clear case of suicide—she locked herself in to do it. They don't go hunting about for keys. As a matter of fact, Miss Plenderleith's sending for the police was lucky. She might have got one or two of the chauffeurs to come and burst in the door—and then the key question would have been overlooked altogether.'

'Yes, I suppose that is true,' said Hercule Poirot. 'It would have been many people's natural reaction. The police, they are the last resource, are they not?'

He was still staring down at the body.

'Anything strike you?' Japp asked.

The question was careless but his eyes were keen and attentive.

Hercule Poirot shook his head slowly.

'I was looking at her wrist-watch.'

He bent over and just touched it with a finger-tip. It was a dainty jewelled affair on a black moiré strap on the wrist of the hand that held the pistol.

'Rather a swell piece that,' observed Japp. 'Must have cost money!' He cocked his head inquiringly at Poirot. 'Something in that maybe?'

'It is possible—yes.'

Poirot strayed across to the writing-bureau. It was the kind that has a front flap that lets down. This was daintily set out to match the general colour scheme.

There was a somewhat massive silver inkstand in the centre, in front of it a handsome green lacquer blotter. To the left of the blotter was an emerald glass pen-tray containing a silver penholder—a stick of green sealing-wax, a pencil and two stamps. On the right of the blotter was a movable calendar giving the day of the week, date and month. There was also a little glass jar of shot and standing in it a flamboyant green quill pen. Poirot seemed interested in the pen. He took it out and looked at it but the quill was innocent of ink. It was clearly a decoration—nothing more. The silver pen-holder with the ink-stained nib was the one in use. His eyes strayed to the calendar.

'Tuesday, November fifth,' said Japp. 'Yesterday. That's all correct.'

He turned to Brett.

'How long has she been dead?'

'She was killed at eleven thirty-three yesterday evening,' said Brett promptly.

Then he grinned as he saw Japp's surprised face.

'Sorry, old boy,' he said. 'Had to do the super doctor of fiction! As a matter of fact eleven is about as near as I can put it—with a margin of about an hour either way.'

'Oh, I thought the wrist-watch might have stopped—or something.'

'It's stopped all right, but it's stopped at a quarter past four.'

'And I suppose she couldn't have been killed possibly at a quarter past four.'

'You can put that right out of your mind.'

Poirot had turned back the cover of the blotter.

'Good idea,' said Japp. 'But no luck.'

The blotter showed an innocent white sheet of blotting-paper. Poirot turned over the leaves but they were all the same.

He turned his attention to the waste-paper basket.

It contained two or three torn-up letters and circulars. They were only torn once and were easily reconstructed. An appeal for money from some society for assisting ex-service men, an invitation to a cocktail party on November 3rd, an appointment with a dressmaker. The circulars were an announcement of a furrier's sale and a catalogue from a department store.

'Nothing there,' said Japp.

'No, it is odd . . .' said Poirot.

'You mean they usually leave a letter when it's suicide?'

'Exactly.'

'In fact, one more proof that it *isn't* suicide.'

He moved away.

'I'll have my men get to work now. We'd better go down and interview this Miss Plenderleith. Coming, Poirot?'

Poirot still seemed fascinated by the writing-bureau and its appointments.

He left the room, but at the door his eyes went back once more to the flaunting emerald quill pen.

At the foot of the narrow flight of stairs a door gave admission to a large-sized living-room—actually the converted stable. In this room, the walls of which were finished in a roughened plaster effect and on which hung etchings and woodcuts, two people were sitting.

One, in a chair near the fireplace, her hand stretched out to the blaze, was a dark efficient-looking young woman of twenty-seven or eight. The other, an elderly woman of ample proportions who carried a string bag, was panting and talking when the two men entered the room.

'—and as I said, Miss, such a turn it gave me I nearly dropped down where I stood. And to think that this morning of all mornings—'

The other cut her short.

'That will do, Mrs Pierce. These gentlemen are police officers, I think.'

'Miss Plenderleith?' asked Japp, advancing.

The girl nodded.

'That is my name. This is Mrs Pierce who comes in to work for us every day.'

The irrepressible Mrs Pierce broke out again.

'And as I was saying to Miss Plenderleith, to think that this morning of all mornings, my sister's Louisa Maud should have been took with a fit and me the only one handy and as I say flesh and blood is flesh and blood, and I didn't think Mrs Allen would mind, though I never likes to disappoint my ladies—'

Japp broke in with some dexterity.

'Quite so, Mrs Pierce. Now perhaps you would take Inspector Jameson into the kitchen and give him a brief statement.'

Having then got rid of the voluble Mrs Pierce, who departed with Jameson talking thirteen to the dozen, Japp turned his attention once more to the girl.

'I am Chief Inspector Japp. Now, Miss Plenderleith, I should like to know all you can tell me about this business.'

'Certainly. Where shall I begin?'

Her self-possession was admirable. There were no signs of grief or shock save for an almost unnatural rigidity of manner.

'You arrived this morning at what time?'

'I think it was just before half-past ten. Mrs Pierce, the old liar, wasn't here, I found—'

'Is that a frequent occurrence?'

Jane Plenderleith shrugged her shoulders.

'About twice a week she turns up at twelve—or not at all. She's supposed to come at nine. Actually, as I say, twice a week she either "comes over queer", or else some member of her family is overtaken by sickness. All these daily women are like that—fail you now and again. She's not bad as they go.'

'You've had her long?'

'Just over a month. Our last one pinched things.'

'Please go on, Miss Plenderleith.'

'I paid off the taxi, carried in my suitcase, looked round for Mrs P., couldn't see her and went upstairs to my room. I tidied up a bit then I went across to Barbara—Mrs Allen—and found the door locked. I rattled the handle and knocked but could get no reply. I came downstairs and rang up the police station.'

'*Pardon!*' Poirot interposed a quick, deft question. 'It did not occur to you to try and break down the door—with the help of one of the chauffeurs in the mews, say?'

Her eyes turned to him—cool, grey-green eyes. Her glance seemed to sweep over him quickly and appraisingly.

'No, I don't think I thought of that. If anything was wrong, it seemed to me that the police were the people to send for.'

'Then you thought—*pardon, mademoiselle*—that there *was* something wrong?'

'Naturally.'

'Because you could not get a reply to your knocks? But possibly your friend might have taken a sleeping draught or something of that kind—'

'She didn't take sleeping draughts.'

The reply came sharply.

'Or she might have gone away and locked her door before going?'

'Why should she lock it? In any case she would have left a note for me.'

'And she did not—leave a note for you? You are quite sure of that?'

'Of course I am sure of it. I should have seen it at once.'

The sharpness of her tone was accentuated.

Japp said:

'You didn't try and look through the keyhole, Miss Plenderleith?'

'No,' said Jane Plenderleith thoughtfully. 'I never thought of that. But I couldn't have seen anything, could I? Because the key would have been in it?'

Her inquiring gaze, innocent, wide-eyed, met Japp's. Poirot smiled suddenly to himself.

'You did quite right, of course, Miss Plenderleith,' said Japp. 'I suppose you'd no reason to believe that your friend was likely to commit suicide?'

'Oh, no.'

'She hadn't seemed worried—or distressed in any way?'

There was a pause—an appreciable pause before the girl answered.

'No.'

'Did you know she had a pistol?'

Jane Plenderleith nodded.

'Yes, she had it out in India. She always kept it in a drawer in her room.'

'H'm. Got a licence for it?'

'I imagine so. I don't know for certain.'

'Now, Miss Plenderleith, will you tell me all you can about Mrs Allen, how long you've known her, where her relations are—everything in fact.'

Jane Plenderleith nodded.

'I've known Barbara about five years. I met her first travelling abroad—in Egypt to be exact. She was on her way home from India. I'd been at the British School in Athens for a bit and was having a few weeks in Egypt before going home. We were on a Nile cruise together. We made friends, decided we liked each other. I was looking at the time for someone to share a flat or a tiny house with me. Barbara was alone in the world. We thought we'd get on well together.'

'And you did get on well together?' asked Poirot.

'Very well. We each had our own friends—Barbara

was more social in her likings—my friends were more of the artistic kind. It probably worked better that way.'

Poirot nodded. Japp went on:

'What do you know about Mrs Allen's family and her life before she met you?'

Jane Plenderleith shrugged her shoulders.

'Not very much really. Her maiden name was Armitage, I believe.'

'Her husband?'

'I don't fancy that he was anything to write home about. He drank, I think. I gather he died a year or two after the marriage. There was one child, a little girl, which died when it was three years old. Barbara didn't talk much about her husband. I believe she married him in India when she was about seventeen. Then they went off to Borneo or one of the God-forsaken spots you send ne'er-do-wells to—but as it was obviously a painful subject I didn't refer to it.'

'Do you know if Mrs Allen was in any financial difficulties?'

'No, I'm sure she wasn't.'

'Not in debt—anything of that kind?'

'Oh, no! I'm sure she wasn't in that kind of a jam.'

'Now there's another question I must ask—and I hope you won't be upset about it, Miss Plenderleith. Had Mrs Allen any particular man friend or men friends?'

Jane Plenderleith answered coolly:

'Well, she was engaged to be married if that answers your question.'

'What is the name of the man she was engaged to?'

'Charles Laverton-West. He's M.P. for some place in Hampshire.'

'Had she known him long?'

'A little over a year.'

'And she has been engaged to him—how long?'

'Two—no—nearer three months.'

'As far as you know there has not been any quarrel?'

Miss Plenderleith shook her head.

'No. I should have been surprised if there had been anything of that sort. Barbara wasn't the quarrelling kind.'

'How long is it since you last saw Mrs Allen?'

'Friday last, just before I went away for the weekend.'

'Mrs Allen was remaining in town?'

'Yes. She was going out with her fiancé on the Sunday, I believe.'

'And you yourself, where did you spend the weekend?'

'At Laidells Hall, Laidells, Essex.'

'And the name of the people with whom you were staying?'

'Mr and Mrs Bentinck.'

'You only left them this morning?'

'Yes.'

'You must have left very early?'

'Mr Bentinck motored me up. He starts early because he has to get to the city by ten.'

'I see.'

Japp nodded comprehendingly. Miss Plenderleith's replies had all been crisp and convincing.

Poirot in his turn put a question.

'What is your own opinion of Mr Laverton-West?'

The girl shrugged her shoulders.

'Does that matter?'

'No, it does not matter, perhaps, but I should like to have your opinion.'

'I don't know that I've thought about him one way or the other. He's young—not more than thirty-one or two—ambitious—a good public speaker—means to get on in the world.'

'That is on the credit side—and on the debit?'

'Well,' Miss Plenderleith considered for a moment or two. 'In my opinion he's commonplace—his ideas are not particularly original—and he's slightly pompous.'

'Those are not very serious faults, mademoiselle,' said Poirot, smiling.

'Don't you think so?'

Her tone was slightly ironic.

'They might be to you.'

He was watching her, saw her look a little disconcerted. He pursued his advantage.

'But to Mrs Allen—no, she would not notice them.'

'You're perfectly right. Barbara thought he was wonderful—took him entirely at his own valuation.'

Poirot said gently:

'You were fond of your friend?'

He saw the hand clench on her knee, the tightening of the line of the jaw, yet the answer came in a matter-of-fact voice free from emotion.

'You are quite right. I was.'

Japp said:

'Just one other thing, Miss Plenderleith. You and she didn't have a quarrel? There was no upset between you?'

'None whatever.'

'Not over this engagement business?'

'Certainly not. I was glad she was able to be so happy about it.'

There was a momentary pause, then Japp said:

'As far as you know, did Mrs Allen have any enemies?'

This time there was a definite interval before Jane Plenderleith replied. When she did so, her tone had altered very slightly.

'I don't know quite what you mean by enemies?'

'Anyone, for instance, who would profit by her death?'

'Oh, no, that would be ridiculous. She had a very small income anyway.'

'And who inherits that income?'

Jane Plenderleith's voice sounded mildly surprised as she said:

'Do you know, I really don't know. I shouldn't be surprised if I did. That is, if she ever made a will.'

'And no enemies in any other sense?' Japp slid off to another aspect quickly. 'People with a grudge against her?'

'I don't think anyone had a grudge against her. She was a very gentle creature, always anxious to please. She had a really sweet, lovable nature.'

For the first time that hard, matter-of-fact voice broke a little. Poirot nodded gently.

Japp said:

'So it amounts to this—Mrs Allen has been in good spirits lately, she wasn't in any financial difficulty, she was engaged to be married and was happy in her engagement. There was nothing in the world to make her commit suicide. That's right, isn't it?'

There was a momentary silence before Jane said:

'Yes.'

Japp rose.

'Excuse me, I must have a word with Inspector Jameson.'

He left the room.

Hercule Poirot remained *tête à tête* with Jane Plenderleith.

For a few minutes there was silence.

Jane Plenderleith shot a swift appraising glance at the little man, but after that she stared in front of her and did not speak. Yet a consciousness of his presence showed itself in a certain nervous tension. Her body was still but not relaxed. When at last Poirot did break the silence the mere sound of his voice seemed to give her a certain relief. In an agreeable everyday voice he asked a question.

'When did you light the fire, mademoiselle?'

'The fire?' Her voice sounded vague and rather absent-minded. 'Oh, as soon as I arrived this morning.'

'Before you went upstairs or afterwards?'

'Before.'

'I see. Yes, naturally . . . And it was already laid—or did you have to lay it?'

'It was laid. I only had to put a match to it.'

There was a slight impatience in her voice. Clearly she suspected him of making conversation. Possibly that was what he was doing. At any rate he went on in quiet conversational tones.

'But your friend—in her room I noticed there was a gas fire only?'

Jane Plenderleith answered mechanically.

'This is the only coal fire we have—the others are all gas fires.'

'And you cook with gas, too?'

'I think everyone does nowadays.'

'True. It is much labour saving.'

The little interchange died down. Jane Plenderleith tapped on the ground with her shoe. Then she said abruptly:

'That man—Chief Inspector Japp—is he considered clever?'

'He is very sound. Yes, he is well thought of. He works hard and painstakingly and very little escapes him.'

'I wonder—' muttered the girl.

Poirot watched her. His eyes looked very green in the firelight. He asked quietly:

'It was a great shock to you, your friend's death?'

'Terrible.'

She spoke with abrupt sincerity.

'You did not expect it—no?'

'Of course not.'

'So that it seemed to you at first, perhaps, that it was impossible—that it could not be?'

The quiet sympathy of his tone seemed to break down Jane Plenderleith's defences. She replied eagerly, naturally, without stiffness.

'That's just it. Even if Barbara *did* kill herself, I can't imagine her *killing herself that way.*'

'Yet she had a pistol?'

Jane Plenderleith made an impatient gesture.

'Yes, but that pistol was a—oh! a hang over. She'd been in out-of-the-way places. She kept it out of habit—not with any other idea. I'm sure of that.'

'Ah! and why are you sure of that?'

'Oh, because of the things she said.'

'Such as—?'

His voice was very gentle and friendly. It led her on subtly.

'Well, for instance, we were discussing suicide once and she said much the easiest way would be to turn the gas on and stuff up all the cracks and just go to bed. I said I thought that would be impossible—to lie there waiting. I said I'd far rather shoot myself. And she said no, she could never shoot herself. She'd be too frightened in case it didn't come off and anyway she said she'd hate the bang.'

'I see,' said Poirot. 'As you say, it is odd . . . Because, as you have just told me, *there was a gas fire in her room.*'

Jane Plenderleith looked at him, slightly startled.

'Yes, there was . . . I can't understand—no, I can't understand why she didn't do it that way.'

Poirot shook his head.

'Yes, it seems—odd—not natural somehow.'

'The whole thing doesn't seem natural. I still can't

believe she killed herself. I suppose it *must* be suicide?'

'Well, there is one other possibility.'

'What do you mean?'

Poirot looked straight at her.

'It might be—murder.'

'Oh, no?' Jane Plenderleith shrank back. 'Oh no! What a horrible suggestion.'

'Horrible, perhaps, but does it strike you as an impossible one?'

'But the door was locked on the inside. So was the window.'

'The door was locked—yes. But there is nothing to show if it were locked from the inside or the outside. You see, *the key was missing.*'

'But then—if it is missing . . .' She took a minute or two. 'Then it must have been locked from the *outside.* Otherwise it would be somewhere in the room.'

'Ah, but it may be. The room has not been thoroughly searched yet, remember. Or it may have been thrown out of the window and somebody may have picked it up.'

'Murder!' said Jane Plenderleith. She turned over the possibility, her dark clever face eager on the scent. 'I believe you're right.'

'But if it were murder there would have been a motive. Do you know of a motive, mademoiselle?'

Slowly she shook her head. And yet, in spite of the denial, Poirot again got the impression that Jane Plenderleith was deliberately keeping something back. The door opened and Japp came in.

Poirot rose.

'I have been suggesting to Miss Plenderleith,' he said, 'that her friend's death was not suicide.'

Japp looked momentarily put out. He cast a glance of reproach at Poirot.

'It's a bit early to say anything definite,' he remarked. 'We've always got to take all possibilities into account, you understand. That's all there is to it at the moment.'

Jane Plenderleith replied quietly.

'I see.'

Japp came towards her.

'Now then, Miss Plenderleith, have you ever seen this before?'

On the palm of his hand he held out a small oval of dark blue enamel.

Jane Plenderleith shook her head.

'No, never.'

'It's not yours nor Mrs Allen's?'

'No. It's not the kind of thing usually worn by our sex, is it?'

'Oh! so you recognize it.'

'Well, it's pretty obvious, isn't it? That's half of a man's cuff link.'

'That young woman's too cocky by half,' Japp complained.

The two men were once more in Mrs Allen's bedroom. The body had been photographed and removed and the fingerprint man had done his work and departed.

'It would be unadvisable to treat her as a fool,' agreed Poirot. 'She most emphatically is *not* a fool. She is, in fact, a particularly clever and competent young woman.'

'Think she did it?' asked Japp with a momentary ray of hope. 'She might have, you know. We'll have to get her alibi looked into. Some quarrel over this young man—this budding M.P. She's rather *too* scathing about him, I think! Sounds fishy. Rather as though she were sweet on him herself and he'd turned her down. She's the kind that would bump anyone off if she felt like it, and keep her head while she was doing it, too. Yes, we'll have to look into that alibi. She had it very pat and after all Essex isn't very far away. Plenty of trains. Or a fast car. It's worthwhile finding out if she went to bed with a headache for instance last night.'

'You are right,' agreed Poirot.

'In any case,' continued Japp, 'she's holding out on us. Eh? Didn't you feel that too? That young woman knows something.'

Poirot nodded thoughtfully.

'Yes, that could be clearly seen.'

'That's always a difficulty in these cases,' Japp complained. 'People *will* hold their tongues—sometimes out of the most honourable motives.'

'For which one can hardly blame them, my friend.'

'No, but it makes it much harder for *us*,' Japp grumbled.

'It merely displays to its full advantage your ingenuity,' Poirot consoled him. 'What about fingerprints, by the way?'

'Well, it's murder all right. No prints whatever on the pistol. Wiped clean before being placed in her hand. Even if she managed to wind her arm round her head in some marvellous acrobatic fashion she could hardly fire off a pistol without hanging on to it and she couldn't wipe it after she was dead.'

'No, no, an outside agency is clearly indicated.'

'Otherwise the prints are disappointing. None on the door-handle. None on the window. Suggestive, eh? Plenty of Mrs Allen's all over the place.'

'Did Jameson get anything?'

'Out of the daily woman? No. She talked a lot but she didn't really know much. Confirmed the fact that Allen and Plenderleith were on good terms. I've sent Jameson out to make inquiries in the mews. We'll have to have a word with Mr Laverton-West too. Find out where he was and what he was doing last night. In the meantime we'll have a look through her papers.'

He set to without more ado. Occasionally he grunted and tossed something over to Poirot. The search did not take long. There were not many papers in the desk and what there were were neatly arranged and docketed.

Finally Japp leant back and uttered a sigh.

'Not very much, is there?'

'As you say.'

'Most of it quite straightforward—receipted bills, a few bills as yet unpaid—nothing particularly outstanding. Social stuff—invitations. Notes from friends. These—' he laid his hand on a pile of seven or eight letters—'and her cheque book and passbook. Anything strike you there?'

'Yes, she was overdrawn.'

'Anything else?'

Poirot smiled.

'Is it an examination that you put me through? But yes, I noticed what you are thinking of. Two hundred pounds drawn to self three months ago—and two hundred pounds drawn out yesterday—'

'And nothing on the counterfoil of the cheque book. No other cheques to self except small sums—fifteen pounds the highest. And I'll tell you this—there's no such sum of money in the house. Four pounds ten in a handbag and an odd shilling or two in another bag. That's pretty clear, I think.'

'Meaning that she paid that sum away yesterday.'

'Yes. Now who did she pay it to?'

The door opened and Inspector Jameson entered.

'Well, Jameson, get anything?'

'Yes, sir, several things. To begin with, nobody actually heard the shot. Two or three women say they did because they want to think they did—but that's all there is to it. With all those fireworks going off there isn't a dog's chance.'

Japp grunted.

'Don't suppose there is. Go on.'

'Mrs Allen was at home most of yesterday afternoon and evening. Came in about five o'clock. Then she went out again about six but only to the post box at the end of the mews. At about nine-thirty a car drove up—Standard Swallow saloon—and a man got out. Description about forty-five, well set up military-looking gent, dark blue overcoat, bowler hat, toothbrush moustache. James Hogg, chauffeur from No. 18 says he's seen him calling on Mrs Allen before.'

'Forty-five,' said Japp. 'Can't very well be Laverton-West.'

'This man, whoever he was, stayed here for just under an hour. Left at about ten-twenty. Stopped in the doorway to speak to Mrs Allen. Small boy, Frederick Hogg, was hanging about quite near and heard what he said.'

'And what did he say?'

'"*Well, think it over and let me know.*" And then she said something and he answered: "*All right. So long.*" After that he got in his car and drove away.'

'That was at ten-twenty,' said Poirot thoughtfully.

Japp rubbed his nose.

'Then at ten-twenty Mrs Allen was still alive,' he said. 'What next?'

'Nothing more, sir, as far as I can learn. The chauffeur at No. 22 got in at half-past ten and he'd promised his kids to let off some fireworks for them. They'd been waiting for him—and all the other kids in the mews too. He let 'em off and everybody around about was busy watching them. After that everyone went to bed.'

'And nobody else was seen to enter No. 14?'

'No—but that's not to say they didn't. Nobody would have noticed.'

'H'm,' said Japp. 'That's true. Well, we'll have to get hold of this "military gentleman with the toothbrush moustache." It's pretty clear that he was the last person to see her alive. I wonder who he was?'

'Miss Plenderleith might tell us,' suggested Poirot.

'She might,' said Japp gloomily. 'On the other hand she might not. I've no doubt she could tell us a good deal if she liked. What about you, Poirot, old boy? You were alone with her for a bit. Didn't you trot out that Father Confessor manner of yours that sometimes makes such a hit?'

Poirot spread out his hands.

'Alas, we talked only of gas fires.'

'Gas fires—gas fires.' Japp sounded disgusted. 'What's the matter with you, old cock? Ever since you've been here the only things you've taken an interest in are quill pens and waste-paper baskets. Oh, yes, I saw you having a quiet look into the one downstairs. Anything in it?'

Poirot sighed.

'A catalogue of bulbs and an old magazine.'

'What's the idea, anyway? If anyone wants to throw away an incriminating document or whatever it is you have in mind they're not likely just to pitch it into a waste-paper basket.'

'That is very true what you say there. Only something quite unimportant would be thrown away like that.'

Poirot spoke meekly. Nevertheless Japp looked at him suspiciously.

'Well,' he said. 'I know what I'm going to do next. What about you?'

'*Eh bien*,' said Poirot. 'I shall complete my search for the unimportant. There is still the dustbin.'

He skipped nimbly out of the room. Japp looked after him with an air of disgust.

'Potty,' he said. 'Absolutely potty.'

Inspector Jameson preserved a respectful silence. His face said with British superiority: 'Foreigners!'

Aloud he said:

'So that's Mr Hercule Poirot! I've heard of him.'

'Old friend of mine,' explained Japp. 'Not half as balmy as he looks, mind you. All the same he's getting on now.'

'Gone a bit gaga as they say, sir,' suggested Inspector Jameson. 'Ah well, age will tell.'

'All the same,' said Japp, 'I wish I knew what he was up to.'

He walked over to the writing-table and stared uneasily at an emerald green quill pen.

Japp was just engaging his third chauffeur's wife in conversation when Poirot, walking noiselessly as a cat, suddenly appeared at his elbow.

'Whew, you made me jump,' said Japp. 'Got anything?'

'Not what I was looking for.'

Japp turned back to Mrs James Hogg.

'And you say you've seen this gentleman before?'

'Oh, yes sir. And my husband too. We knew him at once.'

'Now look here, Mrs Hogg, you're a shrewd woman, I can see. I've no doubt that you know all about everyone in the mews. And you're a woman of judgment—unusually good judgment, I can tell that—' Unblushingly he repeated this remark for the third time. Mrs Hogg bridled slightly and assumed an expression of superhuman intelligence. 'Give me a line on those two young women—Mrs Allen and Miss Plenderleith. What were they like? Gay? Lots of parties? That sort of thing?'

'Oh, no sir, nothing of the kind. They went out a good bit—Mrs Allen especially—but they're *class*, if you know what I mean. Not like some as I could name down the other end. I'm sure the way that Mrs Stevens goes on—if she *is* a Mrs at all which I doubt—well I shouldn't like to tell you what goes on there—I . . .'

'Quite so,' said Japp, dexterously stopping the flow. 'Now that's very important what you've told me. Mrs Allen and Miss Plenderleith were well liked, then?'

'Oh yes, sir, very nice ladies, both of them—especially Mrs Allen. Always spoke a nice word to the children, she did. Lost her own little girl, I believe, poor dear. Ah well, I've buried three myself. And what I say is . . .'

'Yes, yes, very sad. And Miss Plenderleith?'

'Well, of course she was a nice lady too, but much more abrupt if you know what I mean. Just go by with a nod, she would, and not stop to pass the time of day. But I've nothing against her—nothing at all.'

'She and Mrs Allen got on well together?'

'Oh, yes sir. No quarrelling—nothing like that. Very happy and contented they were—I'm sure Mrs Pierce will bear me out.'

'Yes, we've talked to her. Do you know Mrs Allen's fiancé by sight?'

'The gentleman she's going to marry? Oh, yes. He's been here quite a bit off and on. Member of Parliament, they do say.'

'It wasn't he who came last night?'

'No, sir, it was *not*.' Mrs Hogg drew herself up. A note of excitement disguised beneath intense primness came into her voice. 'And if you ask me, sir, what you are thinking is all *wrong*. Mrs Allen wasn't *that* kind of lady, I'm sure. It's true there *was* no one in the house, but I do *not* believe anything of the kind—I said so to Hogg only this morning. "No, Hogg," I said, "Mrs

Allen was a lady—a real lady—so don't go suggesting things"—knowing what a man's mind is, if you'll excuse my mentioning it. Always coarse in their ideas.'

Passing this insult by, Japp proceeded:

'You saw him arrive and you saw him leave—that's so, isn't it?'

'That's so, sir.'

'And you didn't hear anything else? Any sounds of a quarrel?'

'No, sir, nor likely to. Not, that is to say, that such things couldn't be heard—because the contrary to that is well known—and down the other end the way Mrs Stevens goes for that poor frightened maid of hers is common talk—and one and all we've advised her not to stand it, but there, the wages is good—temper of the devil she may have but pays for it—thirty shillings a week ...'

Japp said quickly:

'But you didn't hear anything of the kind at No. 14?'

'No, sir. Nor likely to with fireworks popping off here, there and everywhere and my Eddie with his eyebrows singed off as near as nothing.'

'This man left at ten-twenty—that's right, is it?'

'It might be, sir. I couldn't say myself. But Hogg says so and he's a very reliable, steady man.'

'You actually saw him leave. Did you hear what he said?'

'No, sir. I wasn't near enough for that. Just saw him from my windows, standing in the doorway talking to Mrs Allen.'

'See her too?'

'Yes, sir, she was standing just inside the doorway.'

'Notice what she was wearing?'

'Now really, sir, I couldn't say. Not noticing particularly as it were.'

Poirot said:

'You did not even notice if she was wearing day dress or evening dress?'

'No, sir, I can't say I did.'

Poirot looked thoughtfully up at the window above and then across to No. 14. He smiled and for a moment his eye caught Japp's.

'And the gentleman?'

'He was in a dark-blue overcoat and a bowler hat. Very smart and well set up.'

Japp asked a few more questions and then proceeded to his next interview. This was with Master Frederick Hogg, an impish-faced, bright-eyed lad, considerably swollen with self-importance.

'Yes, sir. I heard them talking. "*Think it over and let me know*," the gent said. Pleasant like, you know. And then she said something and he answered, "*All right. So long.*" And he got into the car—I was holding the door open but he didn't give me nothing,' said Master Hogg with a slight tinge of depression in his tone. 'And he drove away.'

'You didn't hear what Mrs Allen said?'

'No, sir, can't say I did.'

'Can you tell me what she was wearing? What colour, for instance?'

'Couldn't say, sir. You see, I didn't really see her. She must have been round behind the door.'

'Just so,' said Japp. 'Now look here, my boy, I want you to think and answer my next question very carefully. If you don't know and can't remember, say so. Is that clear?'

'Yes, sir.'

Master Hogg looked at him eagerly.

'Which of 'em closed the door, Mrs Allen or the gentleman?'

'The front door?'

'The front door, naturally.'

The child reflected. His eyes screwed themselves up in an effort of remembrance.

'Think the lady probably did—No, she didn't. He did. Pulled it to with a bit of a bang and jumped into the car quick. Looked as though he had a date somewhere.'

'Right. Well, young man, you seem a bright kind of shaver. Here's sixpence for you.'

Dismissing Master Hogg, Japp turned to his friend. Slowly with one accord they nodded.

'Could be!' said Japp.

'There are possibilities,' agreed Poirot.

His eyes shone with a green light. They looked like a cat's.

On re-entering the sitting-room of No. 14, Japp wasted no time in beating about the bush. He came straight to the point.

'Now look here, Miss Plenderleith, don't you think it's better to spill the beans here and now. It's going to come to that in the end.'

Jane Plenderleith raised her eyebrows. She was standing by the mantelpiece, gently warming one foot at the fire.

'I really don't know what you mean.'

'Is that quite true, Miss Plenderleith?'

She shrugged her shoulders.

'I've answered all your questions. I don't see what more I can do.'

'Well, it's my opinion you could do a lot more—if you chose.'

'That's only an opinion, though, isn't it, Chief Inspector?'

Japp grew rather red in the face.

'I think,' said Poirot, 'that mademoiselle would appreciate better the reason for your questions if you told her just how the case stands.'

'That's very simple. Now then, Miss Plenderleith, the facts are as follows. Your friend was found shot through the head with a pistol in her hand and the door and the window fastened. That looked like a plain case of suicide. *But it wasn't suicide.* The medical evidence alone proves that.'

'How?'

All her ironic coolness had disappeared. She leaned forward—intent—watching his face.

'The pistol was in her hand—*but the fingers weren't grasping it.* Moreover there were *no fingerprints at all* on the pistol. And the angle of the wound makes it impossible that the wound should have been self-inflicted. Then again, she left no letter—rather an unusual thing for a suicide. And though the door was locked the key has not been found.'

Jane Plenderleith turned slowly and sat down in a chair facing them.

'So that's it!' she said. 'All along I've felt it was *impossible* that she should have killed herself! I was right! She *didn't* kill herself. Someone else killed her.'

For a moment or two she remained lost in thought. Then she raised her head brusquely.

'Ask me any questions you like,' she said. 'I will answer them to the best of my ability.'

Japp began:

'Last night Mrs Allen had a visitor. He is described as a man of forty-five, military bearing, toothbrush moustache, smartly dressed and driving a Standard Swallow saloon car. Do you know who that is?'

'I can't be sure, of course, but it sounds like Major Eustace.'

'Who is Major Eustace? Tell me all you can about him?'

'He was a man Barbara had known abroad—in India. He turned up about a year ago, and we've seen him on and off since.'

'He was a friend of Mrs Allen's?'

'He behaved like one,' said Jane dryly.

'What was her attitude to him?'

'I don't think she really liked him—in fact, I'm sure she didn't.'

'But she treated him with outward friendliness?'

'Yes.'

'Did she ever seem—think carefully, Miss Plenderleith—afraid of him?'

Jane Plenderleith considered this thoughtfully for a minute or two. Then she said:

'Yes—I think she was. She was always nervous when he was about.'

'Did he and Mr Laverton-West meet at all?'

'Only once, I think. They didn't take to each other much. That is to say, Major Eustace made himself as agreeable as he could to Charles, but Charles wasn't having any. Charles has got a very good nose for anybody who isn't well—quite—quite.'

'And Major Eustace was not—what you call—quite—quite?' asked Poirot.

The girl said dryly:

'No, he wasn't. Bit hairy at the heel. Definitely not out of the top drawer.'

'Alas—I do not know those two expressions. You mean to say he was not the *pukka sahib*?'

A fleeting smile passed across Jane Plenderleith's face, but she replied gravely, 'No.'

'Would it come as a great surprise to you, Miss Plenderleith, if I suggested that this man was blackmailing Mrs Allen?'

Japp sat forward to observe the result of his suggestion. He was well satisfied. The girl started forward, the colour rose in her cheeks, she brought down her hand sharply on the arm of her chair.

'So that was it! What a fool I was not to have guessed. Of course!'

'You think the suggestion feasible, mademoiselle?' asked Poirot.

'I was a fool not to have thought of it! Barbara's borrowed small sums off me several times during the last six months. And I've seen her sitting poring over her passbook. I knew she was living well within her income, so I didn't bother, but, of course, if she was paying out sums of money—'

'And it would accord with her general demeanour—yes?' asked Poirot.

'Absolutely. She was nervous. Quite jumpy sometimes. Altogether different from what she used to be.'

Poirot said gently:

'Excuse me, but that is not just what you told us before.'

'That was different,' Jane Plenderleith waved an impatient hand. 'She wasn't depressed. I mean she wasn't feeling suicidal or anything like that. But blackmail—yes. I wish she'd told *me*. I'd have sent him to the devil.'

'But he might have gone—not to the devil, but to Mr Charles Laverton-West?' observed Poirot.

'Yes,' said Jane Plenderleith slowly. 'Yes . . . that's true . . .'

'You've no idea of what this man's hold over her may have been?' asked Japp.

The girl shook her head.

'I haven't the faintest idea. I can't believe, knowing Barbara, that it could have been anything really serious. On the other hand—' she paused, then went on. 'What

I mean is, Barbara was a bit of a simpleton in some ways. She'd be very easily frightened. In fact, she was the kind of girl who would be a positive gift to a blackmailer! The nasty brute!'

She snapped out the last three words with real venom.

'Unfortunately,' said Poirot, 'the crime seems to have taken place the wrong way round. It is the victim who should kill the blackmailer, not the blackmailer his victim.'

Jane Plenderleith frowned a little.

'No—that is true—but I can imagine circumstances—'

'Such as?'

'Supposing Barbara got desperate. She may have threatened him with that silly little pistol of hers. He tries to wrench it away from her and in the struggle he fires it and kills her. Then he's horrified at what he's done and tries to pretend it was suicide.'

'Might be,' said Japp. 'But there's a difficulty.'

She looked at him inquiringly.

'Major Eustace (if it was him) left here last night at ten-twenty and said goodbye to Mrs Allen on the doorstep.'

'Oh,' the girl's face fell. 'I see.' She paused a minute or two. 'But he might have come back later,' she said slowly.

'Yes, that is possible,' said Poirot.

Japp continued:

'Tell me, Miss Plenderleith, where was Mrs Allen in the habit of receiving guests, here or in the room upstairs?'

'Both. But this room was used for more communal parties or for my own special friends. You see, the arrangement was that Barbara had the big bedroom and used it as a sitting-room as well, and I had the little bedroom and used this room.'

'If Major Eustace came by appointment last night, in which room do you think Mrs Allen would have received him?'

'I think she would probably bring him in here.' The girl sounded a little doubtful. 'It would be less intimate. On the other hand, if she wanted to write a cheque or anything of that kind, she would probably take him upstairs. There are no writing materials down here.'

Japp shook his head.

'There was no question of a cheque. Mrs Allen drew out two hundred pounds in cash yesterday. And so far we've not been able to find any trace of it in the house.'

'And she gave it to that brute? Oh, poor Barbara! Poor, poor Barbara!'

Poirot coughed.

'Unless, as you suggest, it was more or less an accident, it still seems a remarkable fact that he should kill an apparently regular source of income.'

'Accident? It wasn't an accident. He lost his temper and saw red and shot her.'

'That is how you think it happened?'

'Yes.' She added vehemently, 'It was murder—*murder*!'

Poirot said gravely:

'I will not say that you are wrong, mademoiselle.'

Japp said:

'What cigarettes did Mrs Allen smoke?'

'Gaspers. There are some in that box.'

Japp opened the box, took out a cigarette and nodded. He slipped the cigarette into his pocket.

'And you, mademoiselle?' asked Poirot.

'The same.'

'You do not smoke Turkish?'

'Never.'

'Nor Mrs Allen?'

'No. She didn't like them.'

Poirot asked:

'And Mr Laverton-West. What did he smoke?'

She stared hard at him.

'Charles? What does it matter what he smoked? You're not going to pretend that *he* killed her?'

Poirot shrugged his shoulders.

'A man has killed the woman he loved before now, mademoiselle.'

Jane shook her head impatiently.

'Charles wouldn't kill anybody. He's a very careful man.'

'All the same, mademoiselle, it is the careful men who commit the cleverest murders.'

She stared at him.

'But not for the motive you have just advanced, M. Poirot.'

He bowed his head.

'No, that is true.'

Japp rose.

'Well, I don't think that there's much more I can do here. I'd like to have one more look round.'

'In case that money should be tucked away somewhere? Certainly. Look anywhere you like. And in my room too—although it isn't likely Barbara would hide it there.'

Japp's search was quick but efficient. The living-room had given up all its secrets in a very few minutes. Then he went upstairs. Jane Plenderleith sat on the arm of a chair, smoking a cigarette and frowning at the fire. Poirot watched her.

After some minutes, he said quietly:

'Do you know if Mr Laverton-West is in London at present?'

'I don't know at all. I rather fancy he's in Hampshire with his people. I suppose I ought to have wired him. How dreadful. I forgot.'

'It is not easy to remember everything, mademoiselle, when a catastrophe occurs. And after all, the bad news, it will keep. One hears it only too soon.'

'Yes, that's true,' the girl said absently.

Japp's footsteps were heard descending the stairs. Jane went out to meet him.

'Well?'

Japp shook his head.

'Nothing helpful, I'm afraid, Miss Plenderleith. I've been over the whole house now. Oh, I suppose I'd better just have a look in this cupboard under the stairs.'

He caught hold of the handle as he spoke, and pulled.

Jane Plenderleith said:

'It's locked.'

Something in her voice made both men look at her sharply.

'Yes,' said Japp pleasantly. 'I can see it's locked. Perhaps you'll get the key.'

The girl was standing as though carved in stone.

'I—I'm not sure where it is.'

Japp shot a quick glance at her. His voice continued resolutely pleasant and off-hand.

'Dear me, that's too bad. Don't want to splinter the wood, opening it by force. I'll send Jameson out to get an assortment of keys.'

She moved forward stiffly.

'Oh,' she said. 'One minute. It might be—'

She went back into the living-room and reappeared a moment later holding a fair-sized key in her hand.

'We keep it locked,' she explained, 'because one's umbrellas and things have a habit of getting pinched.'

'Very wise precaution,' said Japp, cheerfully accepting the key.

He turned it in the lock and threw the door open. It was dark inside the cupboard. Japp took out his pocket flashlight and let it play round the inside.

Poirot felt the girl at his side stiffen and stop breathing for a second. His eyes followed the sweep of Japp's torch.

There was not very much in the cupboard. Three umbrellas—one broken, four walking sticks, a set of golf clubs, two tennis racquets, a neatly-folded rug and several sofa cushions in various stages of dilapidation. On the top of these last reposed a small, smart-looking attaché-case.

As Japp stretched out a hand towards it, Jane Plenderleith said quickly:

'That's mine. I—it came back with me this morning. So there can't be anything there.'

'Just as well to make quite sure,' said Japp, his cheery friendliness increasing slightly.

The case was unlocked. Inside it was fitted with shagreen brushes and toilet bottles. There were two magazines in it but nothing else.

Japp examined the whole outfit with meticulous attention. When at last he shut the lid and began a cursory examination of the cushions, the girl gave an audible sigh of relief.

There was nothing else in the cupboard beyond what was plainly to be seen. Japp's examination was soon finished.

He relocked the door and handed the key to Jane Plenderleith.

'Well,' he said, 'that concludes matters. Can you give me Mr Laverton-West's address?'

'Farlescombe Hall, Little Ledbury, Hampshire.'

'Thank you, Miss Plenderleith. That's all for the present. I may be round again later. By the way, mum's the word. Leave it at suicide as far as the general public's concerned.'

'Of course, I quite understand.'

She shook hands with them both.

As they walked away down the mews, Japp exploded:

'What the—the hell was there in that cupboard? There was *something*.'

'Yes, there was something.'

'And I'll bet ten to one it was something to do with the attaché-case! But like the double-dyed mutt I must be, I couldn't find anything. Looked in all the bottles—felt the lining—what the devil could it be?'

Poirot shook his head thoughtfully.

'That girl's in it somehow,' Japp went on. 'Brought that case back this morning? Not on your life, she didn't! Notice that there were two magazines in it?'

'Yes.'

'Well, one of them was for *last July*!'

It was the following day when Japp walked into Poirot's flat, flung his hat on the table in deep disgust and dropped into a chair.

'Well,' he growled. '*She's* out of it!'

'Who is out of it?'

'Plenderleith. Was playing bridge up to midnight. Host, hostess, naval-commander guest and two servants can all swear to that. No doubt about it, we've got to give up any idea of her being concerned in the business. All the same, I'd like to know *why* she went all hot and bothered about that little attaché-case under the stairs. That's something in *your* line, Poirot. You like solving the kind of triviality that leads nowhere. The Mystery of the Small Attaché-Case. Sounds quite promising!'

'I will give you yet another suggestion for a title. The Mystery of the Smell of Cigarette Smoke.'

'A bit clumsy for a title. Smell—eh? Was *that* why you were sniffing so when we first examined the body? I saw you—*and* heard you! Sniff—sniff—sniff. Thought you had a cold in your head.'

'You were entirely in error.'

Japp sighed.

'I always thought it was the little grey cells of the brain. Don't tell me the cells of your nose are equally superior to anyone else's.'

'No, no, calm yourself.'

'*I* didn't smell any cigarette smoke,' went on Japp suspiciously.

'No more did I, my friend.'

Japp looked at him doubtfully. Then he extracted a cigarette from his pocket.

'That's the kind Mrs Allen smoked—gaspers. Six of those stubs were hers. *The other three were Turkish.*'

'Exactly.'

'Your wonderful nose knew that without looking at them, I suppose!'

'I assure you my nose does not enter into the matter. My nose registered nothing.'

'But the brain cells registered a lot?'

'Well—there were certain indications—do you not think so?'

Japp looked at him sideways.

'Such as?'

'*Eh bien*, there was very definitely something missing from the room. Also something added, I think ... And then, on the writing-bureau ...'

'I knew it! We're coming to that damned quill pen!'

'*Du tout.* The quill pen plays a purely negative role.'

Japp retreated to safer ground.

'I've got Charles Laverton-West coming to see me at Scotland Yard in half an hour. I thought you might like to be there.'

'I should very much.'

'And you'll be glad to hear we've tracked down Major Eustace. Got a service flat in the Cromwell Road.'

'Excellent.'

'And we've got a little to go on there. Not at all a nice person, Major Eustace. After I've seen Laverton-West, we'll go and see him. That suit you?'

'Perfectly.'

'Well, come along then.'

At half-past eleven, Charles Laverton-West was ushered into Chief Inspector Japp's room. Japp rose and shook hands.

The M.P. was a man of medium height with a very definite personality. He was clean-shaven, with the mobile mouth of an actor, and the slightly prominent eyes that so often go with the gift of oratory. He was good-looking in a quiet, well-bred way.

Though looking pale and somewhat distressed, his manner was perfectly formal and composed.

He took a seat, laid his gloves and hat on the table and looked towards Japp.

'I'd like to say, first of all, Mr Laverton-West, that I fully appreciate how distressing this must be to you.'

Laverton-West waved this aside.

'Do not let us discuss my feelings. Tell me, Chief Inspector, have you any idea what caused my—Mrs Allen to take her own life?'

'You yourself cannot help us in any way?'

'No, indeed.'

'There was no quarrel? No estrangement of any kind between you?'

'Nothing of the kind. It has been the greatest shock to me.'

'Perhaps it will be more understandable, sir, if I tell you that it was not suicide—but murder!'

'Murder?' Charles Laverton-West's eyes popped nearly out of his head. 'You say *murder*?'

'Quite correct. Now, Mr Laverton-West, have you any idea who might be likely to make away with Mrs Allen?'

Laverton-West fairly spluttered out his answer.

'No—no, indeed—nothing of the sort! The mere idea is—is *unimaginable*!'

'She never mentioned any enemies? Anyone who might have a grudge against her?'

'Never.'

'Did you know that she had a pistol?'

'I was not aware of the fact.'

He looked a little startled.

'Miss Plenderleith says that Mrs Allen brought this pistol back from abroad with her some years ago.'

'Really?'

'Of course, we have only Miss Plenderleith's word for that. It is quite possible that Mrs Allen felt herself to be in danger from some source and kept the pistol handy for reasons of her own.'

Charles Laverton-West shook his head doubtfully. He seemed quite bewildered and dazed.

'What is your opinion of Miss Plenderleith, Mr Laverton-West? I mean, does she strike you as a reliable, truthful person?'

The other pondered a minute.

'I think so—yes, I should say so.'

'You don't like her?' suggested Japp, who had been watching him closely.

'I wouldn't say that. She is not the type of young

woman I admire. That sarcastic, independent type is not attractive to me, but I should say she was quite truthful.'

'H'm,' said Japp. 'Do you know a Major Eustace?'

'Eustace? Eustace? Ah, yes, I remember the name. I met him once at Barbara's—Mrs Allen's. Rather a doubtful customer in my opinion. I said as much to my—to Mrs Allen. He wasn't the type of man I should have encouraged to come to the house after we were married.'

'And what did Mrs Allen say?'

'Oh! she quite agreed. She trusted my judgment implicitly. A man knows other men better than a woman can do. She explained that she couldn't very well be rude to a man whom she had not seen for some time—I think she felt especially a horror of being *snobbish*! Naturally, as my wife, she would find a good many of her old associates well—unsuitable, shall we say?'

'Meaning that in marrying you she was bettering her position?' Japp asked bluntly.

Laverton-West held up a well-manicured hand.

'No, no, not quite that. As a matter of fact, Mrs Allen's mother was a distant relation of my own family. She was fully my equal in birth. But of course, in my position, I have to be especially careful in choosing my friends—and my wife in choosing hers. One is to a certain extent in the limelight.'

'Oh, quite,' said Japp dryly. He went on, 'So you can't help us in any way?'

'No indeed. I am utterly at sea. Barbara! Murdered! It seems incredible.'

'Now, Mr Laverton-West, can you tell me what your own movements were on the night of November fifth?'

'My movements? *My* movements?'

Laverton-West's voice rose in shrill protest.

'Purely a matter of routine,' explained Japp. 'We—er—have to ask everybody.'

Charles Laverton-West looked at him with dignity.

'I should hope that a man in my position might be exempt.'

Japp merely waited.

'I was—now let me see ... Ah, yes. I was at the House. Left at half-past ten. Went for a walk along the Embankment. Watched some of the fireworks.'

'Nice to think there aren't any plots of that kind nowadays,' said Japp cheerily.

Laverton-West gave him a fish-like stare.

'Then I—er—walked home.'

'Reaching home—your London address is Onslow Square, I think—at what time?'

'I hardly know exactly.'

'Eleven? Half-past?'

'Somewhere about then.'

'Perhaps someone let you in.'

'No, I have my key.'

'Meet anybody whilst you were walking?'

'No—er—really, Chief Inspector, I *resent* these questions very much!'

'I assure you, it's just a matter of routine, Mr Laverton-West. They aren't personal, you know.'

The reply seemed to soothe the irate M.P.

'If that is all—'

'That is all for the present, Mr Laverton-West.'

'You will keep me informed—'

'Naturally, sir. By the way, let me introduce M. Hercule Poirot. You may have heard of him.'

Mr Laverton-West's eye fastened itself interestedly on the little Belgian.

'Yes—yes—I have heard the name.'

'Monsieur,' said Poirot, his manner suddenly very foreign. 'Believe me, my heart bleeds for you. Such a loss! Such agony as you must be enduring! Ah, but I will say no more. How magnificently the English hide their emotions.' He whipped out his cigarette case. 'Permit me—Ah, it is empty. Japp?'

Japp slapped his pockets and shook his head.

Laverton-West produced his own cigarette case, murmured, 'Er—have one of mine, M. Poirot.'

'Thank you—thank you.' The little man helped himself.

'As you say, M. Poirot,' resumed the other, 'we English do not parade our emotions. A stiff upper lip—that is our motto.'

He bowed to the two men and went out.

'Bit of a stuffed fish,' said Japp disgustedly. '*And* a boiled owl! The Plenderleith girl was quite right about him. Yet he's a good-looking sort of chap—might go down well with some woman who had no sense of humour. What about that cigarette?'

Poirot handed it over, shaking his head.

'Egyptian. An expensive variety.'

'No, that's no good. A pity, for I've never heard a weaker alibi! In fact, it wasn't an alibi at all ... You know, Poirot, it's a pity the boot wasn't on the other leg. If *she'd* been blackmailing him ... He's a lovely type for blackmail—would pay out like a lamb! Anything to avoid a scandal.'

'My friend, it is very pretty to reconstruct the case as you would like it to be, but that is not strictly our affair.'

'No, Eustace is our affair. I've got a few lines on him. Definitely a nasty fellow.'

'By the way, did you do as I suggested about Miss Plenderleith?'

'Yes. Wait a sec, I'll ring through and get the latest.'

He picked up the telephone receiver and spoke through it.

After a brief interchange he replaced it and looked up at Poirot.

'Pretty heartless piece of goods. Gone off to play golf. That's a nice thing to do when your friend's been murdered only the day before.'

Poirot uttered an exclamation.

'What's the matter now?' asked Japp.

But Poirot was murmuring to himself.

'Of course . . . of course . . . but naturally . . . What an imbecile I am—why, it leapt to the eye!'

Japp said rudely:

'Stop jabbering to yourself and let's go and tackle Eustace.'

He was amazed to see the radiant smile that spread over Poirot's face.

'But—yes—most certainly let us tackle him. For now, see you, I know everything—but everything!'

Major Eustace received the two men with the easy assurance of a man of the world.

His flat was small, a mere *pied à terre*, as he explained. He offered the two men a drink and when that was refused he took out his cigarette case.

Both Japp and Poirot accepted a cigarette. A quick glance passed between them.

'You smoke Turkish, I see,' said Japp as he twirled the cigarette between his fingers.

'Yes. I'm sorry, do you prefer a gasper? I've got one somewhere about.'

'No, no, this will do me very well.' Then he leaned forward—his tone changed. 'Perhaps you can guess, Major Eustace, what it was I came to see you about?'

The other shook his head. His manner was nonchalant. Major Eustace was a tall man, good-looking in a somewhat coarse fashion. There was a puffiness round the eyes—small, crafty eyes that belied the good-humoured geniality of his manner.

He said:

'No—I've no idea what brings such a big gun as a chief inspector to see me. Anything to do with my car?'

'No, it is not your car. I think you knew a Mrs Barbara Allen, Major Eustace?'

The major leant back, puffed out a cloud of smoke, and said in an enlightened voice:

'Oh, so that's it! Of course, I might have guessed. Very sad business.'

'You know about it?'

'Saw it in the paper last night. Too bad.'

'You knew Mrs Allen out in India, I think.'

'Yes, that's some years ago now.'

'Did you also know her husband?'

There was a pause—a mere fraction of a second—but during that fraction the little pig eyes flashed a quick look at the faces of the two men. Then he answered:

'No, as a matter of fact, I never came across Allen.'

'But you know something about him?'

'Heard he was by way of being a bad hat. Of course, that was only rumour.'

'Mrs Allen did not say anything?'

'Never talked about him.'

'You were on intimate terms with her?'

Major Eustace shrugged his shoulders.

'We were old friends, you know, old friends. But we didn't see each other very often.'

'But you did see her that last evening? The evening of November fifth?'

'Yes, as a matter of fact, I did.'

'You called at her house, I think.'

Major Eustace nodded. His voice took on a gentle, regretful note.

'Yes, she asked me to advise her about some investments. Of course, I can see what you're driving at—her state of mind—all that sort of thing. Well, really, it's very difficult to say. Her manner seemed normal enough and yet she *was* a bit jumpy, come to think of it.'

'But she gave you no hint as to what she contemplated doing?'

'Not the least in the world. As a matter of fact, when I said goodbye I said I'd ring her up soon and we'd do a show together.'

'You said you'd ring her up. Those were your last words?'

'Yes.'

'Curious. I have information that you said something quite different.'

Eustace changed colour.

'Well, of course, I can't remember the exact words.'

'My information is that what you actually said was, "*Well, think it over and let me know.*"'

'Let me see, yes I believe you're right. Not exactly that. I think I was suggesting she should let me know when she was free.'

'Not quite the same thing, is it?' said Japp.

Major Eustace shrugged his shoulders.

'My dear fellow, you can't expect a man to remember word for word what he said on any given occasion.'

'And what did Mrs Allen reply?'

'She said she'd give me a ring. That is, as near as I can remember.'

'And then you said, "*All right. So long.*"'

'Probably. Something of the kind anyway.'

Japp said quietly:

'You say that Mrs Allen asked you to advise her about her investments. *Did she, by any chance, entrust you with the sum of two hundred pounds in cash to invest for her?*'

Eustace's face flushed a dark purple. He leaned forward and growled out:

'What the devil do you mean by that?'

'Did she or did she not?'

'That's my business, Mr Chief Inspector.'

Japp said quietly:

'Mrs Allen drew out the sum of two hundred pounds in cash from her bank. Some of the money was in five-pound notes. The numbers of these can, of course, be traced.'

'What if she did?'

'*Was* the money for investment—or was it—blackmail, Major Eustace?'

'That's a preposterous idea. What next will you suggest?'

Japp said in his most official manner:

'I think, Major Eustace, that at this point I must ask you if you are willing to come to Scotland Yard and make a statement. There is, of course, no compulsion and you can, if you prefer it, have your solicitor present.'

'Solicitor? What the devil should I want with a solicitor? And what are you cautioning me for?'

'I am inquiring into the circumstances of the death of Mrs Allen.'

'Good God, man, you don't suppose—Why, that's nonsense! Look here, what happened was this. I called round to see Barbara by appointment . . .'

'That was at what time?'

'At about half-past nine, I should say. We sat and talked . . .'

'And smoked?'

'Yes, and smoked. Anything damaging in that?' demanded the major belligerently.

'Where did this conversation take place?'

'In the sitting-room. Left of the door as you go in. We talked together quite amicably, as I say. I left a little before half-past ten. I stayed for a minute on the doorstep for a few last words . . .'

'Last words—precisely,' murmured Poirot.

'Who are *you*, I'd like to know?' Eustace turned and spat the words at him. 'What are *you* butting in for?'

'I am Hercule Poirot,' said the little man with dignity.

'I don't care if you are the Achilles statue. As I say, Barbara and I parted quite amicably. I drove straight to the Far East Club. Got there at five and twenty to eleven and went straight up to the card-room. Stayed there playing bridge until one-thirty. Now then, put that in your pipe and smoke it.'

'I do not smoke the pipe,' said Poirot. 'It is a pretty *alibi* you have there.'

'It should be a pretty cast iron one anyway! Now then, sir,' he looked at Japp. 'Are you satisfied?'

'You remained in the sitting-room throughout your visit?'

'Yes.'

'You did not go upstairs to Mrs Allen's own boudoir?'

'No, I tell you. We stayed in the one room and didn't leave it.'

Japp looked at him thoughtfully for a minute or two. Then he said:

'How many sets of cuff links have you?'

'Cuff links? Cuff links? What's that got to do with it?'

'You are not bound to answer the question, of course.'

'Answer it? I don't mind answering it. I've got nothing to hide. And I shall demand an apology. There are these . . .' he stretched out his arms.

Japp noted the gold and platinum with a nod.

'And I've got these.'

He rose, opened a drawer and taking out a case, he opened it and shoved it rudely almost under Japp's nose.

'Very nice design,' said the chief inspector. 'I see one is broken—bit of enamel chipped off.'

'What of it?'

'You don't remember when that happened, I suppose?'

'A day or two ago, not longer.'

'Would you be surprised to hear that it happened *when you were visiting Mrs Allen*?'

'Why shouldn't it? I've not denied that I was there.' The major spoke haughtily. He continued to bluster, to act the part of the justly indignant man, but his hands were trembling.

Japp leaned forward and said with emphasis:

'Yes, but that bit of cuff link *wasn't found in the sitting-room.* It was found *upstairs* in Mrs Allen's boudoir—there in the room where she was killed, and where a man sat smoking *the same kind of cigarettes as you smoke.*'

The shot told. Eustace fell back into his chair. His eyes went from side to side. The collapse of the bully and the appearance of the craven was not a pretty sight.

'You've got nothing on me.' His voice was almost a whine. 'You're trying to frame me ... But you can't do it. I've got an alibi ... I never came near the house again that night ...'

Poirot in his turn, spoke.

'No, you did not come near the house again ... *You did not need to ...* For perhaps Mrs Allen *was already dead when you left it.*'

'That's impossible—impossible—She was just inside the door—she spoke to me—People must have heard her—seen her ...'

Poirot said softly:

'They heard *you* speaking to her . . . and pretending to wait for her answer and then speaking again . . . It is an old trick that . . . People may have *assumed* she was there, but they did not *see* her, because *they could not even say whether she was wearing evening dress or not—not even mention what colour she was wearing . . .*'

'My God—it isn't true—it isn't true—'

He was shaking now—collapsed . . .

Japp looked at him with disgust. He spoke crisply.

'I'll have to ask you, sir, to come with me.'

'You're arresting me?'

'Detained for inquiry—we'll put it that way.'

The silence was broken with a long, shuddering sigh. The despairing voice of the erstwhile blustering Major Eustace said:

'I'm sunk . . .'

Hercule Poirot rubbed his hands together and smiled cheerfully. He seemed to be enjoying himself.

'Pretty the way he went all to pieces,' said Japp with professional appreciation, later that day.

He and Poirot were driving in a car along the Brompton Road.

'He knew the game was up,' said Poirot absently.

'We've got plenty on him,' said Japp. 'Two or three different aliases, a tricky business over a cheque, and a very nice affair when he stayed at the Ritz and called himself Colonel de Bathe. Swindled half a dozen Piccadilly tradesmen. We're holding him on that charge for the moment—until we get this affair finally squared up. What's the idea of this rush to the country, old man?'

'My friend, an affair must be rounded off properly. Everything must be explained. I am on the quest of the mystery you suggested. The Mystery of the Missing Attaché-Case.'

'The Mystery of the Small Attaché-Case—that's what I called it—It isn't missing that I know of.'

'Wait, *mon ami*.'

The car turned into the mews. At the door of No. 14, Jane Plenderleith was just alighting from a small Austin Seven. She was in golfing clothes.

She looked from one to the other of the two men, then produced a key and opened the door.

'Come in, won't you?'

She led the way. Japp followed her into the sitting-room. Poirot remained for a minute or two in the hall, muttering something about:

'*C'est embêtant*—how difficult to get out of these sleeves.'

In a moment or two he also entered the sitting-room minus his overcoat but Japp's lips twitched under his moustache. He had heard the very faint squeak of an opening cupboard door.

Japp threw Poirot an inquiring glance and the other gave a hardly perceptible nod.

'We won't detain you, Miss Plenderleith,' said Japp briskly.

'Only came to ask if you could tell us the name of Mrs Allen's solicitor.'

'Her solicitor?' The girl shook her head. 'I don't even know that she had one.'

'Well, when she rented this house with you, someone must have drawn up the agreement?'

'No, I don't think so. You see, I took the house, the lease is in my name. Barbara paid me half the rent. It was quite informal.'

'I see. Oh! well, I suppose there's nothing doing then.'

'I'm sorry I can't help you,' said Jane politely.

'It doesn't really matter very much.' Japp turned towards the door. 'Been playing golf?'

'Yes.' She flushed. 'I suppose it seems rather heartless to you. But as a matter of fact it got me down rather, being here in this house. I felt I must go out and *do* something—tire myself—or I'd choke!'

She spoke with intensity.

Poirot said quickly:

'I comprehend, mademoiselle. It is most understandable—most natural. To sit in this house and think—no, it would not be pleasant.'

'So long as you understand,' said Jane shortly.

'You belong to a club?'

'Yes, I play at Wentworth.'

'It has been a pleasant day,' said Poirot.

'Alas, there are few leaves left on the trees now! A week ago the woods were magnificent.'

'It was quite lovely today.'

'Good afternoon, Miss Plenderleith,' said Japp formally. 'I'll let you know when there's anything definite. As a matter of fact we have got a man detained on suspicion.'

'What man?'

She looked at them eagerly.

'Major Eustace.'

She nodded and turned away, stooping down to put a match to the fire.

'Well?' said Japp as the car turned the corner of the mews.

Poirot grinned.

'It was quite simple. The key was in the door this time.'

'And—?'

Poirot smiled.

'*Eh, bien*, the golf clubs had gone—'

'Naturally. The girl isn't a fool, whatever else she is. *Anything else gone*?'

Poirot nodded his head.

'Yes, my friend—*the little attaché-case*!'

The accelerator leaped under Japp's foot.

'Damnation!' he said. 'I knew there was *something*. But what the devil is it? I searched that case pretty thoroughly.'

'My poor Japp—but it is—how do you say, "obvious, my dear Watson"?'

Japp threw him an exasperated look.

'Where are we going?' he asked.

Poirot consulted his watch.

'It is not yet four o'clock. We could get to Wentworth, I think, before it is dark.'

'Do you think she really went there?'

'I think so—yes. She would know that we might make inquiries. Oh, yes, I think we will find that she has been there.'

Japp grunted.

'Oh well, come on.' He threaded his way dexterously through the traffic. 'Though what this attaché-case business has to do with the crime I can't imagine. I can't see that it's got anything at all to do with it.'

'Precisely, my friend, I agree with you—it has nothing to do with it.'

'Then why—No, don't tell me! Order and method and everything nicely rounded off! Oh, well, it's a fine day.'

The car was a fast one. They arrived at Wentworth Golf Club a little after half-past four. There was no great congestion there on a week day. Poirot went straight to the caddie-master and asked for Miss Plenderleith's clubs. She would be playing on a different course tomorrow, he explained.

The caddie-master raised his voice and a boy sorted through some golf clubs standing in a corner. He finally produced a bag bearing the initials, J.P.

'Thank you,' said Poirot. He moved away, then

turned carelessly and asked, 'She did not leave with you a small attaché-case also, did she?'

'Not today, sir. May have left it in the clubhouse.'

'She was down here today?'

'Oh, yes, I saw her.'

'Which caddie did she have, do you know? She's mislaid an attaché-case and can't remember where she had it last.'

'She didn't take a caddie. She came in here and bought a couple of balls. Just took out a couple of irons. I rather fancy she had a little case in her hand then.'

Poirot turned away with a word of thanks. The two men walked round the clubhouse. Poirot stood a moment admiring the view.

'It is beautiful, is it not, the dark pine trees—and then the lake. Yes, the lake—'

Japp gave him a quick glance.

'That's the idea, is it?'

Poirot smiled.

'I think it possible that someone may have seen something. I should set the inquiries in motion if I were you.'

Poirot stepped back, his head a little on one side as he surveyed the arrangement of the room. A chair here—another chair there. Yes, that was very nice. And now a ring at the bell—that would be Japp.

The Scotland Yard man came in alertly.

'Quite right, old cock! Straight from the horse's mouth. A young woman was seen to throw something into the lake at Wentworth yesterday. Description of her answers to Jane Plenderleith. We managed to fish it up without much difficulty. A lot of reeds just there.'

'And it was?'

'It was the attaché-case all right! But *why*, in heaven's name? Well, it beats me! Nothing inside it—not even the magazines. Why a presumably sane young woman should want to fling an expensively-fitted dressing-case into a lake—d'you know, I worried all night because I couldn't get the hang of it.'

'*Mon pauvre Japp*! But you need worry no longer. Here is the answer coming. The bell has just rung.'

George, Poirot's immaculate man-servant, opened the door and announced:

'Miss Plenderleith.'

The girl came into the room with her usual air of complete self-assurance. She greeted the two men.

'I asked you to come here—' explained Poirot. 'Sit here, will you not, and you here, Japp—because I have certain news to give you.'

The girl sat down. She looked from one to the other, pushing aside her hat. She took it off and laid it aside impatiently.

'Well,' she said. 'Major Eustace has been arrested.'

'You saw that, I expect, in the morning paper?'

'Yes.'

'He is at the moment charged with a minor offence,' went on Poirot. 'In the meantime we are gathering evidence in connection with the murder.'

'It *was* murder, then?'

The girl asked it eagerly.

Poirot nodded his head.

'Yes,' he said. 'It was murder. The wilful destruction of one human being by another human being.'

She shivered a little.

'Don't,' she murmured. 'It sounds horrible when you say it like that.'

'Yes—but it is horrible!'

He paused—then he said:

'Now, Miss Plenderleith, I am going to tell you just how I arrived at the truth in this matter.'

She looked from Poirot to Japp. The latter was smiling.

'He has his methods, Miss Plenderleith,' he said. 'I humour him, you know. I think we'll listen to what he has to say.'

Poirot began:

'As you know, mademoiselle, I arrived with my friend at the scene of the crime on the morning of November the sixth. We went into the room where the body of Mrs Allen had been found and I was struck at once by several significant details. There were things, you see, in that room that were decidedly odd.'

'Go on,' said the girl.

'To begin with,' said Poirot, 'there was the smell of cigarette smoke.'

'I think you're exaggerating there, Poirot,' said Japp. '*I* didn't smell anything.'

Poirot turned on him in a flash.

'Precisely. *You did not smell any stale smoke. No more did I.* And that was very, very strange—for the door and the window were both closed and on an ashtray there were the stubs of no fewer than ten cigarettes. It was odd, very odd, that the room should smell—as it did, perfectly fresh.'

'So that's what you were getting at!' Japp sighed. 'Always have to get at things in such a tortuous way.'

'Your Sherlock Holmes did the same. He drew attention, remember, to the curious incident of the dog in the night-time—and the answer to that was there was no curious incident. The dog did nothing in the night-time. To proceed:

'The next thing that attracted my attention was a wrist-watch worn by the dead woman.'

'What about it?'

'Nothing particular about it, but it was worn on the

right wrist. Now in my experience it is more usual for a watch to be worn on the left wrist.'

Japp shrugged his shoulders. Before he could speak, Poirot hurried on:

'But as you say, there is nothing very definite about *that*. Some people *prefer* to wear one on the right hand. And now I come to something really interesting—I come, my friends, to the writing-bureau.'

'Yes, I guessed that,' said Japp.

'That was really *very* odd—*very* remarkable! For wo reasons. The first reason was that something was missing from that writing-table.'

Jane Plenderleith spoke.

'What was missing?'

Poirot turned to her.

'*A sheet of blotting-paper, mademoiselle.* The blotting-book had on top a clean, untouched piece of blotting-paper.'

Jane shrugged her shoulders.

'Really, M. Poirot. People do occasionally tear off a very much used sheet!'

'Yes, but what do they do with it? Throw it into the waste-paper basket, do they not? *But it was not in the waste-paper basket.* I looked.'

Jane Plenderleith seemed impatient.

'Because it had probably been already thrown away the day before. The sheet was clean because Barbara hadn't written any letters that day.'

'That could hardly be the case, mademoiselle. *For Mrs Allen was seen going to the post-box that evening. Therefore she must have been writing letters.* She could not write downstairs—there were no writing materials. She would be hardly likely to go to *your* room to write. So, then, what had happened to the sheet of paper on which she had blotted her letters? It is true that people sometimes throw things in the fire instead of the waste-paper basket, but there was only a gas fire in the room. *And the fire downstairs had not been alight the previous day, since you told me it was all laid ready when you put a match to it.*'

He paused.

'A curious little problem. I looked everywhere, in the waste-paper baskets, in the dustbin, but I could not find a sheet of used blotting-paper—and that seemed to me very important. It looked as though someone had deliberately taken that sheet of blotting-paper away. Why? Because there was writing on it that could easily have been read by holding it up to a mirror.

'But there was a second curious point about the writing-table. Perhaps, Japp, you remember roughly the arrangement of it? Blotter and inkstand in the centre, pen tray to the left, calendar and quill pen to the right. *Eh bien*? You do not see? The quill pen, remember, I examined, it was for show only—it had not been used. Ah! *still* you do not see? I will say it again. Blotter in the centre, pen tray to the left—to the *left*, Japp. But is it not usual to find a pen tray *on the right*, convenient to *the right hand*?

'Ah, now it comes to you, does it not? The pen tray on the *left*—the wrist-watch on the *right* wrist—the blotting-paper removed—and something else brought *into* the room—the ashtray with the cigarette ends!

'That room was fresh and pure smelling, Japp, a room in which the window had been *open*, not closed all night . . . And I made myself a picture.'

He spun round and faced Jane.

'A picture of you, mademoiselle, driving up in your taxi, paying it off, running up the stairs, calling perhaps, "Barbara"—and you open the door and you find your friend there lying dead with the pistol clasped in her hand—the left hand, naturally, *since she is left-handed* and therefore, too, the bullet has entered on the *left side of the head*. There is a note there addressed to you. It tells you what it is that has driven her to take her own life. It was, I fancy, a very moving letter . . . A young, gentle, unhappy woman driven by blackmail to take her life . . .

'I think that, almost at once, the idea flashed into your head. This was a certain man's doing. Let him be punished—fully and adequately punished! You take the pistol, wipe it and place it in the *right* hand. You take the note and you tear off the top sheet of the blotting-paper on which the note has been blotted. You go down, light the fire and put them both on the flames. Then you carry up the ashtray—to further the illusion that two people sat there talking—and you also take up a fragment of enamel cuff link that is on the floor. That is a lucky find and you expect it to clinch matters. Then you close the window and lock the door. There must be no suspicion that you have tampered with the room. The police must see it exactly as it is—so you do not seek help in the mews but ring up the police straightaway.

'And so it goes on. You play your chosen role with judgment and coolness. You refuse at first to say anything but cleverly you suggest doubts of suicide. Later you are quite ready to set us on the trail of Major Eustace . . .

'Yes, mademoiselle, it was clever—a very clever murder—for that is what it is. The attempted murder of Major Eustace.'

Jane Plenderleith sprang to her feet.

'It wasn't murder—it was justice. That man *hounded* poor Barbara to her death! She was so sweet and helpless. You see, poor kid, she got involved with a man in India when she first went out. She was only seventeen and he was a married man years older than her. Then she had a baby. She could have put it in a home but she wouldn't hear of that. She went off to some out of the way spot and came back calling herself Mrs Allen. Later the child died. She came back here and she fell in love with Charles—that pompous, stuffed owl; she adored him—and he took her adoration very complacently. If he had been a different kind of man I'd have advised her to tell him everything. But as it was, I urged her to hold her tongue. After all, nobody knew anything about that business except me.

'And then that devil Eustace turned up! You know the rest. He began to bleed her systematically, but it wasn't till that last evening that she realized that she was exposing Charles too, to the risk of scandal. Once married to Charles, Eustace had got her where he wanted her—married to a rich man with a horror of any scandal! When Eustace had gone with the money she had got for him she sat thinking it over. Then she came up and wrote a letter to me. She said she loved Charles and couldn't live without him, but that for his own sake she mustn't marry him. She was taking the best way out, she said.'

Jane flung her head back.

'Do you wonder I did what I did? And you stand there calling it *murder*!'

'Because it is murder,' Poirot's voice was stern. 'Murder can sometimes seem justified, *but it is murder all the same.* You are truthful and clear-minded—face the truth, mademoiselle! Your friend died, in the last resort, *because she had not the courage to live.* We may sympathize with her. We may pity her. But the fact remains—the act was *hers*—not another.'

He paused.

'And you? That man is now in prison, he will serve a long sentence for other matters. Do you really wish, of your own volition, to destroy the life—the *life*, mind—of *any* human being?'

She stared at him. Her eyes darkened. Suddenly she muttered:

'No. You're right. I don't.'

Then, turning on her heel, she went swiftly from the room. The outer door banged . . .

Japp gave a long—a very prolonged—whistle.

'Well, I'm damned!' he said.

Poirot sat down and smiled at him amiably. It was quite a long time before the silence was broken. Then Japp said:

'Not murder disguised as suicide, but suicide made to look like murder!'

'Yes, and very cleverly done, too. Nothing over-emphasized.'

Japp said suddenly:

'But the attaché-case? Where did that come in?'

'But, my dear, my very dear friend, I have already told you that *it did not come in*.'

'Then why—'

'The golf clubs. The golf clubs, Japp. *They were the golf clubs of a left-handed person.* Jane Plenderleith kept her clubs at Wentworth. Those were Barbara Allen's clubs. No wonder the girl got, as you say, the wind up when we opened that cupboard. Her whole plan might have been ruined. But she is quick, she realized that she had, for one short moment, given herself away. *She* saw that *we* saw. So she does the best thing she can think of on the spur of the moment. She tries to focus our attention on the *wrong object*. She says of the attaché-case "That's mine. I—it came back with me this morning. So there can't be anything there." And, as she hoped, away you go on the false trail. For the same reason, when she sets out the following day to get rid of the golf clubs, she continues to use the attaché-case as a—what is it—kippered herring?'

'Red herring. Do you mean that her real object was—?'

'Consider, my friend. Where is the best place to get rid of a bag of golf clubs? One cannot burn them or put them in a dustbin. If one leaves them somewhere they may be returned to you. Miss Plenderleith took them to a golf course. She leaves them in the clubhouse while she gets a couple of irons from her own bag, and then she goes round without a caddy. Doubtless at judicious intervals she breaks a club in half and throws it into some deep undergrowth, and ends by throwing the empty bag away. If anyone should find a broken golf club here and there it will not create surprise. People have been known to brcak and throw away *all* their clubs in a mood of intense exasperation over the game! It is, in fact, that kind of game!

'But since she realizes that her actions may still be a matter of interest, she throws that useful red herring—the attaché-case—in a somewhat spectacular manner into the lake—and that, my friend, is the truth of "The Mystery of the Attaché-Case."'

Japp looked at his friend for some moments in silence. Then he rose, clapped him on the shoulder, and burst out laughing.

'Not so bad for an old dog! Upon my word, you take the cake! Come out and have a spot of lunch?'

'With pleasure, my friend, but we will not have the cake. Indeed, an Omelette aux Champignons, Blanquette de Veau, Petits pois à la Francaise, and—to follow—a Baba au Rhum.'

'Lead me to it,' said Japp.

The Case of the Rich Woman

The name of Mrs Abner Rymer was brought to Mr Parker Pyne. He knew the name and he raised his eyebrows.

Presently his client was shown into the room.

Mrs Rymer was a tall woman, big-boned. Her figure was ungainly and the velvet dress and the heavy fur coat she wore did not disguise the fact. The knuckles of her large hands were pronounced. Her face was big and broad and highly coloured. Her black hair was fashionably dressed, and there were many tips of curled ostrich in her hat.

She plumped herself down on a chair with a nod. 'Good-morning,' she said. Her voice had a rough accent. 'If you're any good at all you'll tell me how to spend my money!'

'Most original,' murmured Mr Parker Pyne. 'Few ask me that in these days. So you really find it difficult, Mrs Rymer?'

'Yes, I do,' said the lady bluntly. 'I've got three fur coats, a lot of Paris dresses and such like. I've got a car and a house in Park Lane. I've had a yacht but I don't like the sea. I've got a lot of those high-class servants that look down their nose at you. I've travelled a bit and seen foreign parts. And I'm blessed if I can think of anything more to buy or do.' She looked hopefully at Mr Pyne.

'There are hospitals,' he said.

'What? Give it away, you mean? No, that I won't do! That money was worked for, let me tell you, worked for hard. If you think I'm going to hand it out like so much dirt—well, you're mistaken. I want to spend it; spend it and get some good out of it. Now, if you've got any ideas that are worthwhile in that line, you can depend on a good fee.'

'Your proposition interests me,' said Mr Pyne. 'You do not mention a country house.'

'I forgot it, but I've got one. Bores me to death.'

'You must tell me more about yourself. Your problem is not easy to solve.'

'I'll tell you and willing. I'm not ashamed of what I've come from. Worked in a farmhouse, I did, when I was a girl. Hard work it was too. Then I took up with Abner—he was a workman in the mills near by. He courted me for eight years, and then we got married.'

'And you were happy?' asked Mr Pyne.

'I was. He was a good man to me, Abner. We had a hard struggle of it, though; he was out of a job twice, and children coming along. Four we had, three boys and a girl. And none of them lived to grow up. I dare say it would have been different if they had.' Her face softened; looked suddenly younger.

'His chest was weak—Abner's was. They wouldn't take him for the war. He did well at home. He was made foreman. He was a clever fellow, Abner. He worked out a process. They treated him fair, I will say; gave him a good sum for it. He used that money for another idea of his. That brought in money hand over fist. It's still coming in.

'Mind you, it was rare fun at first. Having a house

and a tip-top bathroom and servants of one's own. No more cooking and scrubbing and washing to do. Just sit back on your silk cushions in the drawing-room and ring the bell for tea—like any countess might! Grand fun it was, and we enjoyed it. And then we came up to London. I went to swell dressmakers for my clothes. We went to Paris and the Riviera. Rare fun it was.'

'And then,' said Mr Parker Pyne.

'We got used to it, I suppose,' said Mrs Rymer. 'After a bit it didn't seem so much fun. Why, there were days when we didn't even fancy our meals properly—us, with any dish we fancied to choose from! As for baths—well, in the end, one bath a day's enough for anyone. And Abner's health began to worry him. Paid good money to doctors, we did, but they couldn't do anything. They tried this and they tried that. But it was no use. He died.' She paused. 'He was a young man, only forty-three.'

Mr Pyne nodded sympathetically.

'That was five years ago. Money's still rolling in. It seems wasteful not to be able to do anything with it. But as I tell you, I can't think of anything else to buy that I haven't got already.'

'In other words,' said Mr Pyne, 'your life is dull. You are not enjoying it.'

'I'm sick of it,' said Mrs Rymer gloomily. 'I've no friends. The new lot only want subscriptions, and they laugh at me behind my back. The old lot won't have anything to do with me. My rolling up in a car makes them shy. Can you do anything or suggest anything?'

'It is possible that I can,' said Mr Pyne slowly. 'It will be difficult, but I believe there is a chance of success. I think it's possible I can give you back what you have lost—your interest in life.'

'How?' demanded Mrs Rymer curtly.

'That,' said Mr Parker Pyne, 'is my professional secret. I never disclose my methods beforehand. The question is, will you take a chance? I do not guarantee success, but I do think there is a reasonable possibility of it.

'I shall have to adopt unusual methods, and therefore it will be expensive. My charges will be one thousand pounds, payable in advance.'

'You can open your mouth all right, can't you?' said Mrs Rymer appreciatively. 'Well, I'll risk it. I'm used to paying top price. Only, when I pay for a thing, I take good care that I get it.'

'You shall get it,' said Mr Parker Pyne. 'Never fear.'

'I'll send you the cheque this evening,' said Mrs Rymer, rising. 'I'm sure I don't know why I should trust you. Fools and their money are soon parted, they say. I dare say I'm a fool. You've got nerve, to advertise in all the papers that you can make people happy!'

'Those advertisements cost me money,' said Mr Pyne. 'If I could not make my words good, that money would be wasted. I *know* what causes unhappiness, and consequently I have a clear idea of how to produce an opposite condition.'

Mrs Rymer shook her head doubtfully and departed, leaving a cloud of expensive mixed essences behind her.

The handsome Claude Luttrell strolled into the office. 'Something in my line?'

Mr Pyne shook his head. 'Nothing so simple,' he said. 'No, this is a difficult case. We must, I fear, take a few risks. We must attempt the unusual.'

'Mrs Oliver?'

Mr Pyne smiled at the mention of the world-famous novelist. 'Mrs Oliver,' he said, 'is really the most conventional of all of us. I have in mind a bold and audacious coup. By the way, you might ring up Dr Antrobus.'

'Antrobus?'

'Yes. His services will be needed.'

A week later Mrs Rymer once more entered Mr Parker Pyne's office. He rose to receive her.

'This delay, I assure you, has been necessary,' he said. 'Many things had to be arranged, and I had to secure the services of an unusual man who had to come half-across Europe.'

'Oh!' She said it suspiciously. It was constantly present in her mind that she had paid out a cheque for a thousand pounds and the cheque had been cashed.

Mr Parker Pyne touched a buzzer. A young girl, dark, Oriental looking, but dressed in white nurse's kit, answered it.

'Is everything ready, Nurse de Sara?'

'Yes. Doctor Constantine is waiting.'

'What are you going to do?' asked Mrs Rymer with a touch of uneasiness.

'Introduce you to some Eastern magic, dear lady,' said Mr Parker Pyne.

'Mrs Rymer followed the nurse up to the next floor. Here she was ushered into a room that bore no relation to the rest of the house. Oriental embroideries covered the walls. There were divans with soft cushions and beautiful rugs on the floor. A man was bending over a coffee-pot. He straightened as they entered.

'Doctor Constantine,' said the nurse.

The doctor was dressed in European clothes, but his face was swarthy and his eyes were dark and oblique with a peculiarly piercing power in their glance.

'So this is my patient?' he said in a low, vibrant voice.

'I'm not a patient,' said Mrs Rymer.

'Your body is not sick,' said the doctor, 'but your soul

is weary. We of the East know how to cure that disease. Sit down and drink a cup of coffee.'

Mrs Rymer sat down and accepted a tiny cup of the fragrant brew. As she sipped it the doctor talked.

'Here in the West, they treat only the body. A mistake. The body is only the instrument. A tune is played upon it. It may be a sad, weary tune. It may be a gay tune full of delight. The last is what we shall give you. You have money. You shall spend it and enjoy. Life shall be worth living again. It is easy—easy—so easy . . .'

A feeling of languor crept over Mrs Rymer. The figures of the doctor and the nurse grew hazy. She felt blissfully happy and very sleepy. The doctor's figure grew bigger. The whole world was growing bigger.

The doctor was looking into her eyes. 'Sleep,' he was saying. 'Sleep. Your eyelids are closing. Soon you will sleep. You will sleep. You will sleep . . .'

Mrs Rymer's eyelids closed. She floated with a wonderful great big world . . .

When her eyes opened it seemed to her that a long time had passed. She remembered several things vaguely—strange, impossible dreams; then a feeling of waking; then further dreams. She remembered something about a car and the dark, beautiful girl in a nurse's uniform bending over her.

Anyway, she was properly awake now, and in her own bed.

At least, was it her own bed? It felt different. It lacked the delicious softness of her own bed. It was vaguely reminiscent of days almost forgotten. She moved, and it creaked. Mrs Rymer's bed in Park Lane never creaked.

She looked round. Decidedly, this was not Park Lane. Was it a hospital? No, she decided, not a hospital. Nor was it a hotel. It was a bare room, the walls an uncertain shade of lilac. There was a deal wash-stand with a jug and basin upon it. There was a deal chest of drawers and a tin trunk. There were unfamiliar clothes hanging on pegs. There was the bed covered with a much-mended quilt and there was herself in it.

'Where *am* I?' said Mrs Rymer.

The door opened and a plump little woman bustled in. She had red cheeks and a good-humoured air. Her sleeves were rolled up and she wore an apron.

'There!' she exclaimed. 'She's awake. Come in, doctor.'

Mrs Rymer opened her mouth to say several things—but they remained unsaid, for the man who followed the plump woman into the room was not in the least like the elegant, swarthy Doctor Constantine. He was a bent old man who peered through thick glasses.

'That's better,' he said, advancing to the bed and taking up Mrs Rymer's wrist. 'You'll soon be better now, my dear.'

'What's been the matter with me?' demanded Mrs Rymer.

'You had a kind of seizure,' said the doctor. 'You've been unconscious for a day or two. Nothing to worry about.'

'Gave us a fright you did, Hannah,' said the plump woman. 'You've been raving too, saying the oddest things.'

'Yes, yes, Mrs Gardner,' said the doctor repressively. 'But we musn't excite the patient. You'll soon be up and about again, my dear.'

'But don't you worry about the work, Hannah.' said Mrs Gardner. 'Mrs Roberts has been in to give me a hand and we've got on fine. Just lie still and get well, my dear.'

'Why do you call me Hannah?' said Mrs Rymer.

'Well, it's your name,' said Mrs Gardner, bewildered.

'No, it isn't. My name is Amelia. Amelia Rymer. Mrs Abner Rymer.'

The doctor and Mrs Gardner exchanged glances.

'Well, just you lie still,' said Mrs Gardner.

'Yes, yes; no worry,' said the doctor.

They withdrew. Mrs Rymer lay puzzling. Why did they call her Hannah, and why had they exchanged that glance of amused incredulity when she had given them her name? Where was she and what had happened?

She slipped out of bed. She felt a little uncertain on her legs, but she walked slowly to the small dormer window and looked out—on a farmyard! Completely mystified, she went back to bed. What was she doing in a farmhouse that she had never seen before?

Mrs Gardner re-entered the room with a bowl of soup on a tray.

Mrs Rymer began her questions. 'What am I doing in this house?' she demanded. 'Who brought me here?'

'Nobody brought you, my dear. It's your home. Leastways, you've lived here for the last five years—and me not suspecting once that you were liable to fits.'

'*Lived* here! *Five* years?'

'That's right. Why, Hannah, you don't mean that you still don't remember?'

'I've never lived here! I've never seen you before.'

'You see, you've had this illness and you've forgotten.'

'I've never lived here.'

'But you have, my dear.' Suddenly Mrs Gardner darted across to the chest of drawers and brought to Mrs Rymer a faded photograph in a frame.

It represented a group of four persons: a bearded man, a plump woman (Mrs Gardner), a tall, lank man with a pleasantly sheepish grin, and somebody in a print dress and apron—herself!

Stupefied, Mrs Rymer gazed at the photograph. Mrs Gardner put the soup down beside her and quietly left the room.

Mrs Rymer sipped the soup mechanically. It was good soup, strong and hot. All the time her brain was in a whirl. Who was mad? Mrs Gardner or herself? One of them must be! But there was the doctor too.

'I'm Amelia Rymer,' she said firmly to herself. 'I know I'm Amelia Rymer and nobody's going to tell me different.'

She had finished the soup. She put the bowl back on the tray. A folded newspaper caught her eye and she picked it up and looked at the date on it, October 19. What day had she gone to Mr Parker Pyne's office? Either the fifteenth or the sixteenth. Then she must have been ill for three days.

'That rascally doctor!' said Mrs Rymer wrathfully.

All the same, she was a shade relieved. She had heard of cases where people had forgotten who they were for years at a time. She had been afraid some such thing had happened to her.

She began turning the pages of the paper, scanning the columns idly, when suddenly a paragraph caught her eye.

> Mrs Abner Rymer, widow of Abner Rymer, the 'button shank' king, was removed yesterday to a private home for mental cases. For the past two days she has persisted in declaring she was not herself, but a servant girl named Hannah Moorhouse.

'Hannah Moorhouse! So that's it,' said Mrs Rymer. 'She's me and I'm her. Kind of double, I suppose. Well, we can soon put *that* right! If that oily hypocrite of a Parker Pyne is up to some game or other—'

But at this minute her eye was caught by the name Constantine staring at her from the printed page. This time it was a headline.

DR CONSTANTINE'S CLAIM

> At a farewell lecture given last night on the eve of his departure for Japan, Dr Claudius Constantine advanced some startling theories. He declared that it was possible to prove the existence of the soul by transferring a soul from one body to another. In the course of his experiments in the East he had, he claimed, successfully effected a double transfer—the soul of a hypnotized body A being transferred to a hypnotized body B and the soul of body B to the soul of body A. On recovering from the hypnotic sleep, A declared herself to be B, and B thought herself to be A. For the experiment to succeed, it was necessary to find two people with a great bodily resemblance. It was an undoubted fact that two people resembling each other were *en rapport*. This was very noticeable in the case of twins, but two strangers, varying widely in social position, but with a marked similarity of feature, were found to exhibit the same harmony of structure.

Mrs Rymer cast the paper from her. 'The scoundrel! The black scoundrel!' She saw the whole thing now! It was a dastardly plot to get hold of her money. This Hannah Moorhouse was Mr Pyne's tool—possibly an innocent one. He and that devil Constantine had brought off this fantastic coup.

But she'd expose him! She'd show him up! She'd have the law on him! She'd tell everyone—

Abruptly Mrs Rymer came to a stop in the tide of her indignation. She remembered the first paragraph. Hannah Moorhouse had not been a docile tool. She had protested; had declared her individuality. And what had happened?

'Clapped into a lunatic asylum, poor girl,' said Mrs Rymer.

A chill ran down her spine.

A lunatic asylum. They got you in there and they never let you get out. The more you said you were sane, the less they'd believe you. There you were and there you stayed. No, Mrs Rymer wasn't going to run the risk of that.

The door opened and Mrs Gardner came in.

'Ah, you've drunk your soup, my dear. That's good. You'll soon be better now.'

'When was I taken ill?' demanded Mrs Rymer.

'Let me see. It was three days ago—on Wednesday. That was the fifteenth. You were took bad about four o'clock.'

'Ah!' The ejaculation was fraught with meaning. It had been just about four o'clock when Mrs Rymer had entered the presence of Doctor Constantine.

'You slipped down in your chair,' said Mrs Gardner. "Oh!" you says. "Oh!" just like that. And then: "I'm falling asleep," you says in a dreamy voice. "I'm falling asleep." And fall asleep you did, and we put you to bed and sent for the doctor, and here you've been ever since.'

'I suppose,' Mrs Rymer ventured, 'there isn't any way you could know who I am—apart from my face, I mean.'

'Well, that's a queer thing to say,' said Mrs Gardner. 'What is there to go by better than a person's face, I'd like to know? There's your birthmark, though, if that satisfies you better.'

'A birthmark?' said Mrs Rymer, brightening. She had no such thing. 'Strawberry mark just under the right elbow,' said Mrs Gardner. 'Look for yourself, my dear.'

'This will prove it,' said Mrs Rymer to herself. She knew that she had no strawberry mark under the right elbow. She turned back the sleeve of her nightdress. The strawberry mark was there.

Mrs Rymer burst into tears.

Four days later Mrs Rymer rose from her bed. She had thought out several plans of action and rejected them.

She might show the paragraph in the paper to Mrs Gardner and explain. Would they believe her? Mrs Rymer was sure they would not.

She might go to the police. Would they believe her? Again she thought not.

She might go to Mr Pyne's office. That idea undoubtedly pleased her best. For one thing, she would like to tell that oily scoundrel what she thought of him. She was debarred from putting this plan into operation by a vital obstacle. She was at present in Cornwall (so she had learned), and she had no money for the journey to London. Two and fourpence in a worn purse seemed to represent her financial position.

And so, after four days, Mrs Rymer made a sporting decision. For the present she would accept things! She was Hannah Moorhouse. Very well, she would be Hannah Moorhouse. For the present she would accept that role, and later, when she had saved sufficient money, she would go to London and beard the swindler in his den.

And having thus decided, Mrs Rymer accepted her role with perfect good temper, even with a kind of sardonic amusement. History was repeating itself indeed. This life reminded her of her girlhood. How long ago that seemed!

★ ★ ★

The work was a bit hard after her years of soft living, but after the first week she found herself slipping into the ways of the farm.

Mrs Gardner was a good-tempered, kindly woman. Her husband, a big, taciturn man, was kindly also. The lank, shambling man of the photograph had gone; another farmhand came in his stead, a good-humoured giant of forty-five, slow of speech and thought, but with a shy twinkle in his blue eyes.

The weeks went by. At last the day came when Mrs Rymer had enough money to pay her fare to London. But she did not go. She put it off. Time enough, she thought. She wasn't easy in her mind about asylums yet. That scoundrel, Parker Pyne, was clever. He'd get a doctor to say she was mad and she'd be clapped away out of sight with no one knowing anything about it.

'Besides,' said Mrs Rymer to herself, 'a bit of a change does one good.'

She rose early and worked hard. Joe Welsh, the new farmhand, was ill that winter, and she and Mrs Gardner nursed him. The big man was pathetically dependent on them.

Spring came—lambing time; there were wild flowers in the hedges, a treacherous softness in the air. Joe Welsh gave Hannah a hand with her work. Hannah did Joe's mending.

Sometimes, on Sundays, they went for a walk together. Joe was a widower. His wife had died four years before. Since her death he had, he frankly confessed it, taken a drop too much.

He didn't go much to the Crown nowadays. He bought himself some new clothes. Mr and Mrs Gardner laughed.

Hannah made fun of Joe. She teased him about his clumsiness. Joe didn't mind. He looked bashful but happy.

After spring came summer—a good summer that year. Everyone worked hard.

Harvest was over. The leaves were red and golden on the trees.

It was October eighth when Hannah looked up one day from a cabbage she was cutting and saw Mr Parker Pyne leaning over the fence.

'You!' said Hannah, alias Mrs Rymer. 'You . . .'

It was some time before she got it all out, and when she had said her say, she was out of breath.

Mr Parker Pyne smiled blandly. 'I quite agree with you,' he said.

'A cheat and a liar, that's what you are!' said Mrs Rymer, repeating herself. 'You with your Constantines and your hypnotizing, and that poor girl Hannah Moorhouse shut up with—loonies.'

'No,' said Mr Parker Pyne, 'there you misjudge me. Hannah Moorhouse is not in a lunatic asylum, because Hannah Moorhouse never existed.'

'Indeed?' said Mrs Rymer. 'And what about the photograph of her that I saw with my own eyes?'

'Faked,' said Mr Pyne. 'Quite a simple thing to manage.'

'And the piece in the paper about her?'

'The whole paper was faked so as to include two items in a natural manner which would carry conviction. As it did.'

'That rogue, Doctor Constantine!'

'An assumed name—assumed by a friend of mine with a talent for acting.'

Mrs Rymer snorted. 'Ho! And I wasn't hypnotized either, I suppose?'

'As a matter of fact, you were not. You drank in your coffee a preparation of Indian hemp. After that, other drugs were administered and you were brought down here by car and allowed to recover consciousness.'

'Then Mrs Gardner has been in it all the time?' said Mrs Rymer.

Mr Parker Pyne nodded.

'Bribed by you, I suppose! Or filled up with a lot of lies!'

'Mrs Gardner trusts me,' said Mr Pyne. 'I once saved her only son from penal servitude.'

Something in his manner silenced Mrs Rymer on that tack. 'What about the birthmark!' she demanded.

Mr Pyne smiled. 'It is already fading. In another six months it will have disappeared altogether.'

'And what's the meaning of all this tomfoolery? Making a fool of me, sticking me down here as a servant—me with all that good money in the bank. But I suppose I needn't ask. You've been helping yourself to it, my fine fellow. That's the meaning of all this.'

'It is true,' said Mr Parker Pyne, 'that I did obtain from you, while you were under the influence of drugs, a power of attorney and that during your—er—absence, I have assumed control of your financial affairs, but I can assure you, my dear madam, that apart from that original thousand pounds, no money of yours has found its way into my pocket. As a matter of fact, by judicious investments your financial position is actually improved.' He beamed at her.

'Then why—?' began Mrs Rymer.

'I am going to ask you a question, Mrs Rymer,' said Mr Parker Pyne. 'You are an honest woman. You will answer me honestly, I know. I am going to ask you if you are happy.'

'Happy! That's a pretty question! Steal a woman's money and ask her if she's happy. I like your impudence!'

'You are still angry,' he said. 'Most natural. But leave my misdeeds out of it for the moment. Mrs Rymer, when you came to my office a year ago today, you were an unhappy woman. Will you tell me that you are unhappy now? If so, I apologize, and you are at liberty to take what steps you please against me. Moreover, I will refund the thousand pounds you paid me. Come, Mrs Rymer, are you an unhappy woman now?'

Mrs Rymer looked at Mr Parker Pyne, but she dropped her eyes when she spoke at last.

'No,' she said. 'I'm not unhappy.' A tone of wonder crept into her voice. 'You've got me there. I admit it. I've not been as happy as I am now since Abner died. I—I'm going to marry a man who works here—Joe Welsh. Our banns are going up next Sunday; that, is they *were* going up next Sunday.'

'But now, of course, everything is different.'

Mrs Rymer's face flamed. She took a step forward.

'What do you mean, different? Do you think that if I had all the money in the world it would make me a lady? I don't want to be a lady, thank you; a helpless good-for-nothing lot they are. Joe's good enough for me and I'm good enough for him. We suit each other and we're going to be happy. As you for, Mr Nosey Parker, you take yourself off and don't interfere with what doesn't concern you!'

Mr Parker Pyne took a paper from his pocket and handed it to her. 'The power of attorney,' he said. 'Shall I tear it up? You will assume control of your own fortune now, I take it.'

A strange expression came over Mrs Rymer's face. She thrust back the paper.

'Take it. I've said hard things to you—and some of them you deserved. You're a downy fellow, but all the same I trust you. Seven hundred pounds I'll have in the bank here—that'll buy us a farm we've got our eye on. The rest of it—well, let the hospitals have it.'

'You cannot mean to hand over your entire fortune to hospitals?'

'That's just what I do mean. Joe's a dear, good fellow, but he's weak. Give him money and you'd ruin him. I've got him off the drink now, and I'll keep him off it. Thank God, I know my own mind. I'm not going to let money come between me and happiness.'

'You are a remarkable woman,' said Mr Pyne slowly. 'Only one woman in a thousand would act as you are doing.'

'Then only one woman in a thousand's got sense,' said Mrs Rymer.

'I take my hat off to you,' said Mr Parker Pyne, and there was an unusual note in his voice. He raised his hat with solemnity and moved away.

'And Joe's never to know, mind!' Mrs Rymer called after him.

She stood there with the dying sun behind her, a great blue-green cabbage in her hands, her head thrown back and her shoulders squared. A grand figure of a peasant woman, outlined against the setting sun . . .

While the Light Lasts

The Ford car bumped from rut to rut, and the hot African sun poured down unmercifully. On either side of the so-called road stretched an unbroken line of trees and scrub, rising and falling in gently undulating lines as far as the eye could reach, the colouring a soft, deep yellow-green, the whole effect languorous and strangely quiet. Few birds stirred the slumbering silence. Once a snake wriggled across the road in front of the car, escaping the driver's efforts at destruction with sinuous ease. Once a native stepped out from the bush, dignified and upright, behind him a woman with an infant bound closely to her broad back and a complete household equipment, including a frying pan, balanced magnificently on her head.

All these things George Crozier had not failed to point out to his wife, who had answered him with a monosyllabic lack of attention which irritated him.

'Thinking of that fellow,' he deduced wrathfully. It was thus that he was wont to allude in his own mind to Deirdre Crozier's first husband, killed in the first year of the War. Killed, too, in the campaign against German West Africa. Natural she should, perhaps—he stole a glance at her, her fairness, the pink and white smoothness of her cheek; the rounded lines of her figure—rather more rounded perhaps than they had been in those far-off days when she had passively permitted him to become engaged to her, and then, in that first emotional scare of war, had abruptly cast him aside and made a war wedding of it with that lean, sunburnt boy lover of hers, Tim Nugent.

Well, well, the fellow was dead—gallantly dead—and he, George Crozier, had married the girl he had always meant to marry. She was fond of him, too; how could she help it when he was ready to gratify her every wish and had the money to do it, too! He reflected with some complacency on his last gift to her, at Kimberley, where, owing to his friendship with some of the directors of De Beers, he had been able to purchase a diamond which, in the ordinary way, would not have been in the market, a stone not remarkable as to size, but of a very exquisite and rare shade, a peculiar deep amber, almost old gold, a diamond such as you might not find in a hundred years. And the look in her eyes when he gave it to her! Women were all the same about diamonds.

The necessity of holding on with both hands to prevent himself being jerked out brought George Crozier back to the realities. He cried out for perhaps the fourteenth time, with the pardonable irritation of a man who owns two Rolls-Royce cars and who has exercised his stud on the highways of civilization: 'Good Lord, what a car! What a road!' He went on angrily: 'Where the devil is this tobacco estate, anyway? It's over an hour since we left Bulawayo.'

'Lost in Rhodesia,' said Deirdre lightly between two involuntary leaps into the air.

But the coffee-coloured driver, appealed to, responded with the cheering news that their destination was just round the next bend of the road.

* * *

The manager of the estate, Mr Walters, was waiting on the stoep to receive them with the touch of deference due to George Crozier's prominence in Union Tobacco. He introduced his daughter-in-law, who shepherded Deirdre through the cool, dark inner hall to a bedroom beyond, where she could remove the veil with which she was always careful to shield her complexion when motoring. As she unfastened the pins in her usual leisurely, graceful fashion, Deirdre's eyes swept round the whitewashed ugliness of the bare room. No luxuries here, and Deirdre, who loved comfort as a cat loves cream, shivered a little. On the wall a text confronted her. 'What shall it profit a man if he gain the whole world and lose his own soul?' it demanded of all and sundry, and Deirdre, pleasantly conscious that the question had nothing to do with her, turned to accompany her shy and rather silent guide. She noted, but not in the least maliciously, the spreading hips and the unbecoming cheap cotton gown. And with a glow of quiet appreciation her eyes dropped to the exquisite, costly simplicity of her own French white linen. Beautiful clothes, especially when worn by herself, roused in her the joy of the artist.

The two men were waiting for her.

'It won't bore you to come round, too, Mrs Crozier?'

'Not at all. I've never been over a tobacco factory.'

They stepped out into the still Rhodesian afternoon.

'These are the seedlings here; we plant them out as required. You see—'

The manager's voice droned on, interpolated by her husband's sharp staccato questions—output, stamp duty, problems of labour. She ceased to listen.

This was Rhodesia, this was the land Tim had loved, where he and she were to have gone together after the War was over. If he had not been killed! As always, the bitterness of revolt surged up in her at that thought. Two short months—that was all they had had. Two months of happiness—if that mingled rapture and pain were happiness. Was love ever happiness? Did not a thousand tortures beset the lover's heart? She had lived intensely in that short space, but had she ever known the peace, the leisure, the quiet contentment of her present life? And for the first time she admitted, somewhat unwillingly, that perhaps all had been for the best.

'I wouldn't have liked living out here. I mightn't have been able to make Tim happy. I might have disappointed him. George loves me, and I'm very fond of him, and he's very, very good to me. Why, look at that diamond he bought me only the other day.' And, thinking of it, her eyelids dropped a little in pure pleasure.

'This is where we thread the leaves.' Walters led the way into a low, long shed. On the floor were vast heaps of green leaves, and white-dad black 'boys' squatted round them, picking and rejecting with deft fingers, sorting them into sizes, and stringing them by means of primitive needles on a long line of string. They worked with a cheerful leisureliness, jesting amongst themselves, and showing their white teeth as they laughed.

'Now, out here—'

They passed through the shed into the daylight again, where the lines of leaves hung drying in the sun. Deirdre sniffed delicately at the faint, almost imperceptible fragrance that filled the air.

Walters led the way into other sheds where the tobacco, kissed by the sun into faint yellow discoloration, underwent its further treatment. Dark here, with the brown swinging masses above, ready to fall to powder at a rough touch. The fragrance was stronger, almost overpowering it seemed to Deirdre, and suddenly a sort of terror came upon her, a fear of she knew not what, that drove her from that menacing, scented obscurity out into the sunlight. Crozier noted her pallor.

'What's the matter, my dear, don't you feel well? The sun, perhaps. Better not come with us round the plantations? Eh?'

Walters was solicitous. Mrs Crozier had better go back to the house and rest. He called to a man a little distance away.

'Mr Arden—Mrs Crozier. Mrs Crozier's feeling a little done up with the heat, Arden. Just take her back to the house, will you?'

The momentary feeling of dizziness was passing. Deirdre walked by Arden's side. She had as yet hardly glanced at him.

'Deirdre!'

Her heart gave a leap, and then stood still. Only one person had ever spoken her name like that, with the faint stress on the first syllable that made of it a caress.

She turned and stared at the man by her side. He was burnt almost black by the sun, he walked with a limp, and on the cheek nearer hers was a long scar which altered his expression, but she knew him.

'Tim!'

For an eternity, it seemed to her, they gazed at each other, mute and trembling, and then, without knowing how or why, they were in each other's arms. Time rolled back for them. Then they drew apart again, and Deirdre, conscious as she put it of the idiocy of the question, said:

'Then you're not dead?'

'No, they must have mistaken another chap for me. I was badly knocked on the head, but I came to and managed to crawl into the bush. After that I don't know what happened for months and months, but a friendly tribe looked after me, and at last I got my proper wits again and managed to get back to civilization.' He paused. 'I found you'd been married six months.'

Deirdre cried out:

'Oh, Tim, understand, please understand! It was so awful, the loneliness—and the poverty. I didn't mind being poor with you, but when I was alone I hadn't the nerve to stand up against the sordidness of it all.'

'It's all right, Deirdre; I did understand. I know you always have had a hankering after the flesh-pots. I took you from them once—but the second time, well—my nerve failed. I was pretty badly broken up, you see, could hardly walk without a crutch, and then there was this scar.'

She interrupted him passionately.

'Do you think I would have cared for that?'

'No, I know you wouldn't. I was a fool. Some women did mind, you know. I made up my mind I'd manage to get a glimpse of you. If you looked happy, if I thought you were contented to be with Crozier—why, then I'd remain dead. I did see you. You were just getting into a big car. You had on some lovely sable furs—things I'd never be able to give you if I worked my fingers to the bone—and—well—you seemed happy enough. I hadn't the same strength and courage, the same belief in myself, that I'd had before the War. All I could see was myself, broken and useless, barely able to earn enough to keep you—and you looked so beautiful, Deirdre, such a queen amongst women, so worthy to have furs and jewels and lovely clothes and all the hundred and one luxuries Crozier could give you. That—and—well, the pain—of seeing you together, decided me. Everyone believed me dead. I would stay dead.'

'The pain!' repeated Deirdre in a low voice.

'Well, damn it all, Deirdre, it hurt! It isn't that I blame you. I don't. But it hurt.'

They were both silent. Then Tim raised her face to his and kissed it with a new tenderness.

'But that's all over now, sweetheart. The only thing to decide is how we're going to break it to Crozier.'

'Oh!' She drew herself away abruptly. 'I hadn't thought—' She broke off as Crozier and the manager appeared round the angle of the path. With a swift turn of the head she whispered:

'Do nothing now. Leave it to me. I must prepare him. Where could I meet you tomorrow?'

Nugent reflected.

'I could come in to Bulawayo. How about the Cafe near the Standard Bank? At three o'clock it would be pretty empty.'

Deirdre gave a brief nod of assent before turning her back on him and joining the other two men. Tim Nugent looked after her with a faint frown. Something in her manner puzzled him.

Deirdre was very silent during the drive home. Sheltering behind the fiction of a 'touch of the sun', she deliberated on her course of action. How should she tell him? How would he take it? A strange lassitude seemed to possess her, and a growing desire to postpone the revelation as long as might be. Tomorrow would be soon enough. There would be plenty of time before three o'clock.

The hotel was uncomfortable. Their room was on the ground floor, looking out on to an inner court. Deirdre stood that evening sniffing the stale air and glancing distastefully at the tawdry furniture. Her mind flew to the easy luxury of Monkton Court amidst the Surrey pinewoods. When her maid left her at last, she went slowly to her jewel case. In the palm of her hand the golden diamond returned her stare.

With an almost violent gesture she returned it to

the case and slammed down the lid. Tomorrow morning she would tell George.

She slept badly. It was stifling beneath the heavy folds of the mosquito netting. The throbbing darkness was punctuated by the ubiquitous *ping* she had learnt to dread. She awoke white and listless. Impossible to start a scene so early in the day!

She lay in the small, close room all the morning, resting. Lunchtime came upon her with a sense of shock. As they sat drinking coffee, George Crozier proposed a drive to the Matopos.

'Plenty of time if we start at once.'

Deirdre shook her head, pleading a headache, and she thought to herself: 'That settles it. I can't rush the thing. After all, what does a day more or less matter? I'll explain to Tim.'

She waved goodbye to Crozier as he rattled off in the battered Ford. Then, glancing at her watch, she walked slowly to the meeting place.

The Cafe was deserted at this hour. They sat down at a little table and ordered the inevitable tea that South Africa drinks at all hours of the day and night. Neither of them said a word till the waitress brought it and withdrew to her fastness behind some pink curtains. Then Deirdre looked up and started as she met the intense watchfulness in his eyes.

'Deirdre, have you told him?'

She shook her head, moistening her lips, seeking for words that would not come.

'Why not?'

'I haven't had a chance; there hasn't been time.'

Even to herself the words sounded halting and unconvincing.

'It's not that. There's something else. I suspected it yesterday. I'm sure of it today. Deirdre, what is it?'

She shook her head dumbly.

'There's some reason why you don't want to leave George Crozier, why you don't want to come back to me. What is it?'

It was true. As he said it she knew it, knew it with sudden scorching shame, but knew it beyond any possibility of doubt. And still his eyes searched her.

'It isn't that you love him! You don't. But there's something.'

She thought: 'In another moment he'll see! Oh, God, don't let him!'

Suddenly his face whitened.

'Deirdre—is it—is it that there's going to be a—child?'

In a flash she saw the chance he offered her. A wonderful way! Slowly, almost without her own volition, she bowed her head.

She heard his quick breathing, then his voice, rather high and hard.

'That—alters things. I didn't know. We've got to find a different way out.' He leant across the table and caught both her hands in his. 'Deirdre, my darling, never think—never dream that you were in any way to blame. Whatever happens, remember that. I should have claimed you when I came back to England. I funked it, so it's up to me to do what I can to put things straight now. You see? Whatever happens, don't fret, darling. Nothing has been your fault.'

He lifted first one hand, then the other to his lips. Then she was alone, staring at the untasted tea. And, strangely enough, it was only one thing that she saw—a gaudily illuminated text hanging on a whitewashed wall. The words seemed to spring out from it and hurl themselves at her. 'What shall it profit a man—' She got up, paid for her tea and went out.

On his return George Crozier was met by a request that his wife might not be disturbed. Her headache, the maid said, was very bad.

It was nine o'clock the next morning when he entered her bedroom, his face rather grave. Deirdre was sitting up in bed. She looked white and haggard, but her eyes shone.

'George, I've got something to tell you, something rather terrible—'

He interrupted her brusquely.

'So you've heard. I was afraid it might upset you.'

'Upset me?'

'Yes. You talked to the poor young fellow that day.'

He saw her hand steal to her heart, her eyelids flicker, then she said in a low, quick voice that somehow frightened him:

'I've heard nothing. Tell me quickly.'

'I thought—'

'Tell me!'

'Out at that tobacco estate. Chap shot himself. Badly broken up in the War, nerves all to pieces, I suppose. There's no other reason to account for it.'

'He shot himself—in that dark shed where the tobacco was hanging.' She spoke with certainty, her eyes like a sleep-walker's as she saw before her in the odorous darkness a figure lying there, revolver in hand.

'Why, to be sure; that's where you were taken queer yesterday. Odd thing, that!'

Deirdre did not answer. She saw another picture—a table with tea things on it, and a woman bowing her head in acceptance of a lie.

'Well, well, the War has a lot to answer for,' said Crozier, and stretched out his hand for a match, lighting his pipe with careful puffs.

His wife's cry startled him.

'Ah! don't, don't! I can't bear the smell!'

He stared at her in kindly astonishment.

'My dear girl, you mustn't be nervy. After all, you can't escape from the smell of tobacco. You'll meet it everywhere.'

'Yes, everywhere!' She smiled a slow, twisted smile, and murmured some words that he did not catch, words that she had chosen for the original obituary notice of Tim Nugent's death. 'While the light lasts I shall remember, and in the darkness I shall not forget.'

Her eyes widened as they followed the ascending spiral of smoke, and she repeated in a low, monotonous voice: 'Everywhere, everywhere.'

Triangle at Rhodes

Hercule Poirot sat on the white sand and looked out across the sparkling blue water. He was carefully dressed in a dandified fashion in white flannels and a large panama hat protected his head. He belonged to the old-fashioned generation which believed in covering itself carefully from the sun. Miss Pamela Lyall, who sat beside him and talked ceaselessly, represented the modern school of thought in that she was wearing the barest minimum of clothing on her sun-browned person.

Occasionally her flow of conversation stopped whilst she reanointed herself from a bottle of oily fluid which stood beside her.

On the farther side of Miss Pamela Lyall her great friend, Miss Sarah Blake, lay face downwards on a gaudily-striped towel. Miss Blake's tanning was as perfect as possible and her friend cast dissatisfied glances at her more than once.

'I'm so patchy still,' she murmured regretfully. 'M. Poirot—*would* you mind? Just below the right shoulder-blade—I can't reach to rub it in properly.'

M. Poirot obliged and then wiped his oily hand carefully on his handkerchief. Miss Lyall, whose principal interests in life were the observation of people round her and the sound of her own voice, continued to talk.

'I was right about that woman—the one in the *Chanel* model—it *is* Valentine Dacres—Chantry, I mean. I thought it was. I recognized her at once. She's really rather marvellous, isn't she? I mean I can understand how people go quite crazy about her. She just obviously *expects* them to! That's half the battle. Those other people who came last night are called Gold. He's terribly good-looking.'

'Honeymooners?' murmured Sarah in a stifled voice.

Miss Lyall shook her head in an experienced manner.

'Oh, no—her clothes aren't *new* enough. You can always tell brides! Don't you think it's the most fascinating thing in the world to watch people, M. Poirot, and see what you can find out about them by just looking?'

'Not just looking, darling,' said Sarah sweetly. 'You ask a lot of questions, too.'

'I haven't even spoken to the Golds yet,' said Miss Lyall with dignity. 'And anyway I don't see why one shouldn't be interested in one's fellow-creatures? Human nature is simply fascinating. Don't you think so, M. Poirot?'

This time she paused long enough to allow her companion to reply.

Without taking his eyes off the blue water, M. Poirot replied:

'*Ça depend.*'

Pamela was shocked.

'Oh, M. Poirot! I don't think *anything's* so interesting—so *incalculable* as a human being!'

'Incalculable? That, no.'

'Oh, but they *are*. Just as you think you've got them beautifully taped—they do something completely unexpected.'

Hercule Poirot shook his head.

'No, no, that is not true. It is most rare that anyone does an action that is not *dans son caractère*. It is in the end monotonous.'

'I don't agree with you at all!' said Miss Pamela Lyall.

She was silent for quite a minute and a half before returning to the attack.

'As soon as I see people I begin wondering about them—what they're like—what relations they are to each other—what they're thinking and feeling. It's—oh, it's quite thrilling.'

'Hardly that,' said Hercule Poirot. 'Nature repeats herself more than one would imagine. The sea,' he added thoughtfully, 'has infinitely more variety.'

Sarah turned her head sideways and asked:

'You think that human beings tend to reproduce certain patterns? Stereotyped patterns?'

'*Précisément*,' said Poirot, and traced a design in the sand with his finger.

'What's that you're drawing?' asked Pamela curiously.

'A triangle,' said Poirot.

But Pamela's attention had been diverted elsewhere.

'Here are the Chantrys,' she said.

A woman was coming down the beach—a tall woman, very conscious of herself and her body. She gave a half-nod and smile and sat down a little distance away on the beach. The scarlet and gold silk wrap slipped down from her shoulders. She was wearing a white bathing-dress.

Pamela sighed.

'Hasn't she got a lovely figure?'

But Poirot was looking at her face—the face of a woman of thirty-nine who had been famous since sixteen for her beauty.

He knew, as everyone knew, all about Valentine Chantry. She had been famous for many things—for her caprices, for her wealth, for her enormous sapphire-blue eyes, for her matrimonial ventures and adventures. She had had five husbands and innumerable lovers. She had in turn been the wife of an Italian count, of an American steel magnate, of a tennis professional, of a racing motorist. Of these four the American had died, but the others had been shed negligently in the divorce court. Six months ago she had married a fifth time—a commander in the navy.

He it was who came striding down the beach behind her. Silent, dark—with a pugnacious jaw and a sullen manner. A touch of the primeval ape about him.

She said:

'Tony darling—my cigarette case . . .'

He had it ready for her—lighted her cigarette—helped her to slip the straps of the white bathing-dress from her shoulders. She lay, arms outstretched in the sun. He sat by her like some wild beast that guards its prey.

Pamela said, her voice just lowered sufficiently:

'You know they interest me *frightfully* . . . He's such a brute! So silent and—sort of *glowering.* I suppose a woman of her kind likes that. It must be like controlling a tiger! I wonder how long it will last. She gets tired of them very soon, I believe—especially nowadays. All the same, if she tried to get rid of him, I think he might be dangerous.'

Another couple came down the beach—rather shyly. They were the newcomers of the night before. Mr and Mrs Douglas Gold as Miss Lyall knew from her inspection of the hotel visitors' book. She knew, too, for such were the Italian regulations—their Christian names and their ages as set down from their passports.

Mr Douglas Cameron Gold was thirty-one and Mrs Marjorie Emma Gold was thirty-five.

Miss Lyall's hobby in life, as has been said, was the study of human beings. Unlike most English people, she was capable of speaking to strangers on sight instead of allowing four days to a week to elapse before making the first cautious advance as is the customary British habit. She, therefore, noting the slight hesitancy and shyness of Mrs Gold's advance, called out:

'Good morning, isn't it a lovely day?'

Mrs Gold was a small woman—rather like a mouse. She was not bad-looking, indeed her features were regular and her complexion good, but she had a certain air of diffidence and dowdiness that made her liable to be overlooked. Her husband, on the other hand, was extremely good-looking, in an almost theatrical manner. Very fair, crisply curling hair, blue eyes, broad shoulders, narrow hips. He looked more like a young man on the stage than a young man in real life, but the moment he opened his mouth that impression faded. He was quite natural and unaffected, even, perhaps, a little stupid.

Mrs Gold looked gratefully at Pamela and sat down near her.

'What a lovely shade of brown you are. I feel terribly underdone!'

'One has to take a frightful lot of trouble to brown evenly,' sighed Miss Lyall.

She paused a minute and then went on:

'You've only just arrived, haven't you?'

'Yes. Last night. We came on the Vapo d'Italia boat.'

'Have you ever been to Rhodes before?'

'No. It is lovely, isn't it?'

Her husband said:

'Pity it's such a long way to come.'

'Yes, if it were only nearer England—'

In a muffled voice Sarah said:

'Yes, but then it would be awful. Rows and rows of people laid out like fish on a slab. Bodies everywhere!'

'That's true, of course,' said Douglas Gold. 'It's a nuisance the Italian exchange is so absolutely ruinous at present.'

'It does make a difference, doesn't it?'

The conversation was running on strictly stereotyped lines. It could hardly have been called brilliant.

A little way along the beach, Valentine Chantry stirred and sat up. With one hand she held her bathing-dress in position across her breast.

She yawned, a wide yet delicate cat-like yawn. She glanced casually down the beach. Her eyes slanted past Marjorie Gold—and stayed thoughtfully on the crisp, golden head of Douglas Gold.

She moved her shoulders sinuously. She spoke and her voice was raised a little higher than it need have been.

'Tony darling—isn't it divine—this sun? I simply *must* have been a sun worshipper once—don't you think so?'

Her husband grunted something in reply that failed to reach the others. Valentine Chantry went on in that high, drawling voice.

'Just pull that towel a little flatter, will you, darling?'

She took infinite pains in the resettling of her beautiful body. Douglas Gold was looking now. His eyes were frankly interested.

Mrs Gold chirped happily in a subdued key to Miss Lyall.

'What a beautiful woman!'

Pamela, as delighted to give as to receive information, replied in a lower voice:

'That's Valentine Chantry—you know, who used to be Valentine Dacres—she *is* rather marvellous, isn't she? He's simply crazy about her—won't let her out of his sight!'

Mrs Gold looked once more along the beach. Then she said:

'The sea really is lovely—so blue. I think we ought to go in now, don't you, Douglas?'

He was still watching Valentine Chantry and took a minute or two to answer. Then he said, rather absently:

'Go in? Oh, yes, rather, in a minute.'

Marjorie Gold got up and strolled down to the water's edge.

Valentine Chantry rolled over a little on one side. Her eyes looked along at Douglas Gold. Her scarlet mouth curved faintly into a smile.

The neck of Mr Douglas Gold became slightly red.

Valentine Chantry said:

'Tony darling—would you mind? I want a little pot of face-cream—it's up on the dressing-table. I meant to bring it down. Do get it for me—there's an angel.'

The commander rose obediently. He stalked off into the hotel.

Marjorie Gold plunged into the sea, calling out:

'It's lovely, Douglas—so warm. Do come.'

Pamela Lyall said to him:

'Aren't you going in?'

He answered vaguely:

'Oh! I like to get well hotted up first.'

Valentine Chantry stirred. Her head was lifted for a moment as though to recall her husband—but he was just passing inside the wall of the hotel garden.

'I like my dip the last thing,' explained Mr Gold.

Mrs Chantry sat up again. She picked up a flask of sun-bathing oil. She had some difficulty with it—the screw top seemed to resist her efforts.

She spoke loudly and petulantly.

'Oh, dear—I *can't* get this thing undone!'

She looked towards the other group—

'I wonder—'

Always gallant, Poirot rose to his feet, but Douglas Gold had the advantage of youth and suppleness. He was by her side in a moment.

'Can I do it for you?'

'Oh, thank you—' It was the sweet, empty drawl again.

'You *are* kind. I'm such a *fool* at undoing things—I always seem to screw them the wrong way. Oh! you've done it! Thank you ever so much—'

Hercule Poirot smiled to himself.

He got up and wandered along the beach in the opposite direction. He did not go very far but his progress was leisurely. As he was on his way back, Mrs Gold came out of the sea and joined him. She had been swimming. Her face, under a singularly unbecoming bathing cap, was radiant.

She said breathlessly, 'I do love the sea. And it's so warm and lovely here.'

She was, he perceived, an enthusiastic bather.

She said, 'Douglas and I are simply mad on bathing. He can stay in for hours.'

And at that Hercule Poirot's eyes slid over her shoulder to the spot on the beach where that enthusiastic bather, Mr Douglas Gold, was sitting talking to Valentine Chantry.

His wife said:

'I can't think why he doesn't come . . .'

Her voice held a kind of childish bewilderment.

Poirot's eyes rested thoughtfully on Valentine Chantry. He thought that other women in their time had made that same remark.

Beside him, he heard Mrs Gold draw in her breath sharply.

She said—and her voice was cold:

'She's supposed to be very attractive, I believe. But Douglas doesn't like that type of woman.'

Hercule Poirot did not reply.

Mrs Gold plunged into the sea again.

She swam away from the shore with slow, steady strokes. You could see that she loved the water.

Poirot retraced his steps to the group on the beach.

It had been augmented by the arrival of old General Barnes, a veteran who was usually in the company of the young. He was sitting now between Pamela and Sarah, and he and Pamela were engaged in dishing up various scandals with appropriate embellishments.

Commander Chantry had returned from his errand. He and Douglas Gold were sitting on either side of Valentine.

Valentine was sitting up very straight between the two men and talking. She talked easily and lightly in her sweet, drawling voice, turning her head to take first one man and then the other in the conversation.

She was just finishing an anecdote.

'—and what do you think the foolish man said? "It may have been only a minute, but I'd remember you *anywhere*, Mum!" Didn't he, Tony? And you know, I thought it was so *sweet* of him. I do think it's such a kind world—I mean, everybody is so frightfully kind to *me* always—I don't know why—they just are. But I said to Tony—d'you remember, darling—"Tony, if you want to be a teeny-weeny bit jealous, you can be jealous of that commissionaire." Because he really was too adorable . . .'

There was a pause and Douglas Gold said:

'Good fellows—some of these commissionaires.'

'Oh, yes—but he took such trouble—really an immense amount of trouble—and seemed just pleased to be able to help me.'

Douglas Gold said:

'Nothing odd about that. Anyone would for you, I'm sure.'

She cried delightedly:

'How nice of you! Tony, did you hear that?'

Commander Chantry grunted.

His wife sighed:

'Tony never makes pretty speeches—do you, my lamb?'

Her white hand with its long red nails ruffled up his dark head.

He gave her a sudden sidelong look. She murmured:

'I don't really know how he puts up with me. He's simply frightfully clever—absolutely frantic with brains—and I just go on talking nonsense the whole time, but he doesn't seem to mind. Nobody minds what I do or say—everybody spoils me. I'm sure it's frightfully bad for me.'

Commander Chantry said across her to the other man:

'That your missus in the sea?'

'Yes. Expect it's about time I joined her.'

Valentine murmured:

'But it's so lovely here in the sun. You mustn't go into the sea yet. Tony darling, I don't think I shall actually *bathe* today—not my first day. I might get a chill or something. But why don't you go in now, Tony darling? Mr—Mr Gold will stay and keep me company while you're in.'

Chantry said rather grimly:

'No, thanks. Shan't go in just yet. Your wife seems to be waving to you, Gold.'

Valentine said:

'How well your wife swims. I'm sure she's one of those terribly efficient women who do everything well.

They always frighten me so because I feel they despise me. I'm so frightfully bad at everything—an absolute duffer, aren't I, Tony darling?'

But again Commander Chantry only grunted.

His wife murmured affectionately:

'You're too sweet to admit it. Men are so wonderfully loyal—that's what I like about them. I do think men are so much more loyal than women—and they never say nasty things. Women, I always think, are rather *petty*.'

Sarah Blake rolled over on her side towards Poirot.

She murmured between her teeth.

'Examples of pettiness, to suggest that dear Mrs Chantry is in any way not absolute perfection! What a complete idiot the woman is! I really do think Valentine Chantry is very nearly the most idiotic woman I ever met. She can't do anything but say, "Tony, darling," and roll her eyes. I should fancy she'd got cottonwool padding instead of brains.'

Poirot raised his expressive eyebrows.

'*Un peu sévère!*'

'Oh, yes. Put it down as pure "Cat", if you like. She certainly has her methods! Can't she leave *any* man alone? Her husband's looking like thunder.'

Looking out to sea, Poirot remarked:

'Mrs Gold swims well.'

'Yes, she isn't like us who find it a nuisance to get wet. I wonder if Mrs Chantry will ever go into the sea at all while she's out here.'

'Not she,' said General Barnes huskily. 'She won't risk that make-up of hers coming off. Not that she isn't a fine-looking woman although perhaps a bit long in the tooth.'

'She's looking your way, General,' said Sarah wickedly. 'And you're wrong about the make-up. We're all waterproof and kissproof nowadays.'

'Mrs Gold's coming out,' announced Pamela.

'Here we go gathering nuts and may,' hummed Sarah. 'Here comes his wife to fetch him away—fetch him away—fetch him away . . .'

Mrs Gold came straight up the beach. She had quite a pretty figure but her plain, waterproof cap was rather too serviceable to be attractive.

'Aren't you coming, Douglas?' she demanded impatiently. 'The sea is lovely and warm.'

'Rather.'

Douglas Gold rose hastily to his feet. He paused a moment and as he did so Valentine Chantry looked up at him with a sweet smile.

'Au revoir,' she said.

Gold and his wife went down the beach.

As soon as they were out of earshot, Pamela said critically:

'I don't think, you know, that that was wise. To snatch your husband away from another woman is always bad policy. It makes you seem so possessive. And husbands hate that.'

'You seem to know a lot about husbands, Miss Pamela,' said General Barnes.

'Other people's—not my own!'

'Ah! that's where the difference comes in.'

'Yes, but General, I shall have learnt a lot of Do Nots.'

'Well, darling,' said Sarah, 'I shouldn't wear a cap like that for one thing . . .'

'Seems very sensible to me,' said the General. 'Seems a nice, sensible little woman altogether.'

'You've hit it exactly, General,' said Sarah. 'But you know there's a limit to the sensibleness of sensible women. I have a feeling she won't be so sensible when it's a case of Valentine Chantry.'

She turned her head and exclaimed in a low, excited whisper:

'Look at him now. Just like thunder. That man looks as though he had got the most frightful temper . . .'

Commander Chantry was indeed scowling after the retreating husband and wife in a singularly unpleasant fashion.

Sarah looked up at Poirot.

'Well?' she said. 'What do you make of all this?'

Hercule Poirot did not reply in words, but once again his forefinger traced a design in the sand. The same design—a triangle.

'The eternal triangle,' mused Sarah. 'Perhaps you're right. If so, we're in for an exciting time in the next few weeks.'

M. Hercule Poirot was disappointed with Rhodes. He had come to Rhodes for a rest and for a holiday. A holiday, especially, from crime. In late October, so he had been told, Rhodes would be nearly empty. A peaceful, secluded spot.

That, in itself, was true enough. The Chantrys, the Golds, Pamela and Sarah, the General and himself and two Italian couples were the only guests. But within that restricted circle the intelligent brain of M. Poirot perceived the inevitable shaping of events to come.

'It is that I am criminal-minded,' he told himself reproachfully. 'I have the indigestion! I imagine things.'

But still he worried.

One morning he came down to find Mrs Gold sitting on the terrace doing needlework.

As he came up to her he had the impression that there was the flicker of a cambric handkerchief swiftly whisked out of sight.

Mrs Gold's eyes were dry, but they were suspiciously

bright. Her manner, too, struck him as being a shade too cheerful. The brightness of it was a shade overdone.

She said:

'Good morning, M. Poirot,' with such enthusiasm as to arouse his doubts.

He felt that she could not possibly be quite as pleased to see him as she appeared to be. For she did not, after all, know him very well. And though Hercule Poirot was a conceited little man where his profession was concerned, he was quite modest in his estimate of his personal attractions.

'Good morning, madame,' he responded. 'Another beautiful day.'

'Yes, isn't it fortunate? But Douglas and I are always lucky in our weather.'

'Indeed?'

'Yes. We're really very lucky altogether. You know, M. Poirot, when one sees so much trouble and unhappiness, and so many couples divorcing each other and all that sort of thing, well, one does feel very grateful for one's own happiness.'

'It is pleasant to hear you say so, madame.'

'Yes. Douglas and I are so wonderfully happy together. We've been married five years, you know, and after all, five years is quite a long time nowadays—'

'I have no doubt that in some cases it can seem an eternity, madame,' said Poirot dryly.

'—but I really believe that we're happier now than when we were first married. You see, we're so absolutely suited to each other.'

'That, of course, is everything.'

'That's why I feel so sorry for people who aren't happy.'

'You mean—'

'Oh! I was speaking generally, M. Poirot.'

'I see. I see.'

Mrs Gold picked up a strand of silk, held it to the light, approved of it, and went on:

'Mrs Chantry, for instance—'

'Yes, Mrs Chantry?'

'I don't think she's at all a nice woman.'

'No. No, perhaps not.'

'In fact, I'm quite sure she's not a nice woman. But in a way one feels sorry for her. Because in spite of her money and her good looks and all that'—Mrs Gold's fingers were trembling and she was quite unable to thread her needle—'she's not the sort of woman men really stick to. She's the sort of woman, I think, that men would get tired of very easily. Don't you think so?'

'I myself should certainly get tired of her conversation before any great space of time had passed,' said Poirot cautiously.

'Yes, that's what I mean. She has, of course, a kind of appeal ...' Mrs Gold hesitated, her lips trembled, she stabbed uncertainly at her work. A less acute observer than Hercule Poirot could not have failed to notice her distress. She went on inconsequently:

'Men are just like children! They believe *anything* ...'

She bent over her work. The tiny wisp of cambric came out again unobtrusively.

Perhaps Hercule Poirot thought it well to change the subject.

He said:

'You do not bathe this morning? And monsieur your husband, is he down on the beach?'

Mrs Gold looked up, blinked, resumed her almost defiantly bright manner and replied:

'No, not this morning. We arranged to go round the walls of the old city. But somehow or other we—we missed each other. They started without me.'

The pronoun was revealing, but before Poirot could say anything, General Barnes came up from the beach below and dropped into a chair beside them.

'Good morning, Mrs Gold. Good morning, Poirot. Both deserters this morning? A lot of absentees. You two, and your husband, Mrs Gold—and Mrs Chantry.'

'And Commander Chantry?' inquired Poirot casually.

'Oh, no, he's down there. Miss Pamela's got him in hand.' The General chuckled. 'She's finding him a little bit difficult! One of the strong, silent men you hear about in books.'

Marjorie Gold said with a little shiver:

'He frightens me a little, that man. He—he looks so black sometimes. As though he might do—anything!'

She shivered.

'Just indigestion, I expect,' said the General cheerfully. 'Dyspepsia is responsible for many a reputation for romantic melancholy or ungovernable rages.'

Marjorie Gold smiled a polite little smile.

'And where's your good man?' inquired the General.

Her reply came without hesitation—in a natural, cheerful voice.

'Douglas? Oh, he and Mrs Chantry have gone into the town. I believe they've gone to have a look at the walls of the old city.'

'Ha, yes—very interesting. Time of the knights and all that. You ought to have gone too, little lady.'

Mrs Gold said:

'I'm afraid I came down rather late.'

She got up suddenly with a murmured excuse and went into the hotel.

General Barnes looked after her with a concerned expression, shaking his head gently.

'Nice little woman, that. Worth a dozen painted trollops like someone whose name we won't mention!

Ha! Husband's a fool! Doesn't know when he's well off.'

He shook his head again. Then, rising, he went indoors.

Sarah Blake had just come up from the beach and had heard the General's last speech.

Making a face at the departing warrior's back, she remarked as she flung herself into a chair:

'Nice little woman—nice little woman! Men always approve of dowdy women—but when it comes to brass tacks the dress-up trollops win hands down! Sad, but there it is.'

'Mademoiselle,' said Poirot, and his voice was abrupt. 'I do not like all this!'

'Don't you? Nor do I. No, let's be honest, I suppose I *do* like it really. There is a horrid side of one that enjoys accidents and public calamities and unpleasant things that happen to one's friends.'

Poirot asked:

'Where is Commander Chantry?'

'On the beach being dissected by Pamela (*she's* enjoying herself if you like!) and not being improved in temper by the proceeding. He was looking like a thunder cloud when I came up. There are squalls ahead, believe me.'

Poirot murmured:

'There is something I do not understand—'

'It's not easy to *understand*,' said Sarah. 'But what's going to *happen* that's the question.'

Poirot shook his head and murmured:

'As you say, mademoiselle—it is the future that causes one inquietude.'

'What a nice way of putting it,' said Sarah and went into the hotel.

In the doorway she almost collided with Douglas Gold. The young man came out looking rather pleased with himself but at the same time slightly guilty. He said:

'Hallo, M. Poirot,' and added rather self-consciously, 'Been showing Mrs Chantry the Crusaders' walls. Marjorie didn't feel up to going.'

Poirot's eyebrows rose slightly, but even had he wished he would have had no time to make a comment for Valentine Chantry came sweeping out, crying in her high voice:

'Douglas—a pink gin—positively I must have a pink gin.'

Douglas Gold went off to order the drink. Valentine sank into a chair by Poirot. She was looking radiant this morning.

She saw her husband and Pamela coming up towards them and waved a hand, crying out:

'Have a nice bathe, Tony darling? Isn't it a divine morning?'

Commander Chantry did not answer. He swung up the steps, passed her without a word or a look and vanished into the bar.

His hands were clenched by his sides and that faint likeness to a gorilla was accentuated.

Valentine Chantry's perfect but rather foolish mouth fell open.

She said, 'Oh,' rather blankly.

Pamela Lyall's face expressed keen enjoyment of the situation. Masking it as far as was possible to one of her ingenuous disposition she sat down by Valentine Chantry and inquired:

'Have you had a nice morning?'

As Valentine began, 'Simply marvellous. We—' Poirot got up and in his turn strolled gently towards the bar. He found young Gold waiting for the pink gin with a flushed face. He looked disturbed and angry.

He said to Poirot, 'That man's a brute!' And he nodded his head in the direction of the retreating figure of Commander Chantry.

'It is possible,' said Poirot. 'Yes, it is quite possible. But *les femmes*, they like brutes, remember that!'

Douglas muttered:

'I shouldn't be surprised if he ill-treats her!'

'She probably likes that too.'

Douglas Gold looked at him in a puzzled way, took up the pink gin and went out with it.

Hercule Poirot sat on a stool and ordered a *sirop de cassis*. Whilst he was sipping it with long sighs of enjoyment, Chantry came in and drank several pink gins in rapid succession.

He said suddenly and violently to the world at large rather than to Poirot:

'If Valentine thinks she can get rid of me like she's got rid of a lot of other damned fools, she's mistaken! I've got her and I mean to keep her. No other fellow's going to get her except over my dead body.'

He flung down some money, turned on his heel and went out.

It was three days later that Hercule Poirot went to the Mount of the Prophet. It was a cool, agreeable drive through the golden green fir trees, winding higher and higher, far above the petty wrangling and squabbling of human beings. The car stopped at the restaurant. Poirot got out and wandered into the woods. He came out at last on a spot that seemed truly on top of the world. Far below, deeply and dazzlingly blue, was the sea.

Here at last he was at peace—removed from cares—above the world. Carefully placing his folded overcoat on a tree stump, Hercule Poirot sat down.

'Doubtless *le bon Dieu* knows what he does. But it is odd that he should have permitted himself to fashion certain human beings. *Eh bien*, here for a while at least I am away from these vexing problems.' Thus he mused.

He looked up with a start. A little woman in a brown coat and skirt was hurrying towards him. It was Marjorie Gold and this time she had abandoned all pretence. Her face was wet with tears.

Poirot could not escape. She was upon him.

'M. Poirot. You've got to help me. I'm so miserable I don't know what to do! Oh, what shall I do? What shall I do?'

She looked up at him with a distracted face. Her fingers fastened on his coat sleeve. Then, as something she saw in his face alarmed her, she drew back a little.

'What—what is it?' she faltered.

'You want my advice, madame? It is that you ask?'

She stammered, 'Yes . . . Yes . . .'

'*Eh bien*—here it is.' He spoke curtly—trenchantly. 'Leave this place at once—*before it is too late.*'

'What?' She stared at him.

'You heard me. Leave this island.'

'Leave the island?'

She stared at him stupefied.

'That is what I say.'

'But why—why?'

'It is my advice to you—*if you value your life.*'

She gave a gasp.

'Oh! what do you mean? You're frightening me—you're frightening me.'

'Yes,' said Poirot gravely, 'that is my intention.'

She sank down, her face in her hands.

'But I can't! He wouldn't come! Douglas wouldn't, I mean. She wouldn't let him. She's got hold of him—body and soul. He won't listen to anything against her . . . He's crazy about her . . . He believes everything she tells him—that her husband ill-treats her—that she's an injured innocent— that nobody has ever understood her . . . He doesn't even think about me any more—I don't count—I'm not real to him. He wants me to give him his freedom—to divorce him. He believes that she'll divorce her husband and marry him. But I'm afraid . . . Chantry won't give her up. He's not that kind of man. Last night she showed Douglas bruises on her arm—said her husband had done it. It made Douglas wild. He's so chivalrous . . . Oh! I'm *afraid*! What will come of it all? Tell me what to do!'

Hercule Poirot stood looking straight across the water to the blue line of hills on the mainland of Asia. He said:

'I have told you. Leave the island *before it is too late* . . .'

She shook her head.

'I can't—I can't—unless Douglas . . .'

Poirot sighed.

He shrugged his shoulders.

Hercule Poirot sat with Pamela Lyall on the beach.

She said with a certain amount of gusto, 'The triangle's going strong! They sat one each side of her last night—glowering at each other! Chantry had had too much to drink. He was positively insulting to Douglas Gold. Gold behaved very well. Kept his temper. The Valentine woman enjoyed it, of course. Purred like the man-eating tiger she is. What do you think will happen?'

Poirot shook his head.

'I am afraid. I am very much afraid . . .'

'Oh, we all are,' said Miss Lyall hypocritically. She added, 'This business is rather in *your* line. Or it may come to be. Can't you do anything?'

'I have done what I could.'

Miss Lyall leaned forward eagerly.

'What *have* you done?' she asked with pleasurable excitement.

'I advised Mrs Gold to leave the island before it was too late.'

'Oo-er—so you think—' she stopped.

'Yes, mademoiselle?'

'So *that's* what you think is going to happen!' said Pamela slowly. 'But he couldn't—he'd never do a thing like that ... He's so *nice* really. It's all that Chantry woman. He wouldn't—He wouldn't—do—'

She stopped—then she said softly:

'*Murder*? Is that—is that really the word that's in your mind?'

'It is in someone's mind, mademoiselle. I will tell you that.'

Pamela gave a sudden shiver.

'I don't believe it,' she declared.

The sequence of events on the night of October the twenty-ninth was perfectly clear.

To begin with, there was a scene between the two men—Gold and Chantry. Chantry's voice rose louder and louder and his last words were overheard by four persons—the cashier at the desk, the manager, General Barnes and Pamela Lyall.

'You god-damned swine! If you and my wife think you can put this over on me, you're mistaken! *As long as I'm alive*, Valentine will remain my wife.'

Then he had flung out of the hotel, his face livid with rage.

That was before dinner. After dinner (how arranged no one knew) a reconciliation took place. Valentine asked Marjorie Gold to come out for a moonlight drive. Pamela and Sarah went with them. Gold and Chantry played billiards together. Afterwards they joined Hercule Poirot and General Barnes in the lounge.

For the first time almost, Chantry's face was smiling and good-tempered.

'Have a good game?' asked the General.

The Commander said:

'This fellow's too good for me! Ran out with a break of forty-six.'

Douglas Gold deprecated this modestly.

'Pure fluke. I assure you it was. What'll you have? I'll go and get hold of a waiter.'

'Pink gin for me, thanks.'

'Right. General?'

'Thanks. I'll have a whisky and soda.'

'Same for me. What about you, M. Poirot?'

'You are most amiable. I should like a *sirop de cassis.*'

'A *sirop*—excuse me?'

'*Sirop de cassis.* The syrup of blackcurrants.'

'Oh, a liqueur! I see. I suppose they have it here? I never heard of it.'

'They have it, yes. But it is not a liqueur.'

Douglas Gold said, laughing:

'Sounds a funny taste to me—but every man his own poison! I'll go and order them.'

Commander Chantry sat down. Though not by nature a talkative or a social man, he was clearly doing his best to be genial.

'Odd how one gets used to doing without any news,' he remarked.

The General grunted.

'Can't say the *Continental Daily Mail* four days old is much use to *me.* Of course I get *The Times* sent to me and *Punch* every week, but they're a devilish long time in coming.'

'Wonder if we'll have a general election over this Palestine business?'

'Whole thing's been badly mismanaged,' declared the General just as Douglas Gold reappeared followed by a waiter with the drinks.

The General had just begun on an anecdote of his military career in India in the year 1905. The two Englishmen were listening politely, if without great interest. Hercule Poirot was sipping his *sirop de cassis*.

The General reached the point of his narrative and there was dutiful laughter all round.

Then the women appeared at the doorway of the lounge. They all four seemed in the best of spirits and were talking and laughing.

'Tony, darling, it was too divine,' cried Valentine as she dropped into a chair by his side. 'The most marvellous idea of Mrs Gold's. You all ought to have come!'

Her husband said:

'What about a drink?'

He looked inquiringly at the others.

'Pink gin for me, darling,' said Valentine.

'Gin and gingerbeer,' said Pamela.

'Sidecar,' said Sarah.

'Right.' Chantry stood up. He pushed his own untouched pink gin over to his wife. 'You have this. I'll order another for myself. What's yours, Mrs Gold?'

Mrs Gold was being helped out of her coat by her husband. She turned smiling:

'Can I have an orangeade, please?'

'Right you are. Orangeade.'

He went towards the door. Mrs Gold smiled up in her husband's face.

'It was so lovely, Douglas. I wish you had come.'

'I wish I had too. We'll go another night, shall we?'

They smiled at each other.

Valentine Chantry picked up the pink gin and drained it.

'Oo! I needed that,' she sighed.

Douglas Gold took Marjorie's coat and laid it on a settee.

As he strolled back to the others he said sharply:

'Hallo, what's the matter?'

Valentine Chantry was leaning back in her chair. Her lips were blue and her hand had gone to her heart.

'I feel—rather queer . . .'

She gasped, fighting for breath.

Chantry came back into the room. He quickened his step.

'Hallo, Val, what's the matter?'

'I—I don't know . . . That drink—it tasted queer . . .'

'The pink gin?'

Chantry swung round his face worked. He caught Douglas Gold by the shoulder.

'That was *my* drink . . . Gold, what the hell did you put in it?'

Douglas Gold was staring at the convulsed face of the woman in the chair. He had gone dead white.

'I—I—never—'

Valentine Chantry slipped down in her chair.

General Barnes cried out:

'Get a doctor—quick . . .'

Five minutes later Valentine Chantry died . . .

There was no bathing the next morning.

Pamela Lyall, white-faced, clad in a simple dark dress, clutched at Hercule Poirot in the hall and drew him into the little writing-room.

'It's horrible!' she said. 'Horrible! You said so! You foresaw it! Murder!'

He bent his head gravely.

'Oh!' she cried out. She stamped her foot on the floor. 'You should have stopped it! Somehow! It *could* have been stopped!'

'How?' asked Hercule Poirot.

That brought her up short for the moment.

'Couldn't you go to someone—to the police—?'

'And say what? What is there to say—*before the event*? That someone has murder in their heart? I tell you, *mon enfant*, if one human being is determined to kill another human being—'

'You could warn the victim,' insisted Pamela.

'Sometimes,' said Hercule Poirot, 'warnings are useless.'

Pamela said slowly, 'You could warn the murderer—show him that you knew what was intended . . .'

Poirot nodded appreciatively.

'Yes—a better plan, that. But even then you have to reckon with a criminal's chief vice.'

'What is that?'

'Conceit. A criminal never believes that his crime can fail.'

'But it's absurd—stupid,' cried Pamela. 'The whole crime was childish! Why, the police arrested Douglas Gold at once last night.'

'Yes.' He added thoughtfully, 'Douglas Gold is a very stupid young man.'

'Incredibly stupid! I hear that they found the rest of the poison—whatever it was—?'

'A form of stropanthin. A heart poison.'

'That they actually found the rest of it in his dinner jacket pocket?'

'Quite true.'

'Incredibly stupid!' said Pamela again. 'Perhaps he meant to get rid of it—and the shock of the wrong person being poisoned paralysed him. What a scene it would make on the stage. The lover putting the stropanthin in the husband's glass and then, just when his attention is elsewhere, the wife drinks it instead ... Think of the ghastly moment when Douglas Gold turned round and realized he had killed the woman he loved ...'

She gave a little shiver.

'Your triangle. *The Eternal Triangle!* Who would have thought it would end like this?'

'I was afraid of it,' murmured Poirot.

Pamela turned on him.

'You warned *her*—Mrs Gold. Then why didn't you warn him as well?'

'You mean, why didn't I warn Douglas Gold?'

'No. I mean Commander Chantry. You could have told him that he was in danger—after all, *he* was the real obstacle! I've no doubt Douglas Gold relied on being able to bully his wife into giving him a divorce—she's a meek-spirited little woman and terribly fond of him. But Chantry is a mulish sort of devil. He was determined not to give Valentine her freedom.'

Poirot shrugged his shoulders.

'It would have been no good my speaking to Chantry,' he said.

'Perhaps not,' Pamela admitted. 'He'd probably have said he could lookafter himself and told you to go to the devil. But I do feel there ought to have been *something* one could have done.'

'I did think,' said Poirot slowly, 'of trying to persuade Valentine Chantry to leave the island, but she would not have believed what I had to tell her. She was far too stupid a woman to take in a thing like that. *Pauvre femme*, her stupidity killed her.'

'I don't believe it would have been any good if she *had* left the island,' said Pamela. 'He would simply have followed her.'

'He?'

'Douglas Gold.'

'You think Douglas Gold would have followed her? Oh, no, mademoiselle, you are wrong—you are completely wrong. You have not yet appreciated the truth of this matter. If Valentine Chantry had left the island, her husband would have gone with her.'

Pamela looked puzzled.

'Well, naturally.'

'And then, you see, the crime would simply have taken place somewhere else.'

'I don't understand you?'

'I am saying to you that the same crime would have occurred somewhere else—*that crime being the murder of Valentine Chantry by her husband*.'

Pamela stared.

'Are you trying to say that it was Commander Chantry—Tony Chantry—who murdered Valentine?'

'Yes. You saw him do it! Douglas Gold brought him his drink. He sat with it in front of him. When the women came in we all looked across the room, he had the stropanthin ready, he dropped it into the pink gin and presently, courteously, he passed it along to his wife and she drank it.'

'But the packet of stropanthin was found in Douglas Gold's pocket!'

'A very simple matter to slip it there when we were all crowding round the dying woman.'

It was quite two minutes before Pamela got her breath.

'But I don't understand a word! The triangle—you said yourself—'

Hercule Poirot nodded his head vigorously.

'I said there was a triangle—yes. But you, you imagined *the wrong one*. You were deceived by some very clever acting! You thought, as you were meant to think, that both Tony Chantry and Douglas Gold were in love with Valentine Chantry. You believed, as you were meant to believe, that Douglas Gold, being in love with Valentine Chantry (whose husband refused to divorce her) took the desperate step of administering a powerful heart poison to Chantry and that, by a fatal mistake, Valentine Chantry drank that poison instead. All that is illusion. Chantry has been meaning to do away with his wife for some time. He was bored to death with her, I could see that from the first. He married her for her money. Now he wants to marry another woman—so he planned to get rid of Valentine and keep her money. That entailed murder.'

'Another *woman*?'

Poirot said slowly:

'Yes, yes—*the little Marjorie Gold*. It was the eternal triangle all right! But you saw it the wrong way round. Neither of those two men cared in the least for Valentine Chantry. It was her vanity *and Majorie Gold's very clever stage managing* that made you think they did! A very clever woman, Mrs Gold, and amazingly attractive in her demure Madonna, poor-little-thing-way! I have known four women criminals of the same type. There was Mrs Adams who was acquitted of murdering her husband, but everybody knows she did it. Mary Parker did away with an aunt, a sweetheart and two brothers before she got a little careless and was caught. Then there was Mrs Rowden, she was hanged all right. Mrs Lecray escaped by the skin of her teeth. This woman is exactly the same type. I recognized it as soon as I saw her! That type takes to crime like a duck to water! And a very pretty bit of well-planned work it was. Tell me, what *evidence* did you ever have that Douglas Gold was in love with Valentine Chantry? When you come to think it out, you will realize that there was only Mrs Gold's confidences and Chantry's jealous bluster. Yes? You see?'

'It's horrible,' cried Pamela.

'They were a clever pair,' said Poirot with professional detachment. 'They planned to "meet" here and stage their crime. That Marjorie Gold, she is a cold-blooded devil! She would have sent her poor, innocent fool of a husband to the scaffold without the least remorse.'

Pamela cried out:

'But he was arrested and taken away by the police last night.'

'Ah,' said Hercule Poirot, 'but after that, me, I had a few little words with the police. It is true that I did not see Chantry put the stropanthin in the glass. I, like everyone else, looked up when the ladies came in. But the moment I realized that Valentine Chantry had been poisoned, I watched her husband without taking my eyes off him. And so, you see, I actually saw him slip the packet of stropanthin in Douglas Gold's coat pocket . . .'

He added with a grim expression on his face:

'I am a good witness. My name is well known. The moment the police heard my story they realized that it put an entirely different complexion on the matter.'

'And then?' demanded Pamela, fascinated.

'*Eh bien*, then they asked Commander Chantry a few questions. He tried to bluster it out, but he is not really clever, he soon broke down.'

'So Douglas Gold was set at liberty?'

'Yes.'

'And—Marjorie Gold?'

Poirot's face grew stern.

'I warned her,' he said. 'Yes, I warned her . . . Up on the Mount of the Prophet . . . It was the only chance of averting the crime. I as good as told her that I suspected her. She understood. But she believed herself too clever . . . I told her to leave the island *if* she valued her life. She chose—to remain . . .'

Death by Drowning

Sir Henry Clithering, Ex-Commissioner of Scotland Yard, was staying with his friends the Bantrys at their place near the little village of St Mary Mead.

On Saturday morning, coming down to breakfast at the pleasant guestly hour of ten-fifteen, he almost collided with his hostess, Mrs Bantry, in the doorway of the breakfast room. She was rushing from the room, evidently in a condition of some excitement and distress.

Colonel Bantry was sitting at the table, his face rather redder than usual.

''Morning, Clithering,' he said. 'Nice day. Help yourself.'

Sir Henry obeyed. As he took his seat, a plate of kidneys and bacon in front of him, his host went on:

'Dolly's a bit upset this morning.'

'Yes—er—I rather thought so,' said Sir Henry mildly.

He wondered a little. His hostess was of a placid disposition, little given to moods or excitement. As far as Sir Henry knew, she felt keenly on one subject only—gardening.

'Yes,' said Colonel Bantry. 'Bit of news we got this morning upset her. Girl in the village—Emmott's daughter—Emmott who keeps the Blue Boar.'

'Oh, yes, of course.'

'Ye-es,' said Colonel Bantry ruminatively. 'Pretty girl. Got herself into trouble. Usual story. I've been arguing with Dolly about that. Foolish of me. Women never see sense. Dolly was all up in arms for the girl—you know what women are—men are brutes—all the rest of it, etcetera. But it's not so simple as all that—not in these days. Girls know what they're about. Fellow who seduces a girl's not necessarily a villain. Fifty-fifty as often as not. I rather liked young Sandford myself. A young ass rather than a Don Juan, I should have said.'

'It is this man Sandford who got the girl into trouble?'

'So it seems. Of course I don't know anything personally,' said the Colonel cautiously. 'It's all gossip and chat. You know what this place is! As I say, I *know* nothing. And I'm not like Dolly—leaping to conclusions, flinging accusations all over the place. Damn it all, one ought to be careful in what one says. You know—inquest and all that.'

'Inquest?'

Colonel Bantry stared.

'Yes. Didn't I tell you? Girl drowned herself. That's what all the bother's about.'

'That's a nasty business,' said Sir Henry.

'Of course it is. Don't like to think of it myself. Poor pretty little devil. Her father's a hard man by all accounts. I suppose she just felt she couldn't face the music.'

He paused.

'That's what's upset Dolly so.'

'Where did she drown herself?'

'In the river. Just below the mill it runs pretty fast. There's a footpath and a bridge across. They think she threw herself off that. Well, well, it doesn't bear thinking about.'

And with a portentous rustle, Colonel Bantry opened his newspaper and proceeded to distract his mind from painful matters by an absorption in the newest iniquities of the government.

Sir Henry was only mildly interested by the village tragedy. After breakfast, he established himself on a comfortable chair on the lawn, tilted his hat over his eyes and contemplated life from a peaceful angle.

It was about half past eleven when a neat parlourmaid tripped across the lawn.

'If you please, sir, Miss Marple has called, and would like to see you.'

'Miss Marple?'

Sir Henry sat up and straightened his hat. The name surprised him. He remembered Miss Marple very well—her gentle quiet old-maidish ways, her amazing penetration. He remembered a dozen unsolved and hypothetical cases—and how in each case this typical 'old maid of the village' had leaped unerringly to the right solution of the mystery. Sir Henry had a very deep respect for Miss Marple. He wondered what had brought her to see him.

Miss Marple was sitting in the drawing-room—very upright as always, a gaily coloured marketing basket of foreign extraction beside her. Her cheeks were rather pink and she seemed flustered.

'Sir Henry—I am so glad. So fortunate to find you. I just happened to hear that you were staying down here . . . I do hope you will forgive me . . .'

'This is a great pleasure,' said Sir Henry, taking her hand. 'I'm afraid Mrs Bantry's out.'

'Yes,' said Miss Marple. 'I saw her talking to Footit, the butcher, as I passed. Henry Footit was run over yesterday—that was his dog. One of those smooth-haired fox terriers, rather stout and quarrelsome, that butchers always seem to have.'

'Yes,' said Sir Henry helpfully.

'I was glad to get here when she wasn't at home,' continued Miss Marple. 'Because it was you I wanted to see. About this sad affair.'

'Henry Footit?' asked Sir Henry, slightly bewildered.

Miss Marple threw him a reproachful glance.

'No, no. Rose Emmott, of course. You've heard?'

Sir Henry nodded.

'Bantry was telling me. Very sad.'

He was a little puzzled. He could not conceive why Miss Marple should want to see him about Rose Emmott.

Miss Marple sat down again. Sir Henry also sat. When the old lady spoke her manner had changed. It was grave, and had a certain dignity.

'You may remember, Sir Henry, that on one or two occasions we played what was really a pleasant kind of game. Propounding mysteries and giving solutions. You were kind enough to say that I—that I did not do too badly.'

'You beat us all,' said Sir Henry warmly. 'You displayed an absolute genius for getting to the truth. And you always instanced, I remember, some village parallel which had supplied you with the clue.'

He smiled as he spoke, but Miss Marple did not smile. She remained very grave.

'What you said has emboldened me to come to you now. I feel that if I say something to you—at least you will not laugh at me.'

He realized suddenly that she was in deadly earnest.

'Certainly, I will not laugh,' he said gently.

'Sir Henry—this girl—Rose Emmott. She did not drown herself—*she was murdered* ... And I know who murdered her.'

Sir Henry was silent with sheer astonishment for quite three seconds. Miss Marple's voice had been perfectly quiet and unexcited. She might have been making the most ordinary statement in the world for all the emotion she showed.

'This is a very serious statement to make, Miss Marple,' said Sir Henry when he had recovered his breath.

She nodded her head gently several times.

'I know—I know—that is why I have come to you.'

'But, my dear lady, I am not the person to come to. I am merely a private individual nowadays. If you have knowledge of the kind you claim, you must go to the police.'

'I don't think I can do that,' said Miss Marple.

'But why not?'

'Because, you see, I haven't got any—what you call *knowledge.'*

'You mean it's only a guess on your part?'

'You can call it that, if you like, but it's not really that at all. I *know.* I'm in a position to know; but if I gave my reasons for knowing to Inspector Drewitt—well, he'd simply laugh. And really, I don't know that I'd blame him. It's very difficult to understand what you might call specialized knowledge.'

'Such as?' suggested Sir Henry.

Miss Marple smiled a little.

'If I were to tell you that I know because of a man called Peasegood leaving turnips instead of carrots when he came round with a cart and sold vegetables to my niece several years ago—'

She stopped eloquently.

'A very appropriate name for the trade,' murmured Sir Henry. 'You mean that you are simply judging from the facts in a parallel case.'

'I know human nature,' said Miss Marple. 'It's impossible not to know human nature living in a village all these years. The question is, do you believe me, or don't you?'

She looked at him very straight. The pink flush had heightened on her cheeks. Her eyes met his steadily without wavering.

Sir Henry was a man with a very vast experience of life. He made his decisions quickly without beating about the bush. Unlikely and fantastic as Miss Marple's statement might seem, he was instantly aware that he accepted it.

'I *do* believe you, Miss Marple. But I do not see what you want me to do in the matter, or why you have come to me.'

'I have thought and thought about it,' said Miss Marple. 'As I said, it would be useless going to the police without any facts. I have no facts. What I would ask you to do is to interest yourself in the matter—Inspector Drewitt would be most flattered, I am sure. And, of course, if the matter went farther, Colonel Melchert, the Chief Constable, I am sure, would be wax in your hands.'

She looked at him appealingly.

'And what data are you going to give me to work upon?'

'I thought,' said Miss Marple, 'of writing a name—*the* name—on a piece of paper and giving it to you. Then if, on investigation, you decided that the—the *person*—is not involved in any way—well, I shall have been quite wrong.'

She paused and then added with a slight shiver. 'It would be so dreadful—so very dreadful—if an innocent person were to be hanged.'

'What on earth—' cried Sir Henry, startled.

She turned a distressed face upon him.

'I may be wrong about that—though I don't think so. Inspector Drewitt, you see, is really an intelligent man. But a mediocre amount of intelligence is sometimes most dangerous. It does not take one far enough.'

Sir Henry looked at her curiously.

Fumbling a little, Miss Marple opened a small reticule, took out a little notebook, tore out a leaf, carefully wrote a name on it and folding it in two, handed it to Sir Henry.

He opened it and read the name. It conveyed nothing to him, but his eyebrows lifted a little. He looked across at Miss Marple and tucked the piece of paper in his pocket.

'Well, well,' he said. 'Rather an extraordinary business, this. I've never done anything like it before. But I'm going to back my judgment—of *you,* Miss Marple.'

Sir Henry was sitting in a room with Colonel Melchett, the Chief Constable of the county, and Inspector Drewitt.

The Chief Constable was a little man of aggressively military demeanour. The Inspector was big and broad and eminently sensible.

'I really do feel I'm butting in,' said Sir Henry with his pleasant smile. 'I can't really tell you why I'm doing it.' (Strict truth this!)

'My dear fellow, we're charmed. It's a great compliment.'

'Honoured, Sir Henry,' said the Inspector.

The Chief Constable was thinking: 'Bored to death, poor fellow, at the Bantrys. The old man abusing the government and the old woman babbling on about bulbs.'

The Inspector was thinking: 'Pity we're not up against a real teaser. One of the best brains in England, I've heard it said. Pity it's all such plain sailing.'

Aloud, the Chief Constable said:

'I'm afraid it's all very sordid and straightforward. First idea was that the girl had pitched herself in. She was in the family way, you understand. However, our doctor,

Haydock, is a careful fellow. He noticed the bruises on each arm—upper arm. Caused before death. Just where a fellow would have taken her by the arms and flung her in.'

'Would that require much strength?'

'I think not. There would be no struggle—the girl would be taken unawares. It's a footbridge of slippery wood. Easiest thing in the world to pitch her over—there's no handrail that side.'

'You know for a fact that the tragedy occurred there?'

'Yes. We've got a boy—Jimmy Brown—aged twelve. He was in the woods on the other side. He heard a kind of scream from the bridge and a splash. It was dusk you know—difficult to see anything. Presently he saw something white floating down in the water and he ran and got help. They got her out, but it was too late to revive her.'

Sir Henry nodded.

'The boy saw no one on the bridge?'

'No. But, as I tell you, it was dusk, and there's mist always hanging about there. I'm going to question him as to whether he saw anyone about just afterwards or just before. You see he naturally assumed that the girl had thrown herself over. Everybody did to start with.'

'Still, we've got the note,' said Inspector Drewitt. He turned to Sir Henry.

'Note in the dead girl's pocket, sir. Written with a kind of artist's pencil it was, and all of a sop though the paper was we managed to read it.'

'And what did it say?'

'It was from young Sandford. "All right," that's how it ran. "I'll meet you at the bridge at eight-thirty.—R.S." Well, it was near as might be to eight-thirty—a few minutes after—when Jimmy Brown heard the cry and the splash.'

'I don't know whether you've met Sandford at all?' went on Colonel Melchert. 'He's been down here about a month. One of these modern day young architects who build peculiar houses. He's doing a house for Allington. God knows what it's going to be like—full of new-fangled stuff, I suppose. Glass dinner table and surgical chairs made of steel and webbing. Well, that's neither here nor there, but it shows the kind of chap Sandford is. Bolshie, you know—no morals.'

'Seduction,' said Sir Henry mildly, 'is quite an old-established crime though it does not, of course, date back so far as murder.'

Colonel Melchert stared.

'Oh! yes,' he said. 'Quite. Quite.'

'Well, Sir Henry,' said Drewitt, 'there it is—an ugly business, but plain. This young Sandford gets the girl into trouble. Then he's all for clearing off back to London. He's got a girl there – nice young lady – he's engaged to be married to her. Well, naturally this business, if she gets to hear of it, may cook his goose good and proper. He meets Rose at the bridge—it's a misty evening, no one about—he catches her by the shoulders and pitches her in. A proper young swine—and deserves what's coming to him. That's my opinion.'

Sir Henry was silent for a minute or two. He perceived a strong undercurrent of local prejudice. A new-fangled architect was not likely to be popular in the conservative village of St Mary Mead.

'There is no doubt, I suppose, that this man, Sandford, was actually the father of the coming child?' he asked.

'He's the father all right,' said Drewitt. 'Rose Emmott let out as much to her father. She thought he'd marry her. Marry her! Not he!'

'Dear me,' thought Sir Henry. 'I seem to be back in mid-Victorian melodrama. Unsuspecting girl, the villain from London, the stern father, the betrayal—we only need the faithful village lover. Yes, I think it's time I asked about him.'

And aloud he said:

'Hadn't the girl a young man of her own down here?'

'You mean Joe Ellis?' said the Inspector. 'Good fellow Joe. Carpentering's his trade. Ah! If she'd stuck to Joe—'

Colonel Melchert nodded approval.

'Stick to your own class,' he snapped.

'How did Joe Ellis take this affair?' asked Sir Henry.

'Nobody knew how he was taking it,' said the Inspector. 'He's a quiet fellow, is Joe. Close. Anything Rose did was right in his eyes. She had him on a string all right. Just hoped she'd come back to him some day—that was his attitude, I reckon.'

'I'd like to see him,' said Sir Henry.

'Oh! We're going to look him up,' said Colonel Melchett. 'We're not neglecting any line. I thought myself we'd see Emmott first, then Sandford, and then we can go on and see Ellis. That suits you, Clithering?'

Sir Henry said it would suit him admirably.

They found Tom Emmott at the Blue Boar. He was a big burly man of middle age with a shifty eye and a truculent jaw.

'Glad to see you, gentlemen—good morning, Colonel. Come in here and we can be private. Can I offer you anything, gentlemen? No? It's as you please. You've come about this business of my poor girl. Ah! She was a good girl, Rose was. Always was a good girl—till this bloody swine—beg pardon, but that's what he is—till he came along. Promised her marriage, he did. But I'll have the law on him. Drove her to it, he did. Murdering swine. Bringing disgrace on all of us. My poor girl.'

'Your daughter distinctly told you that Mr Sandford was responsible for her condition?' asked Melchert crisply.

'She did. In this very room she did.'

'And what did you say to her?' asked Sir Henry.

'Say to her?' The man seemed momentarily taken aback.

'Yes. You didn't, for example, threaten to turn her out of the house.'

'I was a bit upset—that's only natural. I'm sure you'll agree that's only natural. But, of course, I didn't turn her out of the house. I wouldn't do such a thing.' He assumed virtuous indignation. 'No. What's the law for—that's what I say. What's the law for? He'd got to do the right by her. And if he didn't, by God, he'd got to pay.'

He brought down his fist on the table.

'What time did you last see your daughter?' asked Melchert.

'Yesterday—tea time.'

'What was her manner then?'

'Well, much as usual. I didn't notice anything. If I'd known—'

'But you didn't know,' said the Inspector drily.

They took their leave.

'Emmott hardly creates a favourable impression,' said Sir Henry thoughtfully.

'Bit of a blackguard,' said Melchert. 'He'd have bled Sandford all right if he'd had the chance.'

Their next call was on the architect. Rex Sandford was very unlike the picture Sir Henry had unconsciously formed of him. He was a tall young man, very fair and very thin. His eyes were blue and dreamy, his hair was untidy and rather too long. His speech was a little too ladylike. Colonel Melchert introduced himself and his companions. Then passing straight to the object of his visit, he invited the architect to make a statement as to his movements on the previous evening.

'You understand,' he said warningly. 'I have no power to compel a statement from you and any statement you make may be used in evidence against you. I want the position to be quite clear to you.'

'I—I don't understand,' said Sandford.

'You understand that the girl Rose Emmott was drowned last night?'

'I know. Oh! it's too, too distressing. Really, I haven't slept a wink. I've been incapable of any work today. I feel responsible—terribly responsible.'

He ran his hands through his hair, making it untidier still.

'I never meant any harm,' he said piteously. 'I never thought. I never dreamt she'd take it that way.'

He sat down at a table and buried his face in his hands.

'Do I understand you to say, Mr Sandford, that you refuse to make a statement as to where you were last night at eight-thirty?'

'No, no—certainly not. I was out. I went for a walk.'

'You went to meet Miss Emmott?'

'No. I went by myself. Through the woods. A long way.'

'Then how do you account for this note, sir, which was found in the dead girl's pocket?'

And Inspector Drewitt read it unemotionally aloud.

'Now, sir,' he finished. 'Do you deny that you wrote that?'

'No—no. You're right. I did write it. Rose asked me to meet her. She insisted. I didn't know what to do. So I wrote that note.'

'Ah, that's better,' said the Inspector.

'But I didn't go!' Sandford's voice rose high and excited. 'I didn't go! I felt it would be much better not to. I was returning to town tomorrow. I felt it would be better not—not to meet. I intended to write from London and—and make—some arrangement.'

'You are aware, sir, that this girl was going to have a child, and that she had named you as its father?'

Sandford groaned, but did not answer.

'Was that statement true, sir?'

Sandford buried his face deeper.

'I suppose so,' he said in a muffled voice.

'Ah!' Inspector Drewitt could not disguise the satisfaction. 'Now about this "walk" of yours. Is there anyone who saw you last night?'

'I don't know. I don't think so. As far as I can remember, I didn't meet anybody.'

'That's a pity.'

'What do you mean?' Sandford stared wildly at him. 'What does it matter whether I was out for a walk or not? What difference does that make to Rose drowning herself?'

'Ah!' said the Inspector. 'But you see, *she didn't.* She was thrown in deliberately, Mr Sandford.'

'She was—' It took him a minute or two to take in all the horror of it. 'My God! Then—'

He dropped into a chair.

Colonel Melchett made a move to depart.

'You understand, Sandford,' he said. 'You are on no account to leave this house.'

The three men left together. The Inspector and the Chief Constable exchanged glances.

'That's enough, I think, sir,' said the Inspector.

'Yes. Get a warrant made out and arrest him.'

'Excuse me,' said Sir Henry, 'I've forgotten my gloves.'

He re-entered the house rapidly. Sandford was sitting just as they had left him, staring dazedly in front of him.

'I have come back,' said Sir Henry, 'to tell you that I personally, am anxious to do all I can to assist you. The motive of my interest in you I am not at liberty to reveal. But I am going to ask you, if you will, to tell me as briefly as possible exactly what passed between you and this girl Rose.'

'She was very pretty,' said Sandford. 'Very pretty and very alluring. And—and she made a dead seat at me. Before God, that's true. She wouldn't let me alone. And it was lonely down here, and nobody liked me much, and—and, as I say she was amazingly pretty and she seemed to know her way about and all that—' His voice died away. He looked up. 'And then this happened. She wanted me to marry her. I didn't know what to do. I'm engaged to a girl in London. If she ever gets to hear of this—and she will, of course—well, it's all up. She won't understand. How could she? And I'm a rotter, of course. As I say, I didn't know what to do. I avoided seeing Rose again. I thought I'd get back to town—see my lawyer—make arrangements about money and so forth, for her. God, what a fool I've been! And it's all so clear—the case against me. But they've made a mistake. She *must* have done it herself.'

'Did she ever threaten to take her life?'

Sandford shook his head.

'Never. I shouldn't have said she was that sort.'

'What about a man called Joe Ellis?'

'The carpenter fellow? Good old village stock. Dull fellow—but crazy about Rose.'

'He might have been jealous?' suggested Sir Henry.

'I suppose he was a bit—but he's the bovine kind. He'd suffer in silence.'

'Well,' said Sir Henry. 'I must be going.'

He rejoined the others.

'You know, Melchert,' he said, 'I feel we ought to have a look at this other fellow—Ellis—before we do anything drastic. Pity if you made an arrest that turned out to be a mistake. After all, jealousy is a pretty good motive for murder—and a pretty common one, too.'

'That's true enough,' said the Inspector. 'But Joe Ellis isn't that kind. He wouldn't hurt a fly. Why, nobody's ever seen him out of temper. Still, I agree we'd better just ask him where he was last night. He'll be at home now. He lodges with Mrs Bartlett—very decent soul—a widow, she takes in a bit of washing.'

The little cottage to which they bent their footsteps was spotlessly clean and neat. A big stout woman of middle age opened the door to them. She had a pleasant face and blue eyes.

'Good morning, Mrs Bartlett,' said the Inspector. 'Is Joe Ellis here?'

'Came back not ten minutes ago,' said Mrs Bartlett. 'Step inside, will you, please, sirs.'

Wiping her hands on her apron she led them into a tiny front parlour with stuffed birds, china dogs, a sofa and several useless pieces of furniture.

She hurriedly arranged seats for them, picked up a whatnot bodily to make further room and went out calling:

'Joe, there's three gentlemen want to see you.'

A voice from the back kitchen replied:

'I'll be there when I've cleaned myself.'

Mrs Bartlett smiled.

'Come in, Mrs Bartlett,' said Colonel Melchett. 'Sit down.'

'Oh, no, sir, I couldn't think of it.'

Mrs Bartlett was shocked at the idea.

'You find Joe Ellis a good lodger?' inquired Melchett in a seemingly careless tone.

'Couldn't have a better, sir. A real steady young fellow. Never touches a drop of drink. Takes a pride in his work. And always kind and helpful about the house. He put up those shelves for me, and he's fixed a new dresser in the kitchen. And any little thing that wants doing in the house—why, Joe does it as a matter of course, and won't hardly take thanks for it. Ah! there aren't many young fellows like Joe, sir.'

'Some girl will be lucky some day,' said Melchett carelessly. 'He was rather sweet on that poor girl, Rose Emmott, wasn't he?'

Mrs Bartlett sighed.

'It made me tired, it did. Him worshipping the ground she trod on and her not caring a snap of the fingers for him.'

'Where does Joe spend his evenings, Mrs Bartlett?'

'Here, sir, usually. He does some odd piece of work in the evenings, sometimes, and he's trying to learn book-keeping by correspondence.'

'Ah! really. Was he in yesterday evening?'

'Yes, sir.'

'You're sure, Mrs Bartlett?' said Sir Henry sharply.

She turned to him.

'Quite sure, sir.'

'He didn't go out, for instance, somewhere about eight to eight-thirty?'

'Oh, no.' Mrs Barlett laughed. 'He was fixing the kitchen dresser for me nearly all the evening, and I was helping him.'

Sir Henry looked at her smiling assured face and felt his first pang of doubt.

A moment later Ellis himself entered the room.

He was a tall broad-shouldered young man, very

good-looking in a rustic way. He had shy, blue eyes and a good-tempered smile. Altogether an amiable young giant.

Melchett opened the conversation. Mrs Bartlett withdrew to the kitchen.

'We are investigating the death of Rose Emmott. You knew her, Ellis.'

'Yes.' He hesitated, then muttered, 'Hoped to marry her one day. Poor lass.'

'You have heard of what her condition was?'

'Yes.' A spark of anger showed in his eyes. 'Let her down, he did. But 'twere for the best. She wouldn't have been happy married to him. I reckoned she'd come to me when this happened. I'd have looked after her.'

'In spite of—'

''Tweren't her fault. He led her astray with fine promises and all. Oh! she told me about it. She'd no call to drown herself. He weren't worth it.'

'Where were you, Ellis, last night at eight-thirty?'

Was it Sir Henry's fancy, or was there really a shade of constraint in the ready—almost too ready—reply.

'I was here. Fixing up a contraption in the kitchen for Mrs B. You ask her. She'll tell you.'

'He was too quick with that,' thought Sir Henry. 'He's a slow-thinking man. That popped out so pat that I suspect he'd got it ready beforehand.'

Then he told himself that it was imagination. He was imagining things—yes, even imagining an apprehensive glint in those blue eyes.

A few more questions and answers and they left. Sir Henry made an excuse to go to the kitchen. Mrs Bartlett was busy at the stove. She looked up with a pleasant smile. A new dresser was fixed against the wall. It was not quite finished. Some tools lay about and some pieces of wood.

'That's what Ellis was at work on last night?' said Sir Henry.

'Yes, sir, it's a nice bit of work, isn't it? He's a very clever carpenter, Joe is.'

No apprehensive gleam in her eye—no embarrassment.

But Ellis—had he imagined it? No, there *had* been something.

'I must tackle him,' thought Sir Henry.

Turning to leave the kitchen, he collided with a perambulator.

'Not woken the baby up, I hope,' he said.

Mrs Bartlett's laugh rang out.

'Oh, no, sir. I've no children—more's the pity. That's what I take the laundry on, sir.'

'Oh! I see—'

He paused then said on an impulse:

'Mrs Bartlett. You knew Rose Emmott. Tell me what you really thought of her.'

She looked at him curiously.

'Well, sir, I thought she was flighty. But she's dead—and I don't like to speak ill of the dead.'

'But I have a reason—a very good reason for asking.'

He spoke persuasively.

She seemed to consider, studying him attentively. Finally she made up her mind.

'She was a bad lot, sir,' she said quietly. 'I wouldn't say so before Joe. She took *him* in good and proper. That kind can—more's the pity. You know how it is, sir.'

Yes, Sir Henry knew. The Joe Ellises of the world were peculiarly vulnerable. They trusted blindly. But for that very cause the shock of discovery might be greater.

He left the cottage baffled and perplexed. He was up against a blank wall. Joe Ellis had been working indoors all yesterday evening. Mrs Bartlett had actually been there watching him. Could one possibly get round that? There was nothing to set against it—except possibly that suspicious readiness in replying on Joe Ellis's part—that suggestion of having a story pat.

'Well,' said Melchett, 'that seems to make the matter quite clear, eh?'

'It does, sir,' agreed the Inspector. 'Sandford's our man. Not a leg to stand upon. The thing's as plain as daylight. It's my opinion as the girl and her father were out to—well—practically blackmail him. He's no money to speak of—he didn't want the matter to get to his young lady's ears. He was desperate and he acted accordingly. What do you say, sir?' he added, addressing Sir Henry deferentially.

'It seems so,' admitted Sir Henry. 'And yet—I can hardly picture Sandford committing any violent action.'

But he knew as he spoke that that objection was hardly valid. The meekest animal, when cornered, is capable of amazing actions.

'I should like to see the boy, though,' he said suddenly. 'The one who heard the cry.'

Jimmy Brown proved to be an intelligent lad, rather small for his age, with a sharp, rather cunning face. He was eager to be questioned and was rather disappointed when checked in his dramatic tale of what he had heard on the fatal night.

'You were on the other side of the bridge, I understand,' said Sir Henry. 'Across the river from the village. Did you see anyone on that side as you came over the bridge?'

'There was someone walking up in the woods. Mr Sandford, I think it was, the architecting gentleman who's building the queer house.'

The three men exchanged glances.

'That was about ten minutes or so before you heard the cry?'

The boy nodded.

'Did you see anyone else—on the village side of the river?'

'A man came along the path that side. Going slow and whistling he was. Might have been Joe Ellis.'

'You couldn't possibly have seen who it was,' said the Inspector sharply. 'What with the mist and its being dusk.'

'It's on account of the whistle,' said the boy. 'Joe Ellis always whistles the same tune—"I wanner be happy"—it's the only tune he knows.'

He spoke with the scorn of the modernist for the old-fashioned.

'Anyone might whistle a tune,' said Melchett. 'Was he going towards the bridge?'

'No. Other way—to village.'

'I don't think we need concern ourselves with this unknown man,' said Melchett. 'You heard the cry and the splash and a few minutes later you saw the body floating downstream and you ran for help, going back to the bridge, crossing it, and making straight for the village. You didn't see anyone near the bridge as you ran for help?'

'I think as there were two men with a wheelbarrow on the river path; but they were some way away and I couldn't tell if they were going or coming and Mr Giles's place was nearest—so I ran there.'

'You did well, my boy,' said Melchett. 'You acted very creditably and with presence of mind. You're a scout, aren't you?'

'Yes, sir.'

'Very good. Very good indeed.'

Sir Henry was silent—thinking. He took a slip of

paper from his pocket, looked at it, shook his head. It didn't seem possible—and yet—

He decided to pay a call on Miss Marple.

She received him in her pretty, slightly overcrowded old-style drawing-room.

'I've come to report progress,' said Sir Henry. 'I'm afraid that from our point of view things aren't going well. They are going to arrest Sandford. And I must say I think they are justified.'

'You have found nothing in—what shall I say—support of my theory, then?' She looked perplexed—anxious. 'Perhaps I have been wrong—quite wrong. You have such wide experience—you would surely detect it if it were so.'

'For one thing,' said Sir Henry, 'I can hardly believe it. And for another we are up against an unbreakable alibi. Joe Ellis was fixing shelves in the kitchen all the evening and Mrs Bartlett was watching him do it.'

Miss Marple leaned forward, taking in a quick breath.

'But that can't be so,' she said. 'It was Friday night.'

'Friday night?'

'Yes—Friday night. On Friday evenings Mrs Bartlett takes the laundry she has done round to the different people.'

Sir Henry leaned back in his chair. He remembered the boy Jimmy's story of the whistling man and—yes—it would all fit in.

He rose, taking Miss Marple warmly by the hand.

'I think I see my way,' he said. 'At least I can try . . .'

Five minutes later he was back at Mrs Bartlett's cottage and facing Joe Ellis in the little parlour among the china dogs.

'You lied to us, Ellis, about last night,' he said crisply. 'You were not in the kitchen here fixing the dresser between eight and eight-thirty. You were seen walking along the path by the river towards the bridge a few minutes before Rose Emmott was murdered.'

The man gasped.

'She weren't murdered—she weren't. I had naught to do with it. She threw herself in, she did. She was desperate like. I wouldn't have harmed a hair on her head, I wouldn't.'

'Then why did you lie as to where you were?' asked Sir Henry keenly.

The man's eyes shifted and lowered uncomfortably.

'I was scared. Mrs B. saw me around there and when we heard just afterwards what had happened—well, she thought it might look bad for me. I fixed I'd say I was working here, and she agreed to back me up. She's a rare one, she is. She's always been good to me.'

Without a word Sir Henry left the room and walked into the kitchen. Mrs Bartlett was washing up at the sink.

'Mrs Bartlett,' he said, 'I know everything. I think you'd better confess—that is, unless you want Joe Ellis hanged for something he didn't do ... No. I see you don't want that. I'll tell you what happened. You were out taking the laundry home. You came across Rose Emmott. You thought she'd given Joe the chuck and was taking up with this stranger. Now she was in trouble—Joe was prepared to come to the rescue—marry her if need be, and if she'd have him. He's lived in your house for four years. You've fallen in love with him. You want him for yourself. You hated this girl—you couldn't bear that this worthless little slut should take your man from you. You're a strong woman, Mrs Bartlett. You caught the girl by the shoulders and shoved her over into the stream. A few minutes later you met Joe Ellis. The boy Jimmy saw you together in the distance but in the darkness and the mist he assumed the perambulator was a wheelbarrow and two men wheeling it. You persuaded Joe that he might be suspected and you concocted what was supposed to be an alibi for him, but which was really an alibi for *you*. Now then, I'm right, am I not?'

He held his breath. He had staked all on this throw.

She stood before him rubbing her hands on her apron, slowly making up her mind.

'It's just as you say, sir,' she said at last, in her quiet subdued voice (a dangerous voice, Sir Henry suddenly felt it to be). 'I don't know what came over me. Shameless—that's what she was. It just came over me—she shan't take Joe from me. I haven't had a happy life, sir. My husband, he was a poor lot—an invalid and cross-grained. I nursed and looked after him true. And then Joe came here to lodge. I'm not such an old woman, sir, in spite of my grey hair. I'm just forty, sir. Joe's one in a thousand. I'd have done anything for him—anything at all. He was like a little child, sir, so gentle and believing. He was mine, sir, to look after and see to. And this—this—' She swallowed—checked her emotion. Even at this moment she was a strong woman. She stood up straight and looked at Sir Henry curiously. 'I'm ready to come, sir. I never thought anyone would find out. I don't know how you knew, sir—I don't, I'm sure.'

Sir Henry shook his head gently.

'It was not I who knew,' he said—and he thought of the piece of paper still reposing in his pocket with the words on it written in neat old-fashioned handwriting.

'Mrs Bartlett, with whom Joe Ellis lodges at
2 Mill Cottages.'

Miss Marple had been right again.

The Bird with the Broken Wing

Mr Satterthwaite looked out of the window. It was raining steadily. He shivered. Very few country houses, he reflected, were really properly heated. It cheered him to think that in a few hours' time he would be speeding towards London. Once one had passed sixty years of age, London was really much the best place.

He was feeling a little old and pathetic. Most of the members of the house party were so young. Four of them had just gone off into the library to do table turning. They had invited him to accompany them, but he had declined. He failed to derive any amusement from the monotonous counting of the letters of the alphabet and the usual meaningless jumble of letters that resulted.

Yes, London was the best place for him. He was glad that he had declined Madge Keeley's invitation when she had rung up to invite him over to Laidell half an hour ago. An adorable young person, certainly, but London was best.

Mr Satterthwaite shivered again and remembered that the fire in the library was usually a good one. He opened the door and adventured cautiously into the darkened room.

'If I'm not in the way—'

'Was that N or M? We shall have to count again. No, of course not, Mr Satterthwaite. Do you know, the most exciting things have been happening. The spirit says her name is Ada Spiers, and John here is going to marry someone called Gladys Bun almost immediately.'

Mr Satterthwaite sat down in a big easy chair in front of the fire. His eyelids drooped over his eyes and he dozed. From time to time he returned to consciousness, hearing fragments of speech.

'It can't be P A B Z L—not unless he's a Russian. John, you're shoving. I *saw* you. I believe it's a new spirit come.'

Another interval of dozing. Then a name jerked him wide awake.

'Q-U-I-N. Is that right?'

'Yes, it's rapped once for "Yes." Quin. Have you a message for someone here? Yes. For me? For John? For Sarah? For Evelyn? No—but there's no one else. Oh! it's for Mr Satterthwaite, perhaps? It says "Yes." Mr Satterthwaite, it's a message for you.'

'What does it say?'

Mr Satterthwaite was broad awake now, sitting taut and erect in his chair, his eyes shining.

The table rocked and one of the girls counted.

'LAI—it can't be—that doesn't make sense. No word begins LAI.'

'Go on,' said Mr Satterthwaite, and the command in his voice was so sharp that he was obeyed without question.

'LAIDEL? and another L—Oh! that seems to be all.'

'Go on.'

'Tell us some more, please.'

A pause.

'There doesn't seem to be any more. The table's gone quite dead. How silly.'

'No,' said Mr Satterthwaite thoughtfully. 'I don't think it's silly.'

He rose and left the room. He went straight to the telephone. Presently he was through.

'Can I speak to Miss Keeley? Is that you, Madge, my dear? I want to change my mind, if I may, and accept your kind invitation. It is not so urgent as I thought that I should get back to town. Yes—yes—I will arrive in time for dinner.'

He hung up the receiver, a strange flush on his withered cheeks. Mr Quin—the mysterious Mr Harley Quin. Mr Satterthwaite counted over on his fingers the times he had been brought into contact with that man of mystery. Where Mr Quin was concerned—things happened! What had happened or was going to happen—at Laidell?

Whatever it was, there was work for him, Mr Satterthwaite, to do. In some way or other, he would have an active part to play. He was sure of that.

Laidell was a large house. Its owner, David Keeley, was one of those quiet men with indeterminate personalities who seem to count as part of the furniture. Their inconspicuousness has nothing to do with brain power—David Keeley was a most brilliant mathematician, and had written a book totally incomprehensible to ninety-nine hundreds of humanity. But like so many men of brilliant intellect, he radiated no bodily vigour or magnetism. It was a standing joke that David Keeley was a real 'invisible man'. Footmen passed him by with the vegetables, and guests forgot to say how do you do or goodbye.

His daughter Madge was very different. A fine upstanding young woman, bursting with energy and life. Thorough, healthy and normal, and extremely pretty.

It was she who received Mr Satterthwaite when he arrived.

'How nice of you to come—after all.'

'Very delightful of you to let me change my mind. Madge, my dear, you're looking very well.'

'Oh! I'm always well.'

'Yes, I know. But it's more than that. You look—well, blooming is the word I have in mind. Has anything happened my dear? Anything—well—special?'

She laughed—blushed a little.

'It's too bad, Mr Satterthwaite. You always guess things.'

He took her hand.

'So it's that, is it? Mr Right has come along?'

It was an old-fashioned term, but Madge did not object to it. She rather liked Mr Satterthwaite's old-fashioned ways.

'I suppose so—yes. But nobody's supposed to know. It's a secret. But I don't really mind your knowing, Mr Satterthwaite. You're always so nice and sympathetic.'

Mr Satterthwaite thoroughly enjoyed romance at second hand. He was sentimental and Victorian.

'I mustn't ask who the lucky man is? Well, then all I can say is that I hope he is worthy of the honour you are conferring on him.'

Rather a duck, old Mr Satterthwaite, thought Madge.

'Oh! we shall get on awfully well together, I think,' she said. 'You see, we like doing the same things, and that's so awfully important, isn't it? We've really got a lot in common—and we know all about each other and all that. It's really been coming on for a long time. That gives one such a nice safe feeling, doesn't it?'

'Undoubtedly,' said Mr Satterthwaite. 'But in my experience one can never really know all about anyone else. That is part of the interest and charm of life.'

'Oh! I'll risk it,' said Madge, laughing, and they went up to dress for dinner.

Mr Satterthwaite was late. He had not brought a valet, and having his things unpacked for him by a stranger always flurried him a little. He came down to find everyone assembled, and in the modern style Madge merely said: 'Oh! here's Mr Satterthwaite. I'm starving. Let's go in.'

She led the way with a tall grey-haired woman—a woman of striking personality. She had a very clear rather incisive voice, and her face was clear cut and rather beautiful.

'How d'you do, Satterthwaite,' said Mr Keeley.

Mr Satterthwaite jumped.

'How do you do,' he said. 'I'm afraid I didn't see you.'

'Nobody does,' said Mr Keeley sadly.

They went in. The table was a low oval of mahogany. Mr Satterthwaite was placed between his young hostess and a short dark girl—a very hearty girl with a loud voice and a ringing determined laugh that expressed more the determination to be cheerful at all costs than any real mirth. Her name seemed to be Doris, and she was the type of young woman Mr Satterthwaite most disliked. She had, he considered, no artistic justification for existence.

On Madge's other side was a man of about thirty, whose likeness to the grey-haired woman proclaimed them mother and son.

Next to him—

Mr Satterthwaite caught his breath.

He didn't know what it was exactly. It was not beauty. It was something else—something much more elusive and intangible than beauty.

She was listening to Mr Keeley's rather ponderous dinner-table conversation, her head bent a little sideways. She was there, it seemed to Mr Satterthwaite—and yet she was not there! She was somehow a great deal less substantial than anyone else seated round the oval table. Something in the droop of her body sideways was beautiful—was more than beautiful. She looked up—her eyes met Mr Satterthwaite's for a moment across the table—and the word he wanted leapt to his mind.

Enchantment—that was it. She had the quality of enchantment. She might have been one of those creatures who are only half-human—one of the Hidden People from the Hollow Hills. She made everyone else look rather too real . . .

But at the same time, in a queer way, she stirred his pity. It was as though semi-humanity handicapped her. He sought for a phrase and found it.

'A bird with a broken wing,' said Mr Satterthwaite.

Satisfied, he turned his mind back to the subject of Girl Guides and hoped that the girl Doris had not noticed his abstraction. When she turned to the man on the other side of her—a man Mr Satterthwaite had hardly noticed, he himself turned to Madge.

'Who is the lady sitting next to your father?' he asked in a low voice.

'Mrs Graham? Oh, no! you mean Mabelle. Don't you know her? Mabelle Annesley. She was a Clydesley—one of the illfated Clydesleys.'

He started. The ill-fated Clydesleys. He remembered. A brother had shot himself, a sister had been drowned, another had perished in an earthquake. A queer doomed family. This girl must be the youngest of them.

His thoughts were recalled suddenly. Madge's hand touched his under the table. Everyone else was talking. She gave a faint inclination of her head to her left.

'That's him,' she murmured ungrammatically.

Mr Satterthwaite nodded quickly in comprehension. So this young Graham was the man of Madge's choice. Well, she could hardly have done better as far as appearances went—and Mr Satterthwaite was a shrewd observer. A pleasant, likeable, rather matter-of-fact young fellow. They'd make a nice pair—no nonsense about either of them—good healthy sociable young folk.

Laidell was run on old-fashioned lines. The ladies left the dining-room first. Mr Satterthwaite moved up to Graham and began to talk to him. His estimate of the young man was confirmed, yet there was something that struck him as being not quite true to type. Roger Graham was distrait, his mind seemed far away, his hand shook as he replaced the glass on the table.

'He's got something on his mind,' thought Mr Satterthwaite acutely. 'Not nearly as important as he thinks it is, I dare say. All the same, I wonder what it is.'

Mr Satterthwaite was in the habit of swallowing a couple of digestive pastilles after meals. Having neglected to bring them down with him, he went up to his room to fetch them.

On his way down to the drawing-room, he passed along the long corridor on the ground floor. About half-way along it was a room known as the terrace room. As Mr Satterthwaite looked through the open doorway in passing, he stopped short.

Moonlight was streaming into the room. The latticed panes gave it a queer rhythmic pattern. A figure was sitting on the low window sill, drooping a little sideways and softly twanging the string of a ukelele—not in a jazz rhythm, but in a far older rhythm, the beat of fairy horses riding on fairy hills.

Mr Satterthwaite stood fascinated. She wore a dress of dull dark blue chiffon, ruched and pleated so that it looked like the feathers of a bird. She bent over the instrument crooning to it.

He came into the room—slowly, step by step. He was

close to her when she looked up and saw him. She didn't start, he noticed, or seem surprised.

'I hope I'm not intruding,' he began.

'Please—sit down.'

He sat near her on a polished oak chair. She hummed softly under her breath.

'There's a lot of magic about tonight,' she said. 'Don't you think so?'

'Yes, there was a lot of magic about.'

'They wanted me to fetch my uke,' she explained. 'And as I passed here, I thought it would be so lovely to be alone here—in the dark and the moon.'

'Then I—' Mr Satterthwaite half rose, but she stopped him.

'Don't go. You—you fit in, somehow. It's queer, but you do.'

He sat down again.

'It's been a queer sort of evening,' she said. 'I was out in the woods late this afternoon, and I met a man—such a strange sort of man—tall and dark, like a lost soul. The sun was setting, and the light of it through the trees made him look like a kind of Harlequin.'

'Ah!' Mr Satterthwaite leant forward—his interest quickened.

'I wanted to speak to him—he—he looked so like somebody I know. But I lost him in the trees.'

'I think I know him,' said Mr Satterthwaite.

'Do you? He is—interesting, isn't he?'

'Yes, he is interesting.'

There was a pause. Mr Satterthwaite was perplexed. There was something, he felt, that he ought to do—and he didn't know what it was. But surely—surely, it had to do with this girl. He said rather clumsily:

'Sometimes—when one is unhappy—one wants to get away—'

'Yes. That's true.' She broke off suddenly. 'Oh! I see what you mean. But you're wrong. It's just the other way round. I wanted to be alone because I'm happy.'

'Happy?'

'Terribly happy.'

She spoke quite quietly, but Mr Satterthwaite had a sudden sense of shock. What this strange girl meant by being happy wasn't the same as Madge Keeley would have meant by the same words. Happiness, for Mabelle Annesley, meant some kind of intense and vivid ecstasy . . . something that was not only human, but more than human. He shrank back a little.

'I—didn't know,' he said clumsily.

'Of course you couldn't. And it's not—the actual thing—I'm not happy yet—but I'm going to be.' She leaned forward. 'Do you know what it's like to stand in a wood—a big wood with dark shadows and trees very close all round you—a wood you might never get out of—and then, suddenly—just in front of you, you see the country of your dreams—shining and beautiful—you've only got to step out from the trees and the darkness and you've found it . . .'

'So many things look beautiful,' said Mr Satterthwaite, 'before we've reached them. Some of the ugliest things in the world look the most beautiful . . .'

There was a step on the floor. Mr Satterthwaite turned his head. A fair man with a stupid, rather wooden face, stood there. He was the man Mr Satterthwaite had hardly noticed at the dinner-table.

'They're waiting for you, Mabelle,' he said.

She got up, the expression had gone out of her face, her voice was flat and calm.

'I'm coming, Gerard,' she said. 'I've been talking to Mr Satterthwaite.'

She went out of the room, Mr Satterthwaite following.

He turned his head over his shoulder as he went and caught the expression on her husband's face. A hungry, despairing look.

'Enchantment,' thought Mr Satterthwaite. 'He feels it right enough. Poor fellow—poor fellow.'

The drawing-room was well lighted. Madge and Doris Coles were vociferous in reproaches.

'Mabelle, you little beast—you've been ages.'

She sat on a low stool, tuned the ukelele and sang. They all joined in.

'Is it possible,' thought Mr Satterthwaite, 'that so many idiotic songs could have been written about My Baby.'

But he had to admit that the syncopated wailing tunes were stirring. Though, of course, they weren't a patch on the old-fashioned waltz.

The air got very smoky. The syncopated rhythm went on.

'No conversation,' thought Mr Satterthwaite. 'No good music. No *peace*.' He wished the world had not become definitely so noisy.

Suddenly Mabelle Annesley broke off, smiled across the room at him, and began to sing a song of Grieg's.

'My swan—my fair one . . .'

It was a favourite of Mr Satterthwaite's. He liked the note of ingenuous surprise at the end.

'Wert only a swan then? A swan then?'

After that, the party broke up. Madge offered drinks whilst her father picked up the discarded ukelele and began twanging it absent-mindedly. The party exchanged goodnights, drifted nearer and nearer to the door.

Everyone talked at once. Gerard Annesley slipped away unostentatiously, leaving the others.

Outside the drawing-room door, Mr Satterthwaite bade Mrs Graham a ceremonious goodnight. There were two staircases, one close at hand, the other at the end of a long corridor. It was by the latter that Mr Satterthwaite reached his room. Mrs Graham and her son passed by the stairs near at hand whence the quiet Gerard Annesley had already preceded them.

'You'd better get your ukelele, Mabelle,' said Madge. 'You'll forget it in the morning if you don't. You've got to make such an early start.'

'Come on, Mr Satterthwaite,' said Doris Coles, seizing him boisterously by one arm. 'Early to bed—etcetera.'

Madge took him by the other arm and all three ran down the corridor to peals of Doris's laughter. They paused at the end to wait for David Keeley, who was following at a much more sedate pace, turning out electric lights as he came. The four of them went upstairs together.

Mr Satterthwaite was just preparing to descend to the dining-room for breakfast on the following morning, when there was a light tap on the door and Madge Keeley entered. Her face was dead white, and she was shivering all over.

'Oh, Mr Satterthwaite.'

'My dear child, what's happened?' He took her hand.

'Mabelle—Mabelle Annesley . . .'

'Yes?'

What had happened? What? Something terrible—he knew that. Madge could hardly get the words out.

'She—she hanged herself last night . . . On the back of her door. Oh! it's too horrible.' She broke down—sobbing.

Hanged herself. Impossible. Incomprehensible!

He said a few soothing old-fashioned words to Madge, and hurried downstairs. He found David Keeley looking perplexed and incompetent.

'I've telephoned to the police, Satterthwaite. Apparently that's got to be done. So the doctor said. He's just finished examining the—the—good lord, it's a beastly business. She must have been desperately unhappy—to do it that way—Queer that song last night. Swan song, eh? She looked rather like a swan—a black swan.'

'Yes.'

'Swan Song,' repeated Keeley. 'Shows it was in her mind, eh?'

'It would seem so—yes, certainly it would seem so.'

He hesitated, then asked if he might see—if, that is . . .

His host comprehended the stammering request.

'If you want to—I'd forgotten you have a *penchant* for human tragedies.'

He led the way up the broad staircase. Mr Satterthwaite followed him. At the head of the stairs was the room occupied by Roger Graham and opposite it, on the other side of the passage, his mother's room. The latter door was ajar and a faint wisp of smoke floated through it.

A momentary surprise invaded Mr Satterthwaite's mind. He had not judged Mrs Graham to be a woman who smoked so early in the day. Indeed, he had had the idea that she did not smoke at all.

They went along the passage to the end door but one. David Keeley entered the room and Mr Satterthwaite followed him.

The room was not a very large one and showed signs of a man's occupation. A door in the wall led into a second room. A bit of cut rope still dangled from a hook high up on the door. On the bed . . .

Mr Satterthwaite stood for a minute looking down on the heap of huddled chiffon. He noticed that it was ruched and pleated like the plumage of a bird. At the face, after one glance, he did not look again.

He glanced from the door with its dangling rope to the communicating door through which they had come.

'Was that open?'

'Yes. At least the maid says so.'

'Annesley slept in there? Did he hear anything?'

'He says—nothing.'

'Almost incredible,' murmured Mr Satterthwaite. He looked back at the form on the bed.

'Where is he?'

'Annesley? He's downstairs with the doctor.'

They went downstairs to find an Inspector of police had arrived. Mr Satterthwaite was agreeably surprised to recognize in him an old acquaintance, Inspector Winkfield. The Inspector went upstairs with the doctor, and a few minutes later a request came that all members of the house party should assemble in the drawing-room.

The blinds had been drawn, and the whole room had a funereal aspect. Doris Coles looked frightened and subdued. Every now and then she dabbed her eyes with a handkerchief. Madge was resolute and alert, her feelings fully under control by now. Mrs Graham was composed, as always, her face grave and impassive. The tragedy seemed to have affected her son more keenly than anyone. He looked a positive wreck this morning. David Keeley, as usual, had subsided into the background.

The bereaved husband sat alone, a little apart from the others. There was a queer dazed looked about him, as though he could hardly realize what had taken place.

Mr Satterthwaite, outwardly composed, was inwardly seething with the importance of a duty shortly to be performed.

Inspector Winkfield, followed by Dr Morris, came in and shut the door behind him. He cleared his throat and spoke.

'This is a very sad occurrence—very sad, I'm sure. It's necessary, under the circumstances, that I should ask everybody a few questions. You'll not object, I'm sure. I'll begin with Mr Annesley. You'll forgive my asking, sir, but had your good lady ever threatened to take her life?'

Mr Satterthwaite opened his lips impulsively, then closed them again. There was plenty of time. Better not speak too soon.

'I—no, I don't think so.'

His voice was so hesitating, so peculiar, that everyone shot a covert glance at him.

'You're not sure, sir?'

'Yes—I'm—quite sure. She didn't.'

'Ah! Were you aware that she was unhappy in any way?'

'No. I—no, I wasn't.'

'She said nothing to you. About feeling depressed, for instance?'

'I—no, nothing.'

Whatever the Inspector thought, he said nothing. Instead he proceeded to his next point.

'Will you describe to me briefly the events of last night?'

'We—all went up to bed. I fell asleep immediately and heard nothing. The housemaid's scream aroused me this morning. I rushed into the adjoining room and found my wife—and found her—'

His voice broke. The Inspector nodded.

'Yes, yes, that's quite enough. We needn't go into that. When did you last see your wife the night before?'

'I—downstairs.'

'Downstairs?'

'Yes, we all left the drawing-room together. I went straight up leaving the others talking in the hall.'

'And you didn't see your wife again? Didn't she say goodnight when she came up to bed?'

'I was asleep when she came up.'

'But she only followed you a few minutes later. That's right, isn't it, sir?' He looked at David Keeley, who nodded.

'She hadn't come up half an hour later.'

Annesley spoke stubbornly. The Inspector's eyes strayed gently to Mrs Graham.

'She didn't stay in your room talking, Madam?'

Did Mr Satterthwaite fancy it, or was there a slight pause before Mrs Graham said with her customary quiet decision of manner:

'No, I went straight into my room and closed the door. I heard nothing.'

'And you say, sir'—the Inspector had shifted his attention back to Annesley—'that you slept and heard nothing. The communicating door was open, was it not?'

'I—I believe so. But my wife would have entered her room by the other door from the corridor.'

'Even so, sir, there would have been certain sounds—a choking noise, a drumming of heels on the door—'

'*No*.'

It was Mr Satterthwaite who spoke, impetuously, unable to stop himself. Every eye turned towards him in surprise. He himself became nervous, stammered, and turned pink.

'I—I beg your pardon, Inspector. But I must speak. You are on the wrong track—the wrong track altogether. Mrs Annesley did not kill herself—I am sure of it. She was murdered.'

There was a dead silence, then Inspector Winkfield said quietly:

'What leads you to say that, sir?'

'I—it is a feeling. A very strong feeling.'

'But I think, sir, there must be more than that to it. There must be some particular reason.'

Well, of course there *was* a particular reason. There was the mysterious message from Mr Quin. But you couldn't tell a police inspector that. Mr Satterthwaite cast about desperately, and found nothing.

'Last night—when we were talking together, she said she was very happy. Very happy—just that. That wasn't like a woman thinking of committing suicide.'

He was triumphant. He added:

'She went back to the drawing-room to fetch her ukelele, so that she wouldn't forget it in the morning. That didn't look like suicide either.'

'No,' admitted the Inspector. 'No, perhaps it didn't.' He turned to David Keeley. 'Did she take the ukelele upstairs with her?'

The mathematician tried to remember.

'I think—yes, she did. She went upstairs carrying it in her hand. I remember seeing it just as she turned the corner of the staircase before I turned off the light down here.'

'Oh!' cried Madge. 'But it's here now.'

She pointed dramatically to where the ukelele lay on a table.

'That's curious,' said the Inspector. He stepped swiftly across and rang the bell.

A brief order sent the butler in search of the housemaid

whose business it was to do the rooms in the morning. She came, and was quite positive in her answer. The ukelele had been there first thing that morning when she had dusted.

Inspector Winkfield dismissed her and then said curtly:

'I would like to speak to Mr Satterthwaite in private, please. Everyone may go. But no one is to leave the house.'

Mr Satterthwaite twittered into speech as soon as the door had closed behind the others.

'I—I am sure, Inspector, that you have the case excellently in hand. Excellently. I just felt that—having, as I say, a very strong feeling—'

The Inspector arrested further speech with an upraised hand.

'You're quite right, Mr Satterthwaite. The lady was murdered.'

'You knew it?' Mr Satterthwaite was chagrined.

'There were certain things that puzzled Dr Morris.' He looked across at the doctor, who had remained, and the doctor assented to his statement with a nod of the head. 'We made a thorough examination. The rope that was round her neck wasn't the rope that she was strangled with—it was something much thinner that did the job, something more like a wire. It had cut right into the flesh. The mark of the rope was superimposed on it. She was strangled and then hung up on the door afterwards to make it look like suicide.'

'But who—?'

'Yes,' said the Inspector. 'Who? That's the question. What about the husband sleeping next door, who never said goodnight to his wife and who heard nothing? I should say we hadn't far to look. Must find out what terms they were on That's where you can be useful to us, Mr Satterthwaite. You've the *ongtray* here, and you can get the hang of things in a way we can't. Find out what relations there were between the two.'

'I hardly like—' began Mr Satterthwaite, stiffening.

'It won't be the first murder mystery you've helped us with. I remember the case of Mrs Strangeways. You've got a *flair* for that sort of thing, sir. An absolute *flair*.'

Yes, it was true—he *had a flair*. He said quietly:

'I will do my best, Inspector.'

Had Gerard Annesley killed his wife? Had he? Mr Satterthwaite recalled that look of misery last night. He loved her—and he was suffering. Suffering will drive a man to strange deeds.

But there was something else—some other factor. Mabelle had spoken of herself as coming out of a wood—she was looking forward to happiness—not a quiet rational happiness—but a happiness that was irrational—a wild ecstasy . . .

If Gerard Annesley had spoken the truth, Mabelle had not come to her room till at least half an hour later than he had done. Yet David Keeley had seen her going up those stairs. There were two other rooms occupied in that wing. There was Mrs Graham's, and there was her son's.

Her son's. But he and Madge . . .

Surely Madge would have guessed . . . But Madge wasn't the guessing kind. All the same, no smoke without fire—Smoke!

Ah! he remembered. *A wisp of smoke curling out through Mrs Graham's bedroom door.*

He acted on impulse. Straight up the stairs and into her room. It was empty. He closed the door behind him and locked it.

He went across to the grate. A heap of charred fragments. Very gingerly he raked them over with his finger. His luck was in. In the very centre were some unburnt fragments—fragments of letters . . .

Very disjointed fragments, but they told him something of value.

'Life can be wonderful, Roger darling. I never knew . . . all my life has been a dream till I met you, Roger . . .'

'. . . Gerard knows, I think . . . I am sorry but what can I do? Nothing is real to me but you, Roger . . . We shall be together, soon.'

'What are you going to tell him at Laidell, Roger? You write strangely—but I am not afraid . . .'

Very carefully, Mr Satterthwaite put the fragments into an envelope from the writing-table. He went to the door, unlocked it and opened it to find himself face to face with Mrs Graham.

It was an awkward moment, and Mr Satterthwaite was momentarily out of countenance. He did what was, perhaps, the best thing, attacked the situation with simplicity.

'I have been searching your room, Mrs Graham. I have found something—a packet of letters imperfectly burnt.'

A wave of alarm passed over her face. It was gone in a flash, but it had been there.

'Letters from Mrs Annesley to your son.'

She hesitated for a minute, then said quietly: 'That is so. I thought they would be better burnt.'

'For what reason?'

'My son is engaged to be married. These letters—if they had been brought into publicity through the poor girl's suicide—might have caused much pain and trouble.'

'Your son could burn his own letters.'

She had no answer ready for that. Mr Satterthwaite pursued his advantage.

'You found these letters in his room, brought them into your room and burnt them. Why? You were afraid, Mrs Graham.'

'I am not in the habit of being afraid, Mr Satterthwaite.'

'No—but this was a desperate case.'

'Desperate?'

'Your son might have been in danger of arrest—for murder.'

'Murder!'

He saw her face go white. He went on quickly:

'You heard Mrs Annesley go into your son's room last night. He had told her of his engagement? No, I see he hadn't. He told her then. They quarrelled, and he—'

'That's a lie!'

They had been so absorbed in their duel of words that they had not heard approaching footsteps. Roger Graham had come up behind them unperceived by either.

'It's all right, Mother. Don't—worry. Come into my room, Mr Satterthwaite.'

Mr Sattherwaite followed him into his room. Mrs Graham had turned away and did not attempt to follow them. Roger Graham shut the door. 'Listen, Mr Satterthwaite, you think I killed Mabelle. You think I strangled her—here—and took her along and hung her up on that door—later—when everyone was asleep?'

Mr Satterthwaite stared at him. Then he said surprisingly:

'No, I do not think so.'

'Thank God for that. I couldn't have killed Mabelle. I—I loved her. Or didn't I? I don't know. It's a tangle that I can't explain. I'm fond of Madge—I always have been. And she's such a good sort. We suit each other. But Mabelle was different. It was—I can't explain it—a sort of enchantment. I was, I think—afraid of her.'

Mr Satterthwaite nodded.

'It was madness—a kind of bewildering ecstasy ... But it was impossible. It wouldn't have worked. That sort of thing—doesn't last. I know what it means now to have a spell cast over you.'

'Yes, it must have been like that,' said Mr Satterthwaite thoughtfully.

'I—I wanted to get out of it all. I was going to tell Mabelle—last night.'

'But you didn't?'

'No, I didn't,' said Graham slowly. 'I swear to you, Mr Satterthwaite, that I never saw her after I said goodnight downstairs.'

'I believe you,' said Mr Satterthwaite.

He got up. It was not Roger Graham who had killed Mabelle Annesley. He could have fled from her, but he could not have killed her. He had been afraid of her, afraid of that wild intangible fairy-like quality of hers. He had known enchantment—and turned his back on it. He had gone for the safe sensible thing that he had known 'would work' and had relinquished the intangible dream that might lead him he knew not where.

He was a sensible young man, and, as such, uninteresting to Mr Satterthwaite, who was an artist and a connoisseur in life.

He left Roger Graham in his room and went downstairs. The drawing-room was empty. Mabelle's ukelele lay on a stool by the window. He took it up and twanged it absent-mindedly. He knew nothing of the instrument, but his ear told him that it was abominably out of tune. He turned a key experimentally.

Doris Coles came into the room. She looked at him reproachfully.

'Poor Mabelle's uke,' she said.

Her clear condemnation made Mr Satterthwaite feel obstinate.

'Tune it for me,' he said, and added: 'If you can.'

'Of course I can,' said Doris, wounded at the suggestion of incompetence in any direction.

She took it from him, twanged a string, turned a key briskly—and the string snapped.

'Well, I never. Oh! I see—but how extraordinary! It's the wrong string—a size too big. It's an A string. How stupid to put that on. Of course it snaps when you try to tune it up. How stupid people are.'

'Yes,' said Mr Satterthwaite. 'They are—even when they try to be clever . . .'

His tone was so odd that she stared at him. He took the ukelele from her and removed the broken string. He went out of the room holding it in his hand. In the library he found David Keeley.

'Here,' he said.

He held out the string. Keeley took it.

'What's this?'

'A broken ukelele string.' He paused and then went on: '*What did you do with the other one*?'

'The other one?'

'*The one you strangled her with*. Your were very clever, weren't you? It was done very quickly—just in that moment we were all laughing and talking in the hall.

'Mabelle came back into this room for her ukelele. You had taken the string off as you fiddled with it just before. You caught her round the throat with it and strangled her. Then you came out and locked the door and joined us. Later, in the dead of night, you came down and—and disposed of the body by hanging it on the door of her room. And you put another string on the ukelele—*but it was the wrong string*, that's why you were stupid.'

There was a pause.

'But why did you do it?' said Mr Satterthwaite. 'In God's name, *why*?'

Mr Keeley laughed, a funny giggling little laugh that made Mr Satterthwaite feel rather sick.

'It was so very simple,' he said. 'That's why! And then—nobody ever noticed me. Nobody ever noticed what I was doing. I thought—I thought I'd have the laugh of them . . .'

And again he gave that furtive little giggle and looked at Mr Satterthwaite with mad eyes.

Mr Satterthwaite was glad that at that moment Inspector Winkfield came into the room.

It was twenty-four hours later, on his way to London, that Mr Satterthwaite awoke from a doze to find a tall dark man sitting opposite to him in the railway carriage. He was not altogether surprised.

'My dear Mr Quin!'

'Yes—I am here.'

Mr Satterthwaite said slowly: 'I can hardly face you. I am ashamed—I failed.'

'Are you sure of that?'

'I did not save her.'

'But you discovered the truth?'

'Yes—that is true. One or other of those young men might have been accused—might even have been found guilty. So, at any rate, I saved a man's life. But, she—she—that strange enchanting creature . . .' His voice broke off.

Mr Quin looked at him.

'Is death the greatest evil that can happen to anyone?'

'I—well—perhaps—No . . .'

Mr Satterthwaite remembered . . . Madge and Roger Graham . . . Mabelle's face in the moonlight—its serene unearthly happiness . . .

'No,' he admitted. 'No—perhaps death is not the greatest evil . . .'

He remembered the ruffled blue chiffon of her dress that had seemed to him like the plumage of a bird . . . A bird with a broken wing . . .

When he looked up, he found himself alone. Mr Quin was no longer there.

But he had left something behind.

On the seat was a roughly carved bird fashioned out of some dim blue stone. It had, possibly, no great artistic merit. But it had something else.

It had the vague quality of enchantment.

So said Mr Satterthwaite—and Mr Satterthwaite was a connoisseur.

The Lemesurier Inheritance

In company with Poirot, I have investigated many strange cases, but none, I think, to compare with that extraordinary series of events which held our interest over a period of many years, and which culminated in the ultimate problem brought to Poirot to solve. Our attention was first drawn to the family history of the Lemesuriers one evening during the war. Poirot and I had but recently come together again, renewing the old days of our acquaintanceship in Belgium. He had been handling some little matter for the War Office—disposing of it to their entire satisfaction; and we had been dining at the Carlton with a Brass Hat who paid Poirot heavy compliments in the intervals of the meal. The Brass Hat had to rush away to keep an appointment with someone, and we finished our coffee in a leisurely fashion before following his example.

As we were leaving the room, I was hailed by a voice which struck a familiar note, and turned to see Captain Vincent Lemesurier, a young fellow whom I had known in France. He was with an older man whose likeness to him proclaimed him to be of the same family. Such proved to be the case, and he was introduced to us as Mr Hugo Lemesurier, uncle of my young friend.

I did not really know Captain Lemesurier at all intimately, but he was a pleasant young fellow, somewhat dreamy in manner, and I remembered hearing that he belonged to an old and exclusive family with a property in Northumberland which dated from before the Reformation. Poirot and I were not in a hurry, and at the younger man's invitation, we sat down at the table with our two new-found friends, and chattered pleasantly enough on various matters. The elder Lemesurier was a man of about forty, with a touch of the scholar in his stooping shoulders; he was engaged at the moment upon some chemical research work for the Government, it appeared.

Our conversation was interrupted by a tall dark young man who strode up to the table, evidently labouring under some agitation of mind.

'Thank goodness I've found you both!' he exclaimed.

'What's the matter, Roger?'

'Your guv'nor, Vincent. Bad fall. Young horse.' The rest trailed off, as he drew the other aside.

In a few minutes our two friends had hurriedly taken leave of us. Vincent Lemesurier's father had had a serious accident while trying a young horse, and was not expected to live until morning. Vincent had gone deadly white, and appeared almost stunned by the news. In a way, I was surprised—for from the few words he had let fall on the subject while in France, I had gathered that he and his father were not on particularly friendly terms, and so his display of filial feeling now rather astonished me.

The dark young man, who had been introduced to us as a cousin, Mr Roger Lemesurier, remained behind, and we three strolled out together.

'Rather a curious business, this,' observed the young man. 'It would interest M. Poirot, perhaps. I've heard of you, you know, M. Poirot—from Higginson.' (Higginson was our Brass Hat friend.) 'He says you're a whale on psychology.'

'I study the psychology, yes,' admitted my friend cautiously.

'Did you see my cousin's face? He was absolutely bowled over, wasn't he? Do you know why? A good old-fashioned family curse! Would you care to hear about it?'

'It would be most kind of you to recount it to me.'

Roger Lemesurier looked at his watch.

'Lots of time. I'm meeting them at King's Cross. Well, M. Poirot, the Lemesuriers are an old family. Way back in medieval times, a Lemesurier became suspicious of his wife. He found the lady in a compromising situation. She swore that she was innocent, but old Baron Hugo didn't listen. She had one child, a son—and he swore that the boy was no child of his and should never inherit. I forget what he did—some pleasing medieval fancy like walling up the mother and son alive; anyway, he killed them both, and she died protesting her innocence and solemnly cursing the Lemesuriers forever. No first-born son of a Lemesurier should ever inherit—so the curse ran. Well, time passed, and the lady's innocence was established beyond doubt. I believe that Hugo wore a hair shirt and ended up his days on his knees in a monk's cell. But the curious thing is that from that day to this, no first-born son ever has succeeded to the estate. It's gone to brothers, to nephews, to second sons—never to the eldest son. Vincent's father was the second of five sons, the eldest of whom died in infancy. Of course, all through the war, Vincent has been convinced that whoever else was doomed, he certainly was. But strangely enough, his two younger brothers have been killed, and he himself has remained unscathed.'

'An interesting family history,' said Poirot thoughtfully. 'But now his father is dying, and he, as the eldest son, succeeds?'

'Exactly. A curse has gone rusty—unable to stand the strain of modern life.'

Poirot shook his head, as though deprecating the other's jesting tone. Roger Lemesurier looked at his watch again, and declared that he must be off.

The sequel to the story came on the morrow, when we learned of the tragic death of Captain Vincent Lemesurier. He had been travelling north by the Scotch mail-train, and during the night must have opened the door of the compartment and jumped out on the line. The shock of his father's accident coming on top of the shell-shock was deemed to have caused temporary mental aberration. The curious superstition prevalent in the Lemesurier family was mentioned, in connection with the new heir, his father's brother, Ronald Lemesurier, whose only son had died on the Somme.

I suppose our accidental meeting with young Vincent on the last evening of his life quickened our interest in anything that pertained to the Lemesurier family, for we noted with some interest two years later the death of Ronald Lemesurier, who had been a confirmed invalid at the time of his succession to the family estates. His brother John succeeded him, a hale, hearty man with a boy at Eton.

Certainly an evil destiny overshadowed the Lemesuriers. On his very next holiday the boy managed to shoot himself fatally. His father's death, which occurred quite suddenly after being stung by a wasp, gave the estate over to the youngest brother of the five—Hugo, whom we remembered meeting on the fatal night at the Carlton.

Beyond commenting on the extraordinary series of

misfortunes which befell the Lemesuriers, we had taken no personal interest in the matter, but the time was now close at hand when we were to take a more active part.

One morning 'Mrs Lemesurier' was announced. She was a tall, active woman, possibly about thirty years of age, who conveyed by her demeanour a great deal of determination and strong common sense. She spoke with a faint transatlantic accent.

'M. Poirot? I am pleased to meet you. My husband, Hugo Lemesurier, met you once many years ago, but you will hardly remember the fact.'

'I recollect it perfectly, madame. It was at the Carlton.'

'That's quite wonderful of you. M. Poirot, I'm very worried.'

'What about, madame?'

'My elder boy—I've two boys, you know. Ronald's eight, and Gerald's six.'

'Proceed, madame: why should you be worried about little Ronald?'

'M. Poirot, within the last six months he has had three narrow escapes from death: once from drowning—when we were all down at Cornwall this summer; once when he fell from the nursery window; and once from ptomaine poisoning.'

Perhaps Poirot's face expressed rather too eloquently what he thought, for Mrs Lemesurier hurried on with hardly a moment's pause: 'Of course I know you think I'm just a silly fool of a woman, making mountains out of molehills.'

'No, indeed, madame. Any mother might be excused for being upset at such occurrences, but I hardly see where I can be of any assistance to you. I am not *le bon Dieu* to control the waves; for the nursery window

I should suggest some iron bars; and for the food—what can equal a mother's care?'

'But why should these things happen to Ronald and not to Gerald?'

'The chance, madame—*le hasard*!'

'You think so?'

'What do you think, madame—you and your husband?'

A shadow crossed Mrs Lemesurier's face.

'It's no good going to Hugo—he won't listen. As perhaps you may have heard, there's supposed to be a curse on the family—no eldest son can succeed. Hugo believes in it. He's wrapped up in the family history, and he's superstitious to the last degree. When I go to him with my fears, he just says it's the curse, and we can't escape it. But I'm from the States, M. Poirot, and over there we don't believe much in curses. We like them as belonging to a real high-toned old family—it gives a sort of *cachet*, don't you know. I was just a musical comedy actress in a small part when Hugo met me—and I thought his family curse was just too lovely for words. That kind of thing's all right for telling round the fire on a winter's evening, but when it comes to one's own children—I just adore my children, M. Poirot. I'd do anything for them.'

'So you decline to believe in the family legend, madame?'

'Can a legend saw through an ivy stem?'

'What is that you are saying, madame?' cried Poirot, an expression of great astonishment on his face.

'I said, can a legend—or a ghost, if you like to call it that—saw through an ivy stem? I'm not saying anything about Cornwall. Any boy might go out too far and get into difficulties—though Ronald could swim when he was four years old. But the ivy's different. Both the boys were very naughty. They'd discovered they could climb up and down by the ivy. They were always doing it. One day—Gerald was away at the time—Ronald did it once too often, and the ivy gave way and he fell. Fortunately he didn't damage himself seriously. But I went out and examined the ivy: it was cut through, M. Poirot—deliberately cut through.'

'It is very serious what you are telling me there, madame. You say your younger boy was away from home at the moment?'

'Yes.'

'And at the time of the ptomaine poisoning, was he still away?'

'No, they were both there.'

'Curious,' murmured Poirot. 'Now, madame, who are the inmates of your establishment?'

'Miss Saunders, the children's governess, and John Gardiner, my husband's secretary—'

Mrs Lemesurier paused, as though slightly embarrassed.

'And who else, madame?'

'Major Roger Lemesurier, whom you also met on that night, I believe, stays with us a good deal.'

'Ah, yes—he is a cousin is he not?'

'A distant cousin. He does not belong to our branch of the family. Still, I suppose now he is my husband's nearest relative. He is a dear fellow, and we are all very fond of him. The boys are devoted to him.'

'It was not he who taught them to climb up the ivy?'

'It might have been. He incites them to mischief often enough.'

'Madame, I apologize for what I said to you earlier. The danger is real, and I believe that I can be of assistance. I propose that you should invite us both to stay with you. Your husband will not object?'

'Oh no. But he will believe it to be all of no use. It makes me furious the way he just sits around and expects the boy to die.'

'Calm yourself, madame. Let us make our arrangements methodically.'

Our arrangements were duly made, and the following day saw us flying northward. Poirot was sunk in a reverie. He came out of it, to remark abruptly: 'It was from a train such as this that Vincent Lemesurier fell?'

He put a slight accent on the 'fell'.

'You don't suspect foul play there, surely?' I asked.

'Has it struck you, Hastings, that some of the Lemesurier deaths were, shall we say, capable of being arranged? Take that of Vincent, for instance. Then the Eton boy—an accident with a gun is always ambiguous. Supposing this child had fallen from the nursery window and been dashed to death—what more natural and unsuspicious? But why only the one child, Hastings? Who profits by the death of the elder child? His younger brother, a child of seven! Absurd!'

'They mean to do away with the other later,' I suggested, though with the vaguest ideas as to who 'they' were.

Poirot shook his head as though dissatisfied.

'Ptomaine poisoning,' he mused. 'Atropine will produce much the same symptoms. Yes, there is need for our presence.'

Mrs Lemesurier welcomed us enthusiastically. Then she took us to her husband's study and left us with him. He had changed a good deal since I saw him last. His shoulders stooped more than ever, and his face had a curious pale grey tinge. He listened while Poirot explained our presence in the house.

'How exactly like Sadie's practical common sense!' he

said at last. 'Remain by all means, M. Poirot, and I thank you for coming; but—what is written, is written. The way of the transgressor is hard. We Lemesuriers *know*—none of us can escape the doom.'

Poirot mentioned the sawn-through ivy, but Hugo seemed very little impressed.

'Doubtless some careless gardener—yes, yes, there may be an instrument, but the purpose behind is plain; and I will tell you this, M. Poirot, it cannot be long delayed.'

Poirot looked at him attentively.

'Why do you say that?'

'Because I myself am doomed. I went to a doctor last year. I am suffering from an incurable disease—the end cannot be much longer delayed; but before I die, Ronald will be taken. Gerald will inherit.'

'And if anything were to happen to your second son also?'

'Nothing will happen to him; he is not threatened.'

'But if it did?' persisted Poirot.

'My cousin Roger is the next heir.'

We were interrupted. A tall man with a good figure and crispy curling auburn hair entered with a sheaf of papers.

'Never mind about those now, Gardiner,' said Hugo Lemesurier, then he added: 'My secretary, Mr Gardiner.'

The secretary bowed, uttered a few pleasant words and then went out. In spite of his good looks, there was something repellent about the man. I said so to Poirot shortly afterward when we were walking round the beautiful old grounds together, and rather to my surprise, he agreed.

'Yes, yes, Hastings, you are right. I do not like him. He is too good-looking. He would be one for the soft job always. Ah, here are the children.'

Mrs Lemesurier was advancing towards us, her two children beside her. They were fine-looking boys, the younger dark like his mother, the elder with auburn curls. They shook hands prettily enough, and were soon absolutely devoted to Poirot. We were next introduced to Miss Saunders, a nondescript female, who completed the party.

For some days we had a pleasant, easy existence—ever vigilant, but without result. The boys led a happy normal life and nothing seemed to be amiss. On the fourth day after our arrival Major Roger Lemesurier came down to stay. He was little changed, still care-free and debonair as of old, with the same habit of treating all things lightly. He was evidently a great favourite with the boys, who greeted his arrival with shrieks of delight and immediately dragged him off to play wild Indians in the garden. I noticed that Poirot followed them unobtrusively.

On the following day we were all invited to tea, boys included, with Lady Claygate, whose place adjoined that of the Lemesuriers. Mrs Lemesurier suggested that we also should come, but seemed rather relieved when Poirot refused and declared he would much prefer to remain at home.

Once everyone had started, Poirot got to work. He reminded me of an intelligent terrier. I believe that there was no corner of the house that he left unsearched; yet it was all done so quietly and methodically that no attention was directed to his movements. Clearly, at the end, he remained unsatisfied. We had tea on the terrace with Miss Saunders, who had not been included in the party.

'The boys will enjoy it,' she murmured in her faded way, 'though I hope they will behave nicely, and not damage the flower-beds, or go near the bees—'

Poirot paused in the very act of drinking. He looked like a man who has seen a ghost.

'Bees?' he demanded in a voice of thunder.

'Yes, M. Poirot, bees. Three hives. Lady Claygate is very proud of her bees—'

'Bees?' cried Poirot again. Then he sprang from the table and walked up and down the terrace with his hands to his head. I could not imagine why the little man should be so agitated at the mere mention of bees.

At that moment we heard the car returning. Poirot was on the doorstep as the party alighted.

'Ronald's been stung,' cried Gerald excitedly.

'It's nothing,' said Mrs Lemesurier. 'It hasn't even swollen. We put ammonia on it.'

'Let me see, my little man,' said Poirot. 'Where was it?'

'Here, on the side of my neck,' said Ronald importantly. 'But it doesn't hurt. Father said: "Keep still—there's a bee on you." And I kept still, and he took it off, but it stung me first, though it didn't really hurt, only like a pin, and I didn't cry, because I'm so big and going to school next year.'

Poirot examined the child's neck, then drew away again. He took me by the arm and murmured:

'Tonight, *mon ami*, tonight we have a little affair on! Say nothing—to anyone.'

He refused to be more communicative, and I went through the evening devoured by curiosity. He retired early and I followed his example. As we went upstairs, he caught me by the arm and delivered his instructions:

'Do not undress. Wait a sufficient time, extinguish your light and join me here.'

I obeyed, and found him waiting for me when the time came. He enjoined silence on me with a gesture, and we crept quietly along the nursery wing. Ronald occupied a small room of his own. We entered it and took up our position in the darkest corner. The child's breathing sounded heavy and undisturbed.

'Surely he is sleeping very heavily?' I whispered.

Poirot nodded.

'Drugged,' he murmured.

'Why?'

'So that he should not cry out at—'

'At what?' I asked, as Poirot paused.

'At the prick of the hypodermic needle, *mon ami*! Hush, let us speak no more—not that I expect anything to happen for some time.'

But in this Poirot was wrong. Hardly ten minutes had elapsed before the door opened softly, and someone entered the room. I heard a sound of quick hurried breathing. Footsteps moved to the bed, and then there was a sudden click. The light of a little electric lantern fell on the sleeping child—the holder of it was still invisible in the shadow. The figure laid down the lantern. With the right hand it brought forth a syringe; with the left it touched the boy's neck—

Poirot and I sprang at the same minute. The lantern rolled to the floor, and we struggled with the intruder in the dark. His strength was extraordinary. At last we overcame him.

'The light, Hastings, I must see his face—though I fear I know only too well whose face it will be.'

So did I, I thought as I groped for the lantern. For a moment I had suspected the secretary, egged on by my secret dislike of the man, but I felt assured by now that the man who stood to gain by the death of his two childish cousins was the monster we were tracking.

My foot struck against the lantern. I picked it up and switched on the light. It shone full on the face of—Hugo Lemesurier, the boy's father!

The lantern almost dropped from my hand. 'Impossible,' I murmured hoarsely. 'Impossible!'

Lemesurier was unconscious. Poirot and I between us carried him to his room and laid him on the bed. Poirot bent and gently extricated something from his right hand. He showed it to me. It was a hypodermic syringe. I shuddered.

'What is in it? Poison?'

'Formic acid, I fancy.'

'Formic acid?'

'Yes. Probably obtained by distilling ants. He was a chemist, you remember. Death would have been attributed to the bee sting.'

'My God,' I muttered. 'His own son! And you expected this?'

Poirot nodded gravely.

'Yes. He is insane, of course. I imagine that the family history has become a mania with him. His intense longing to succeed to the estate led him to commit the long series of crimes. Possibly the idea occurred to him first when travelling north that night with Vincent. He couldn't bear the prediction to be falsified. Ronald's son was already dead, and Ronald himself was a dying man—they are a weakly lot. He arranged the accident to the gun, and—which I did not suspect until now—contrived the death of his brother John by this same method of injecting formic acid into the jugular vein. His ambition was realized then, and he became the master of the family acres. But his triumph was short-lived—he found that he was suffering from an incurable disease. And he had the madman's fixed idea—the eldest son of a Lemesurier could not inherit. I suspect that the bathing accident was due to him—he encouraged the child to go out too far. That failing, he sawed through the ivy, and afterwards poisoned the child's food.'

'Diabolical!' I murmured with a shiver. 'And so cleverly planned!'

'Yes, *mon ami*, there is nothing more amazing than the extraordinary sanity of the insane! Unless it is the extraordinary eccentricity of the sane! I imagine that it is only lately that he has completely gone over the borderline, there was method in his madness to begin with.'

'And to think that I suspected Roger—that splendid fellow.'

'It was the natural assumption, *mon ami*. We knew that he also travelled north with Vincent that night. We knew, too, that he was the next heir after Hugo and Hugo's children. But our assumption was not borne out by the facts. The ivy was sawn through when only little Ronald was at home—but it would be to Roger's interest that both children should perish. In the same way, it was only Ronald's food that was poisoned. And today when they came home and I found that there was only his father's word for it that Ronald had been stung, I remembered the other death from a wasp sting—and I knew!'

Hugo Lemesurier died a few months later in the private asylum to which he was removed. His widow was remarried a year later to Mr John Gardiner, the auburn-haired secretary. Ronald inherited the broad acres of his father, and continues to flourish.

'Well, well,' I remarked to Poirot. 'Another illusion gone. You have disposed very successfully of the curse of the Lemesuriers.'

'I wonder,' said Poirot very thoughtfully. 'I wonder very much indeed.'

'What do you mean?'

'*Mon ami*, I will answer you with one significant word—*red*!'

'Blood?' I queried, dropping my voice to an awe-stricken whisper.

'Always you have the imagination melodramatic, Hastings! I refer to something much more prosaic—the colour of little Ronald Lemesurier's hair.'

The House of Lurking Death

'What—' began Tuppence, and then stopped.

She had just entered the private office of Mr Blunt from the adjoining one marked 'Clerks,' and was surprised to behold her lord and master with his eye riveted to the private peep-hole into the outer office.

'Ssh,' said Tommy warningly. 'Didn't you hear the buzzer? It's a girl—rather a nice girl—in fact she looks to me a frightfully nice girl. Albert is telling her all that tosh about my being engaged with Scotland Yard.'

'Let *me* see,' demanded Tuppence.

Somewhat unwillingly, Tommy moved aside. Tuppence in her turn glued her eye to the peep-hole.

'She's not bad,' admitted Tuppence. 'And her clothes are simply the lastest shout.'

'She's perfectly lovely,' said Tommy. 'She's like those girls Mason writes about—you know, frightfully sympathetic, and beautiful, and distinctly intelligent without being too saucy. I think, yes—I certainly think—I shall be the great Hanaud this morning.'

'H'm,' said Tuppence. 'If there is one detective out of all the others whom you are most unlike—I should say it was Hanaud. Can you do the lightning changes of personality? Can you be the great comedian, the little gutter boy, the serious and sympathetic friend—all in five minutes?'

'I know this,' said Tommy, rapping sharply on the desk, 'I am the Captain of the Ship—and don't you forget it, Tuppence. I'm going to have her in.'

He pressed the buzzer on his desk. Albert appeared ushering in the client.

The girl stopped in the doorway as though undecided. Tommy came forward.

'Come in, mademoiselle,' he said kindly, 'and seat yourself here.'

Tuppence choked audibly and Tommy turned upon her with a swift change of manner. His tone was menacing.

'You spoke, Miss Robinson? Ah, no, I thought not.'

He turned back to the girl.

'We will not be serious or formal,' he said. 'You will just tell me about it, and then we will discuss the best way to help you.'

'You are very kind,' said the girl. 'Excuse me, but are you a foreigner?'

A fresh choke from Tuppence. Tommy glared in her direction out of the corner of his eye.

'Not exactly,' he said with difficulty. 'But of late years I have worked a good deal abroad. My methods are the methods of the Sûreté.'

'Oh!' The girl seemed impressed.

She was, as Tommy had indicated, a very charming girl. Young and slim, with a trace of golden hair peeping out from under her little brown felt hat, and big serious eyes.

That she was nervous could be plainly seen. Her little hands were twisting themselves together, and she kept clasping and unclasping the catch of her lacquered handbag.

'First of all, Mr Blunt, I must tell you that my name is Lois Hargreaves. I live in a great rambling old-fashioned house called Thurnly Grange. It is in the heart of the country. There is the village of Thurnly nearby, but it is very small and insignificant. There is plenty of hunting in winter, and we get tennis in summer, and I have never felt lonely there. Indeed I much prefer country to town life.

'I tell you this so that you may realise that in a country village like ours, everything that happens is of supreme importance. About a week ago, I got a box of chocolates sent through the post. There was nothing inside to indicate who they came from. Now I myself am not particularly fond of chocolates, but the others in the house are, and the box was passed round. As a result, everyone who had eaten any chocolates was taken ill. We sent for the doctor, and after various inquiries as to what other things had been eaten, he took the remains of the chocolates away with him, and had them analysed. Mr Blunt, those chocolates contained arsenic! Not enough to kill anyone, but enough to make anyone quite ill.'

'Extraordinary,' commented Tommy.

'Dr Burton was very excited over the matter. It seems that this was the third occurrence of the kind in the neighbourhood. In each case a big house was selected, and the inmates were taken ill after eating the mysterious chocolates. It looked as though some local person of weak intellect was playing a particularly fiendish practical joke.'

'Quite so, Miss Hargreaves.'

'Dr Burton put it down to Socialist agitation—rather absurdly, I thought. But there are one or two malcontents in Thurnly village, and it seemed possible that they might have had something to do with it. Dr Burton was very keen that I should put the whole thing in the hands of the police.'

'A very natural suggestion,' said Tommy. 'But you have not done so, I gather, Miss Hargreaves?'

'No,' admitted the girl. 'I hate the fuss and the publicity that would ensue—and you see, I know our local Inspector. I can never imagine him finding out anything! I have often seen your advertisements, and I told Dr Burton that it would be much better to call in a private detective.'

'I see.'

'You say a great deal about discretion in your advertisement. I take that to mean—that—that—well, that you would not make anything public without my consent?'

Tommy looked at her curiously, but it was Tuppence who spoke.

'I think,' she said quietly, 'that it would be as well if Miss Hargreaves told us *everything*.'

She laid especial stress upon the last word, and Lois Hargreaves flushed nervously.

'Yes,' said Tommy quickly, 'Miss Robinson is right. You must tell us everything.'

'You will not—' she hesitated.

'Everything you say is understood to be strictly in confidence.'

'Thank you. I know that I ought to have been quite frank with you. I have a reason for not going to the police. Mr Blunt, that box of chocolates was sent by someone in our house!'

'How do you know that, mademoiselle?'

'It's very simple. I've got a habit of drawing a little silly thing—three fish intertwined—whenever I have a pencil in my hand. A parcel of silk stockings arrived from a certain shop in London not long ago. We were at the breakfast table. I'd just been marking something in the newspaper, and without thinking, I began to draw my silly little fish on the label of the parcel before cutting the string and opening it. I thought no more about the matter, but when I was examining the piece of brown paper in which the chocolates had been sent, I caught sight of the corner of the original label—most of which had been torn off. My silly little drawing was on it.'

Tommy drew his chair forward.

'That is very serious. It creates, as you say, a very strong presumption that the sender of the chocolates is a member of your household. But you will forgive me if I say that I still do not see why that fact should render you indisposed to call in the police?'

Lois Hargreaves looked him squarely in the face.

'I will tell you, Mr Blunt. I may want the whole thing hushed up.'

Tommy retired gracefully from the position.

'In that case,' he murmured, 'we know where we are. I see, Miss Hargreaves, that you are not disposed to tell me who it is you suspect?'

'I suspect no one—but there are possibilities.'

'Quite so. Now will you describe the household to me in detail?'

'The servants, with the exception of the parlourmaid, are all old ones who have been with us many years. I must explain to you, Mr Blunt, that I was brought up by my aunt, Lady Radclyffe, who was extremely wealthy. Her husband made a big fortune, and was knighted. It was he who bought Thurnly Grange, but he died two years after going there, and it was then that Lady Radclyffe sent for me to come and make my home with her. I was her only living relation. The other inmate of the house was Dennis Radclyffe, her husband's nephew. I have always called him cousin, but of course he is really nothing of the kind. Aunt Lucy always said openly that she intended to leave her money, with the exception of a small provision for me, to Dennis. It was Radclyffe money, she said, and it ought to go to a Radclyffe. However, when Dennis was twenty-two, she quarrelled violently with him—over some debts that he had run up, I think. When she died, a year later, I was astonished to find that she had made a will leaving all her money to me. It was, I know, a great blow to Dennis, and I felt very badly about it. I would have given him the money if he would have taken it, but it seems that kind of thing can't be done. However, as soon as I was twenty-one, I made a will leaving it all to him. That's the least I can do. So if I'm run over by a motor, Dennis will come into his own.'

'Exactly,' said Tommy. 'And when were you twenty-one, if I may ask the question?'

'Just three weeks ago.'

'Ah!' said Tommy. 'Now will you give me fuller particulars of the members of your household at this minute?'

'Servants—or—others?'

'Both.'

'The servants, as I say, have been with us some time. There is old Mrs Holloway, the cook, and her niece Rose, the kitchenmaid. Then there are two elderly housemaids, and Hannah who was my aunt's maid and who has always been devoted to me. The parlourmaid is called Esther Quant, and seems a very nice quiet girl. As for ourselves, there is Miss Logan, who was Aunt Lucy's companion, and who runs the house for me, and Captain Radclyffe—Dennis, you know, whom I told you about, and there is a girl called Mary Chilcott, an old school friend of mine who is staying with us.'

Tommy thought for a moment.

'That all seems fairly clear and straightforward, Miss

Hargreaves,' he said after a minute or two. 'I take it that you have no special reason for attaching suspicion more to one person than another? You are only afraid it might prove to be—well—not a servant, shall we say?'

'That's it exactly, Mr Blunt. I have honestly no idea who used that piece of brown paper. The handwriting was printed.'

'There seems only one thing to be done,' said Tommy. 'I must be on the spot.'

The girl looked at him inquiringly.

Tommy went on after a moment's thought.

'I suggest that you prepare the way for the arrival of—say, Mr and Miss Van Dusen—American friends of yours. Will you be able to do that quite naturally?'

'Oh, yes. There will be no difficulty at all. When will you come down—tomorrow—or the day after?'

'Tomorrow, if you please. There is no time to waste.'

'That is settled then.'

The girl rose and held out her hand.

'One thing, Miss Hargreaves, not a word, mind, to anyone—anyone at all, that we are not what we seem.'

'What do you think of it, Tuppence?' he asked, when he returned from showing the visitor out.

'I don't like it,' said Tuppence decidedly. 'Especially I don't like the chocolates having so little arsenic in them.'

'What *do* you mean?'

'Don't you see? All those chocolates being sent round the neighbourhood were a blind. To establish the idea of a local maniac. Then, when the girl was really poisoned, it would be thought to be the same thing. You see, but for a stroke of luck, no one would ever have guessed that the chocolates were actually sent by someone in the house itself.'

'That was a stroke of luck. You're right. You think it's a deliberate plot against the girl herself?'

'I'm afraid so. I remember reading about old Lady Radclyffe's will. That girl has come into a terrific lot of money.'

'Yes, and she came of age and made a will three weeks ago. It looks bad—for Dennis Radclyffe. He gains by her death.'

Tuppence nodded.

'The worst of it is—that she thinks so too! That's why she won't have the police called in. Already she suspects him. And she must be more than half in love with him to act as she has done.'

'In that case,' said Tommy thoughtfully, 'why the devil doesn't he marry her? Much simpler and safer.'

Tuppence stared at him.

'You've said a mouthful,' she observed. 'Oh, boy! I'm getting ready to be Miss Van Dusen, you observe.'

'Why rush to crime, when there is a lawful means near at hand?'

Tuppence reflected for a minute or two.

'I've got it,' she announced. 'Clearly he must have married a barmaid whilst at Oxford. Origin of the quarrel with his aunt. That explains everything.'

'Then why not send the poisoned sweets to the barmaid?' suggested Tommy. 'Much more practical. I wish you wouldn't jump to these wild conclusions, Tuppence.'

'They're deductions,' said Tuppence, with a good deal of dignity. 'This is your first *corrida*, my friend, but when you have been twenty minutes in the arena—'

Tommy flung the office cushion at her.

'Tuppence, I say, Tuppence, come here.'

It was breakfast time the next morning. Tuppence hurried out of her bedroom and into the dining-room. Tommy was striding up and down, the open newspaper in his hand.

'What's the matter?'

Tommy wheeled round, and shoved the paper into her hand, pointing to the headlines.

MYSTERIOUS POISONING CASE
DEATHS FROM FIG SANDWICHES

Tuppence read on. This mysterious outbreak of ptomaine poisoning had occurred at Thurnly Grange. The deaths so far reported were those of Miss Lois Hargreaves, the owner of the house, and the parlourmaid, Esther Quant. A Captain Radclyffe and a Miss Logan were reported to be seriously ill. The cause of the outbreak was supposed to be some fig paste used in sandwiches, since another lady, a Miss Chilcott, who had not partaken of these was reported to be quite well.

'We must get down there at once,' said Tommy. 'That girl! That perfectly ripping girl! Why the devil didn't I go straight down there with her yesterday?'

'If you had,' said Tuppence, 'you'd probably have eaten fig sandwiches too for tea, and then you'd have been dead. Come on, let's start at once. I see it says that Dennis Radclyffe is seriously ill also.'

'Probably shamming, the dirty blackguard.'

They arrived at the small village of Thurnly about midday. An elderly woman with red eyes opened the door to them when they arrived at Thurnly Grange.

'Look here,' said Tommy quickly before she could speak. 'I'm not a reporter or anything like that. Miss Hargreaves came to see me yesterday, and asked me to come down here. Is there anyone I can see?'

'Dr Burton is here now, if you'd like to speak to him,' said the woman doubtfully. 'Or Miss Chilcott. She's making all the arrangements.'

But Tommy had caught at the first suggestion.

'Dr Burton,' he said authoritatively. 'I should like to see him at once if he is here.'

The woman showed them into a small morning-room. Five minutes later the door opened, and a tall, elderly man with bent shoulders and a kind, but worried face, came in.

'Dr Burton,' said Tommy. He produced his professional card. 'Miss Hargreaves called on me yesterday with reference to those poisoned chocolates. I came down to investigate the matter at her request—alas! too late.'

The doctor looked at him keenly.

'You are Mr Blunt himself?'

'Yes. This is my assistant, Miss Robinson.'

The doctor bowed to Tuppence.

'Under the circumstances, there is no need for reticence. But for the episode of the chocolates, I might have believed these deaths to be the result of severe ptomaine poisoning—but ptomaine poisoning of an unusually virulent kind. There is gastro-intestinal inflammation and haemorrhage. As it is, I am taking the fig paste to be analysed.'

'You suspect arsenic poisoning?'

'No. The poison, if a poison has been employed, is something far more potent and swift in its action. It looks more like some powerful vegetable toxin.'

'I see. I should like to ask you, Dr Burton, whether you are thoroughly convinced that Captain Radclyffe is suffering from the same form of poisoning?'

The doctor looked at him.

'Captain Radclyffe is not suffering from any sort of poisoning now.'

'Aha,' said Tommy. 'I—'

'Captain Radclyffe died at five o'clock this morning.'

Tommy was utterly taken aback. The doctor prepared to depart.

'And the other victim, Miss Logan?' asked Tuppence.

'I have every reason to hope that she will recover since she has survived so far. Being an older woman, the poison seems to have had less effect on her. I will let you know the result of the analysis, Mr Blunt. In the meantime, Miss Chilcott, will, I am sure, tell you anything you want to know.'

As he spoke, the door opened, and a girl appeared. She was tall, with a tanned face, and steady blue eyes.

Dr Burton performed the necessary introductions.

'I am glad you have come, Mr Blunt,' said Mary Chilcott. 'This affair seems too terrible. Is there anything you want to know that I can tell you?'

'Where did the fig paste come from?'

'It is a special kind that comes from London. We often have it. No one suspected that this particular pot differed from any of the others. Personally I dislike the flavour of figs. That explains my immunity. I cannot understand how Dennis was affected, since he was out for tea. He must have picked up a sandwich when he came home, I suppose.'

Tommy felt Tuppence's hand press his arm ever so slightly.

'What time did he come in?' he asked.

'I don't really know. I could find out.'

'Thank you, Miss Chilcott. It doesn't matter. You have no objection, I hope, to my questioning the servants?'

'Please do anything you like, Mr Blunt. I am nearly distraught. Tell me—you don't think there has been—foul play?'

Her eyes were very anxious, as she put the question.

'I don't know what to think. We shall soon know.'

'Yes, I suppose Dr Burton will have the paste analysed.'

Quickly excusing herself, she went out by the window to speak to one of the gardeners.

'You take the housemaids, Tuppence,' said Tommy, 'and I'll find my way to the kitchen. I say, Miss Chilcott may feel very distraught, but she doesn't look it.'

Tuppence nodded assent without replying.

Husband and wife met half an hour later.

'Now to pool results,' said Tommy. 'The sandwiches came out for tea, and the parlourmaid ate one—that's how she got it in the neck. Cook is positive Dennis Radclyffe hadn't returned when tea was cleared away. Query—how did *he* get poisoned?'

'He came in at a quarter to seven,' said Tuppence. 'Housemaid saw him from one of the windows. He had a cocktail before dinner—in the library. She was just clearing away the glass now, and luckily I got it from her before she washed it. It was after that that he complained of feeling ill.'

'Good,' said Tommy. 'I'll take that glass along to Burton, presently. Anything else?'

'I'd like you to see Hannah, the maid. She's—she's queer.'

'How do you mean—queer?'

'She looks to me as though she were going off her head.'

'Let me see her.'

Tuppence led the way upstairs. Hannah had a small sitting-room of her own. The maid sat upright on a high chair. On her knees was an open Bible. She did not look towards the two strangers as they entered. Instead she continued to read aloud to herself.

'Let hot burning coals fall upon them, let them be cast into the fire and into the pit, that they never rise up again.'

'May I speak to you a minute?' asked Tommy.

Hannah made an impatient gesture with her hand.

'This is no time. The time is running short, I say. *I will follow upon mine enemies and overtake them, neither will I turn again till I have destroyed them*. So it is written. The word of the Lord has come to me. I am the scourge of the Lord.'

'Mad as a hatter,' murmured Tommy.

'She's been going on like that all the time,' whispered Tuppence.

Tommy picked up a book that was lying open, face downwards on the table. He glanced at the title and slipped it into his pocket.

Suddenly the old woman rose and turned towards them menacingly.

'Go out from here. The time is at hand! I am the flail of the Lord. The wind bloweth where it listeth—so do I destroy. The ungodly shall perish. This is a house of evil—of evil, I tell you! Beware of the wrath of the Lord whose handmaiden I am.'

She advanced upon them fiercely. Tommy thought it best to humour her and withdrew. As he closed the door, he saw her pick up the Bible again.

'I wonder if she's always been like that,' he muttered.

He drew from his pocket the book he had picked up off the table.

'Look at that. Funny reading for an ignorant maid.'

Tuppence took the book.

'Materia Medica,' she murmured. She looked at the flyleaf, 'Edward Logan. It's an old book. Tommy, I wonder if we could see Miss Logan? Dr Burton said she was better.'

'Shall we ask Miss Chilcott?'

'No. Let's get hold of a housemaid, and send her in to ask.'

After a brief delay, they were informed that Miss Logan would see them. They were taken into a big bedroom facing over the lawn. In the bed was an old lady with white hair, her delicate face drawn by suffering.

'I have been very ill,' she said faintly. 'And I can't talk much, but Ellen tells me you are detectives. Lois went to consult you then? She spoke of doing so.'

'Yes, Miss Logan,' said Tommy. 'We don't want to tire you, but perhaps you can answer a few questions. The maid, Hannah, is she quite right in her head?'

Miss Logan looked at them with obvious surprise.

'Oh, yes. She is very religious—but there is nothing wrong with her.'

Tommy held out the book he had taken from the table.

'Is this yours, Miss Logan?'

'Yes. It was one of my father's books. He was a great doctor, one of the pioneers of serum therapeutics.'

The old lady's voice rang with pride.

'Quite so,' said Tommy. 'I thought I knew his name.' he added mendaciously. 'This book now, did you lend it to Hannah?'

'To Hannah?' Miss Logan raised herself in bed with indignation. 'No, indeed. She wouldn't understand the first word of it. It is a highly technical book.'

'Yes. I see that. Yet I found it in Hannah's room.'

'Disgraceful,' said Miss Logan. 'I will not have the servants touching my things.'

'Where ought it to be?'

'In the bookshelf in my sitting-room—or—stay, I lent it to Mary. The dear girl is very interested in herbs. She has made one or two experiments in my little kitchen. I have a little place of my own, you know, where I brew liqueurs and make preserves in the old-fashioned way. Dear Lucy, Lady Radclyffe, you know, used to swear by my tansy tea—a wonderful thing for a cold in the head. Poor Lucy, she was subject to colds. So is Dennis. Dear boy, his father was my first cousin.'

Tommy interrupted these reminiscences.

'This kitchen of yours? Does anyone else use it except you and Miss Chilcott?'

'Hannah clears up there. And she boils the kettle there for our early morning tea.'

'Thank you, Miss Logan,' said Tommy. 'There is nothing more I want to ask you at present. I hope we haven't tired you too much.'

He left the room and went down the stairs, frowning to himself. 'There is something here, my dear Mr Ricardo, that I do not understand.'

'I hate this house,' said Tuppence with a shiver. 'Let's go for a good long walk and try to think things out.'

Tommy complied and they set out. First they left the cocktail glass at the doctor's house, and then set off for a good tramp across the country, discussing the case as they did so.

'It makes it easier somehow if one plays the fool,' said Tommy. 'All this Hanaud business. I suppose some people would think I didn't care. But I do, most awfully. I feel that somehow or other we ought to have prevented this.'

'I think that's foolish of you,' said Tuppence. 'It is not as though we advised Lois Hargreaves not to go to Scotland Yard or anything like that. Nothing would have induced her to bring the police into the matter. If she hadn't come to us, she would have done nothing at all.'

'And the result would have been the same. Yes, you are right, Tuppence. It's morbid to reproach oneself over something one couldn't help. What I would like to do is to make good now.'

'And that's not going to be easy.'

'No, it isn't. There are so many possibilities, and yet all of them seem wild and improbable. Supposing Dennis Radclyffe put the poison in the sandwiches. He knew he would be out to tea. That seems fairly plain sailing.'

'Yes,' said Tuppence, 'that's all right so far. Then we can put against that the fact that he was poisoned himself—so that seems to rule him out. There is one person we mustn't forget—and that is Hannah.'

'Hannah?'

'People do all sorts of queer things when they have religious mania.'

'She is pretty far gone with it too,' said Tommy. 'You ought to drop a word to Dr Burton about it.'

'It must have come on very rapidly,' said Tuppence. 'That is if we go by what Miss Logan said.'

'I believe religious mania does,' said Tommy. 'I mean, you go on singing hymns in your bedroom with the door open for years, and then you go suddenly right over the line and become violent.'

'There is certainly more evidence against Hannah than against anybody else,' said Tuppence thoughtfully. 'And yet I have an idea—' She stopped.

'Yes?' said Tommy encouragingly.

'It is not really an idea. I suppose it is just a prejudice.'

'A prejudice against someone?'

Tuppence nodded.

'Tommy—did *you* like Mary Chilcott?'

Tommy considered.

'Yes, I think I did. She struck me as extremely capable and businesslike—perhaps a shade too much so—but very reliable.'

'You didn't think it was odd that she didn't seem more upset?'

'Well, in a way that is a point in her favour. I mean, if she had done anything, she would make a point of being upset—lay it on rather thick.'

'I suppose so,' said Tuppence. 'And anyway there doesn't seem to be any motive in her case. One doesn't see what good this wholesale slaughter can do her.'

'I suppose none of the servants are concerned?'

'It doesn't seem likely. They seem a quiet, reliable lot. I wonder what Esther Quant, the parlourmaid, was like.'

'You mean, that if she was young and good-looking there was a chance that she was mixed up in it some way.'

'That is what I mean,' Tuppence sighed. 'It is all very discouraging.'

'Well, I suppose the police will get down to it all right,' said Tommy.

'Probably. I should like it to be us. By the way, did you notice a lot of small red dots on Miss Logan's arm?'

'I don't think I did. What about them?'

'They looked as though they were made by a hypodermic syringe,' said Tuppence.

'Probably Dr Burton gave her a hypodermic injection of some kind.'

'Oh, very likely. But he wouldn't give her about forty.'

'The cocaine habit,' suggested Tommy helpfully.

'I thought of that,' said Tuppence, 'but her eyes were all right. You could see at once if it was cocaine or morphia. Besides, she doesn't look that sort of old lady.'

'Most respectable and God-fearing,' agreed Tommy.

'It is all very difficult,' said Tuppence. 'We have talked and talked and we don't seem any nearer now than we were. Don't let's forget to call at the doctor's on our way home.'

The doctor's door was opened by a lanky boy of about fifteen.

'Mr Blunt?' he inquired. 'Yes, the doctor is out, but he left a note for you in case you should call.'

He handed them the note in question and Tommy tore it open.

Dear Mr Blunt,

There is reason to believe that the poison employed was Ricin, a vegetable toxalbumose of tremendous potency. Please keep this to yourself for the present.

Tommy let the note drop, but picked it up quickly.

'Ricin,' he murmured. 'Know anything about it, Tuppence? You used to be rather well up in these things.'

'Ricin,' said Tuppence, thoughtfully. 'You get it out of castor oil, I believe.'

'I never did take kindly to castor oil,' said Tommy. 'I am more set against it than ever now.'

'The oil's all right. You get Ricin from the seeds of the castor oil plant. I believe I saw some castor oil plants in the garden this morning—big things with glossy leaves.'

'You mean that someone extracted the stuff on the premises. Could Hannah do such a thing?'

Tuppence shook her head.

'Doesn't seem likely. She wouldn't know enough.'

Suddenly Tommy gave an exclamation.

'That book. Have I got it in my pocket still? Yes.' He took it out, and turned over the leaves vehemently. 'I thought so. Here's the page it was open at this morning. Do you see, Tuppence? Ricin!'

Tuppence seized the book from him.

'Can you make head or tail of it? I can't.'

'It's clear enough to me,' said Tuppence. She walked along, reading busily, with one hand on Tommy's arm to steer herself. Presently she shut the book with a bang. They were just approaching the house again.

'Tommy, will you leave this to me? Just for once, you see, I am the bull that has been more than twenty minutes in the arena.'

Tommy nodded.

'You shall be the Captain of the Ship, Tuppence,' he said gravely. 'We've got to get to the bottom of this.'

'First of all,' said Tuppence as they entered the house, 'I must ask Miss Logan one more question.'

She ran upstairs. Tommy followed her. She rapped sharply on the old lady's door and went in.

'Is that you, my dear?' said Miss Logan. 'You know you are much too young and pretty to be a detective. Have you found out anything?'

'Yes,' said Tuppence. 'I have.'

Miss Logan looked at her questioningly.

'I don't know about being pretty,' went on Tuppence, 'but being young, I happened to work in a hospital during the War. I know something about serum therapeutics. I happen to know that when Ricin is injected in small doses hypodermically, immunity is produced, antiricin is formed. That fact paved the way for the foundation of serum therapeutics. You knew that, Miss Logan. You injected Ricin for some time hypodermically into yourself. Then you let yourself be poisoned with the rest. You helped your father in his work, and you knew all about Ricin and how to obtain it and extract it from the seeds. You chose a day when Dennis Radclyffe was out for tea. It wouldn't do for him to be poisoned at the same time—he might die before Lois Hargreaves. So long as she died first, he inherited her money, and at his death it passes to you, his next-of-kin. You remember, you told us this morning that his father was your first cousin.'

The old lady stared at Tuppence with baleful eyes.

Suddenly a wild figure burst in from the adjoining room. It was Hannah. In her hand she held a lighted torch which she waved frantically.

'Truth has been spoken. That is the wicked one. I saw her reading the book and smiling to herself and I knew. I found the book and the page—but it said nothing to me. But the voice of the Lord spoke to me. She hated my mistress, her ladyship. She was always jealous and envious. She hated my own sweet Miss Lois. But the wicked shall perish, the fire of the Lord shall consume them.'

Waving her torch she sprang forward to the bed.

A cry arose from the old lady.

'Take her away—take her away. It's true—but take her away.'

Tuppence flung herself upon Hannah, but the woman managed to set fire to the curtains of the bed before Tuppence could get the torch from her and stamp on it. Tommy, however, had rushed in from the landing outside. He tore down the bed hangings and managed to stifle the flames with a rug. Then he rushed to Tuppence's assistance, and between them they subdued Hannah just as Dr Burton came hurrying in.

A very few words sufficed to put him *au courant* of the situation.

He hurried to the bedside, lifted Miss Logan's hand, then uttered a sharp exclamation.

'The shock of fire has been too much for her. She's dead. Perhaps it is as well under the circumstances.'

He paused, and then added, 'There was Ricin in the cocktail glass as well.'

'It's the best thing that could have happened,' said Tommy, when they had relinquished Hannah to the doctor's care, and were alone together. 'Tuppence, you were simply marvellous.'

'There wasn't much Hanaud about it,' said Tuppence.

'It was too serious for play-acting. I still can't bear to think of that girl. I won't think of her. But, as I said before, you were marvellous. The honours are with you. To use a familiar quotation, "It is a great advantage to be intelligent and not to look it."'

'Tommy,' said Tuppence, 'you're a beast.'

Tape-Measure Murder

Miss Politt took hold of the knocker and rapped politely on the cottage door. After a discreet interval she knocked again. The parcel under her left arm shifted a little as she did so, and she readjusted it. Inside the parcel was Mrs Spenlow's new green winter dress, ready for fitting. From Miss Politt's left hand dangled a bag of black silk, containing a tape measure, a pincushion, and a large, practical pair of scissors.

Miss Politt was tall and gaunt, with a sharp nose, pursed lips, and meagre iron-grey hair. She hesitated before using the knocker for the third time. Glancing down the street, she saw a figure rapidly approaching. Miss Hartnell, jolly, weather-beaten, fifty-five, shouted out in her usual loud bass voice, 'Good afternoon, Miss Politt!'

The dressmaker answered, 'Good afternoon, Miss Hartnell.' Her voice was excessively thin and genteel in its accents. She had started life as a lady's maid. 'Excuse me,' she went on, 'but do you happen to know if by any chance Mrs Spenlow isn't at home?'

'Not the least idea,' said Miss Hartnell.

'It's rather awkward, you see. I was to fit on Mrs Spenlow's new dress this afternoon. Three-thirty, she said.'

Miss Hartnell consulted her wrist watch. 'It's a little past the half-hour now.'

'Yes. I have knocked three times, but there doesn't seem to be any answer, so I was wondering if perhaps Mrs Spenlow might have gone out and forgotten. She doesn't forget appointments as a rule, and she wants the dress to wear the day after tomorrow.'

Miss Hartnell entered the gate and walked up the path to join Miss Politt outside the door of Laburnum Cottage.

'Why doesn't Gladys answer the door?' she demanded. 'Oh, no, of course, it's Thursday—Gladys's day out. I expect Mrs Spenlow has fallen asleep. I don't expect you've made enough noise with this thing.'

Seizing the knocker, she executed a deafening *rat-a-tat-tat,* and in addition thumped upon the panels of the door. She also called out in a stentorian voice, 'What ho, within there!'

There was no response.

Miss Politt murmured, 'Oh, I think Mrs Spenlow must have forgotten and gone out, I'll call round some other time.' She began edging away down the path.

'Nonsense,' said Miss Hartnell firmly. 'She can't have gone out. I'd have met her. I'll just take a look through the windows and see if I can find any signs of life.'

She laughed in her usual hearty manner, to indicate that it was a joke, and applied a perfunctory glance to the nearest window-pane—perfunctory because she knew quite well that the front room was seldom used, Mr and Mrs Spenlow preferring the small back sitting-room.

Perfunctory as it was, though, it succeeded in its object. Miss Hartnell, it is true, saw no signs of life. On the contrary, she saw, through the window, Mrs Spenlow lying on the hearthrug—dead.

'Of course,' said Miss Hartnell, telling the story afterwards, 'I managed to keep my head. That Politt creature wouldn't have had the least idea of what to do. "Got to keep our heads," I said to her. "*You* stay here, and I'll go for Constable Palk." She said something about not wanting to be left, but I paid no attention at all. One has to be firm with that sort of person. I've always found they enjoy making a fuss. So I was just going off when, at that very moment, Mr Spenlow came round the corner of the house.'

Here Miss Hartnell made a significant pause. It enabled her audience to ask breathlessly, 'Tell me, how did he *look?*'

Miss Hartnell would then go on, 'Frankly, *I* suspected something at once! He was *far* too calm. He didn't seem surprised in the least. And you may say what you like, it isn't natural for a man to hear that his wife is dead and display no emotion whatever.'

Everybody agreed with this statement.

The police agreed with it, too. So suspicious did they consider Mr Spenlow's detachment, that they lost no time in ascertaining how that gentleman was situated as a result of his wife's death. When they discovered that Mrs Spenlow had been the monied partner, and that her money went to her husband under a will made soon after their marriage, they were more suspicious than ever.

Miss Marple, that sweet-faced—and, some said, vinegar-tongued—elderly spinster who lived in the house next to the rectory, was interviewed very early—within half an hour of the discovery of the crime. She was approached by Police Constable Palk, importantly thumbing a notebook. 'If you don't mind, ma'am, I've a few questions to ask you.'

Miss Marple said, 'In connection with the murder of Mrs Spenlow?'

Palk was startled. 'May I ask, madam, how you got to know of it?'

'The fish,' said Miss Marple.

The reply was perfectly intelligible to Constable Palk. He assumed correctly that the fishmonger's boy had brought it, together with Miss Marple's evening meal.

Miss Marple continued gently. 'Lying on the floor in the sitting-room, strangled—possibly by a very narrow belt. But whatever it was, it was taken away.'

Palk's face was wrathful. 'How that young Fred gets to know everything—'

Miss Marple cut him short adroitly. She said, 'There's a pin in your tunic.'

Constable Palk looked down, startled. He said, 'They do say, "See a pin and pick it up, all the day you'll have good luck."'

'I hope that will come true. Now what is it you want me to tell you?'

Constable Palk cleared his throat, looked important, and consulted his notebook. 'Statement was made to me by Mr Arthur Spenlow, husband of the deceased. Mr Spenlow says that at two-thirty, as far as he can say, he was rung up by Miss Marple, and asked if he would come over at a quarter past three as she was anxious to consult him about something. Now, ma'am, is that true?'

'Certainly not,' said Miss Marple.

'You did not ring up Mr Spenlow at two-thirty?'

'Neither at two-thirty nor any other time.'

'Ah,' said Constable Palk, and sucked his moustache with a good deal of satisfaction.

'What else did Mr Spenlow say?'

'Mr Spenlow's statement was that he came over here as requested, leaving his own house at ten minutes past three; that on arrival here he was informed by the maid-servant that Miss Marple was "not at 'ome".'

'That part of it is true,' said Miss Marple. 'He did come here, but I was at a meeting at the Women's Institute.'

'Ah,' said Constable Palk again.

Miss Marple exclaimed, 'Do tell me, Constable, do you suspect Mr Spenlow?'

'It's not for me to say at this stage, but it looks to me as though somebody, naming no names, has been trying to be artful.'

Miss Marple said thoughtfully, 'Mr Spenlow?'

She liked Mr Spenlow. He was a small, spare man, stiff and conventional in speech, the acme of respectability. It seemed odd that he should have come to live in the country, he had so clearly lived in towns all his life. To Miss Marple he confided the reason. He said, 'I have always intended, ever since I was a small boy, to live in the country some day and have a garden of my own. I have always been very much attached to flowers. My wife, you know, kept a flower shop. That's where I saw her first.'

A dry statement, but it opened up a vista of romance. A younger, prettier Mrs Spenlow, seen against a background of flowers.

Mr Spenlow, however, really knew nothing about flowers. He had no idea of seeds, of cuttings, of bedding out, of annuals or perennials. He had only a vision—a vision of a small cottage garden thickly planted with sweet-smelling, brightly coloured blossoms. He had asked, almost pathetically, for instruction, and had noted down Miss Marple's replies to questions in a little book.

He was a man of quiet method. It was, perhaps, because of this trait, that the police were interested in him when his wife was found murdered. With patience and perseverance they learned a good deal about the late Mrs Spenlow—and soon all St Mary Mead knew it, too.

The late Mrs Spenlow had begun life as a between-maid in a large house. She had left that position to marry the second gardener, and with him had started a flower shop in London. The shop had prospered. Not so the gardener, who before long had sickened and died.

His widow carried on the shop and enlarged it in an ambitious way. She had continued to prosper. Then she had sold the business at a handsome price and embarked upon matrimony for the second time—with Mr Spenlow, a middle-aged jeweller who had inherited a small and struggling business. Not long afterwards, they had sold the business and came down to St Mary Mead.

Mrs Spenlow was a well-to-do woman. The profits from her florist's establishment she had invested—'under spirit guidance', as she explained to all and sundry. The spirits had advised her with unexpected acumen.

All her investments had prospered, some in quite a sensational fashion. Instead, however, of this increasing her belief in spiritualism, Mrs Spenlow basely deserted mediums and sittings, and made a brief but wholehearted plunge into an obscure religion with Indian affinities which was based on various forms of deep breathing. When, however, she arrived at St Mary Mead, she had relapsed into a period of orthodox Church-of-England beliefs. She was a good deal at the vicarage, and attended church services with assiduity. She patronized the village shops, took an interest in the local happenings, and played village bridge.

A humdrum, everyday life. And—suddenly—murder.

Colonel Melchert, the chief constable, had summoned Inspector Slack.

Slack was a positive type of man. When he had made up his mind, he was sure. He was quite sure now.

'Husband did it, sir,' he said.

'You think so?'

'Quite sure of it. You've only got to look at him. Guilty as hell. Never showed a sign of grief or emotion. He came back to the house knowing she was dead.'

'Wouldn't he at least have tried to act the part of the distracted husband?'

'Not him, sir. Too pleased with himself. Some gentlemen can't act. Too stiff.'

'Any other woman in his life?' Colonel Melchett asked.

'Haven't been able to find any trace of one. Of course, he's the artful kind. He'd cover his tracks. As I see it, he was just fed up with his wife. She'd got the money, and I should say was a trying woman to live with - always taking up with some "ism" or other. He cold-bloodedly decided to do away with her and live comfortably on his own.'

'Yes, that could be the case, I suppose.'

'Depend upon it, that was it. Made his plans careful. Pretended to get a phone call—'

Melchert interrupted him. 'No call been traced?'

'No, sir. That means either that he lied, or that the call was put through from a public telephone booth. The only two public phones in the village are at the station and the post office. Post office it certainly wasn't. Mrs Blade sees everyone who comes in. Station it might be. Train arrives at two twenty-seven and there's a bit of a bustle then. But the main thing is *he* says it was Miss Marple who called him up, and that certainly isn't true. The call didn't come from her house, and she herself was away at the Institute.'

'You're not overlooking the possibility that the husband was deliberately got out of the way—by someone who wanted to murder Mrs Spenlow?'

'You're thinking of young Ted Gerard, aren't you,

sir? I've been working on him—what we're up against there is lack of motive. He doesn't stand to gain anything.'

'He's an undesirable character, though. Quite a pretty little spot of embezzlement to his credit.'

'I'm not saying he isn't a wrong 'un. Still, he did go to his boss and own up to that embezzlement. And his employers weren't wise to it.'

'An Oxford Grouper,' said Melchett.

'Yes, sir. Became a convert and went off to do the straight thing and own up to having pinched money. I'm not saying, mind you, that it mayn't have been astuteness. He may have thought he was suspected and decided to gamble on honest repentance.'

'You have a sceptical mind, Slack,' said Colonel Melchett. 'By the way, have you talked to Miss Marple at all?'

'What's *she* got to do with it, sir?'

'Oh, nothing. But she hears things, you know. Why don't you go and have a chat with her? She's a very sharp old lady.'

Slack changed the subject. 'One thing I've been meaning to ask you, sir. That domestic-service job where the deceased started her career—Sir Robert Abercrombie's place. That's where that jewel robbery was—emeralds—worth a packet. Never got them. I've been looking it up—must have happened when the Spenlow woman was there, though she'd have been quite a girl at the time. Don't think she was mixed up in it, do you, sir? Spenlow, you know, was one of those little tuppenny-ha'penny jewellers—just the chap for a fence.'

Melchett shook his head. 'Don't think there's anything in that. She didn't even know Spenlow at the time. I remember the case. Opinion in police circles was that a son of the house was mixed up in it—Jim Abercrombie—

awful young waster. Had a pile of debts, and just after the robbery they were all paid off—some rich woman, so they said, but I don't know—Old Abercrombie hedged a bit about the case—tried to call the police off.'

'It was just an idea, sir,' said Slack.

Miss Marple received Inspector Slack with gratification, especially when she heard that he had been sent by Colonel Melchert.

'Now, really, that is very kind of Colonel Melchert. I didn't know he remembered me.'

'He remembers you, all right. Told me that what you didn't know of what goes on in St Mary Mead isn't worth knowing.'

'Too kind of him, but really I don't know anything at all. About this murder, I mean.'

'You know what the talk about it is.'

'Oh, of course—but it wouldn't do, would it, to repeat just idle talk?'

Slack said, with an attempt at geniality, 'This isn't an official conversation, you know. It's in confidence, so to speak.'

'You mean you really want to know what people are saying? Whether there's any truth in it or not?'

'That's the idea.'

'Well, of course, there's been a great deal of talk and speculation. And there are really two distinct camps, if you understand me. To begin with, there are the people who think that the husband did it. A husband or a wife is, in a way, the natural person to suspect, don't you think so?'

'Maybe,' said the inspector cautiously.

'Such close quarters, you know. Then, so often, the money angle. I hear that it was Mrs Spenlow who had the money, and therefore Mr Spenlow does benefit by her death. In this wicked world I'm afraid the most uncharitable assumptions are often justified.'

'He comes into a tidy sum, all right.'

'Just so. It would seem quite plausible, wouldn't it, for him to strangle her, leave the house by the back, come across the fields to my house, ask for me and pretend he'd had a telephone call from me, then go back and find his wife murdered in his absence—hoping, of course, that the crime would be put down to some tramp or burglar.'

The inspector nodded. 'What with the money angle—and if they'd been on bad terms lately—'

But Miss Marple interrupted him. 'Oh, but they hadn't.'

'You know that for a fact?'

'Everyone would have known if they'd quarrelled! The maid, Gladys Brent—she'd have soon spread it round the village.'

The inspector said feebly, 'She mightn't have known—' and received a pitying smile in reply.

Miss Marple went on. 'And then there's the other school of thought. Ted Gerard. A good-looking young man. I'm afraid, you know, that good looks are inclined to influence one more than they should. Our last curate but one—quite a magical effect! All the girls came to church—evening service as well as morning. And many older women became unusually active in parish work—and the slippers and scarfs that were made for him! Quite embarrassing for the poor young man.

'But let me see, where was I? Oh, yes, this young man, Ted Gerard. Of course, there has been talk about him. He's come down to see her so often. Though Mrs Spenlow told me herself that he was a member of what I think they call the Oxford Group. A religious movement. They are quite sincere and very earnest, I believe, and Mrs Spenlow was impressed by it all.'

Miss Marple took a breath and went on. 'And I'm sure there was no reason to believe that there was anything more in it than that, but you know what people are. Quite a lot of people are convinced that Mrs Spenlow was infatuated with the young man, and that she'd lent him quite a lot of money. And it's perfectly true that he was actually seen at the station that day. In the train—the two twenty-seven down train. But of course it would be quite easy, wouldn't it, to slip out of the other side of the train and go through the cutting and over the fence and round by the hedge and never come out of the station entrance at all. So that he need not have been seen going to the cottage. And, of course, people do think that what Mrs Spenlow was wearing was rather peculiar.'

'Peculiar?'

'A kimono. Not a dress.' Miss Marple blushed. 'That sort of thing, you know, is, perhaps, rather suggestive to some people.'

'You think it was suggestive?'

'Oh, no, *I* don't think so, I think it was perfectly natural.'

'You think it was natural?'

'Under the circumstances, yes.' Miss Marple's glance was cool and reflective.

Inspector Slack said, 'It might give us another motive for the husband. Jealousy.'

'Oh, no, Mr Spenlow would never be jealous. He's not the sort of man who notices things. If his wife had gone away and left a note on the pincushion, it would be the first he'd know of anything of that kind.'

Inspector Slack was puzzled by the intent way she was looking at him. He had an idea that all her conversation was intended to hint at something he didn't understand. She said now, with some emphasis, 'Didn't *you* find any clues, Inspector—on the spot?'

'People don't leave fingerprints and cigarette ash nowadays, Miss Marple.'

'But this, I think,' she suggested, 'was an old-fashioned crime—'

Slack said sharply, 'Now what do you mean by that?'

Miss Marple remarked slowly, 'I think, you know, that Constable Palk could help you. He was the first person on the—on the "scene of the crime", as they say.'

Mr Spenlow was sitting in a deck chair. He looked bewildered. He said, in his thin, precise voice, 'I may, of course, be imagining what occurred. My hearing is not as good as it was. But I distinctly think I heard a small boy call after me, "Yah, who's a Crippen?" It—it conveyed the impression to me that he was of the opinion that I had—had killed my dear wife.'

Miss Marple, gently snipping off a dead rose head, said, 'That was the impression he meant to convey, no doubt.'

'But what could possibly have put such an idea into a child's head?'

Miss Marple coughed. 'Listening, no doubt, to the opinions of his elders.'

'You—you really mean that other people think that, also?'

'Quite half the people in St Mary Mead.'

'But—my dear lady—what can possibly have given rise to such an idea? I was sincerely attached to my wife. She did not, alas, take to living in the country as much as I had hoped she would do, but perfect agreement on every subject is an impossible idea. I assure you I feel her loss very keenly.'

'Probably. But if you will excuse my saying so, you don't sound as though you do.'

Mr Spenlow drew his meagre frame up to its full height. 'My dear lady, many years ago I read of a certain Chinese philosopher who, when his dearly loved wife was taken from him, continued calmly to beat a gong in the street—a customary Chinese pastime, I presume—exactly as usual. The people of the city were much impressed by his fortitude.'

'But,' said Miss Marple, 'the people of St Mary Mead react rather differently. Chinese philosophy does not appeal to them.'

'But you understand?'

Miss Marple nodded. 'My Uncle Henry,' she explained, 'was a man of unusual self-control. His motto was "Never display emotion". He, too, was very fond of flowers.'

'I was thinking,' said Mr Spenlow with something like eagerness, 'that I might, perhaps, have a pergola on the west side of the cottage. Pink roses and, perhaps, wisteria. And there is a white starry flower, whose name for the moment escapes me—'

In the tone in which she spoke to her grandnephew, aged three, Miss Marple said, 'I have a very nice catalogue here, with pictures. Perhaps you would like to look through it—I have to go up to the village.'

Leaving Mr Spenlow sitting happily in the garden with his catalogue, Miss Marple went up to her room, hastily rolled up a dress in a piece of brown paper, and, leaving the house, walked briskly up to the post office. Miss Politt, the dressmaker, lived in the rooms over the post office.

But Miss Marple did not at once go through the door and up the stairs. It was just two-thirty, and, a minute late, the Much Benham bus drew up outside the post office door. It was one of the events of the day in St Mary Mead. The postmistress hurried out with parcels, parcels connected with the shop side of her business, for the post office also dealt in sweets, cheap books, and children's toys.

For some four minutes Miss Marple was alone in the post office.

Not till the postmistress returned to her post did Miss Marple go upstairs and explain to Miss Politt that she wanted her old grey crepe altered and made more fashionable if that were possible. Miss Politt promised to see what she could do.

The chief constable was rather astonished when Miss Marple's name was brought to him. She came in with many apologies. 'So sorry—so very sorry to disturb you. You are so busy, I know, but then you have always been so very kind, Colonel Melchett, and I felt I would rather come to you instead of Inspector Slack. For one thing, you know, I should hate Constable Palk to get into any trouble. Strictly speaking, I suppose he shouldn't have touched anything at all.'

Colonel Melchett was slightly bewildered. He said, 'Palk? That's the St Mary Mead constable, isn't it? What has he been doing?'

'He picked up a pin, you know. It was in his tunic. And it occurred to me at the time that it was quite probable he had actually picked it up in Mrs Spenlow's house.'

'Quite, quite. But after all, you know, what's a pin? Matter of fact he did pick the pin up just by Mrs Spenlow's body. Came and told Slack about it yesterday—you put him up to that, I gather? Oughtn't to have touched anything, of course, but as I said, what's a pin? It was only a common pin. Sort of thing any woman might use.'

'Oh, no, Colonel Melchett, that's where you're wrong. To a man's eye, perhaps, it looked like an ordinary pin, but it wasn't. It was a special pin, a very thin pin, the kind you buy by the box, the kind used mostly by dressmakers.'

Melchett stared at her, a faint light of comprehension breaking in on him. Miss Marple nodded her head several times, eagerly.

'Yes, of course. It seems to me so obvious. She was in her kimono because she was going to try on her new dress, and she went into the front room, and Miss Politt just said something about measurements and put the tape measure round her neck—and then all she'd have to do was to cross it and pull—quite easy, so I've heard. And then, of course, she'd go outside and pull the door to and stand there knocking as though she'd just arrived. But the pin shows she'd *already been in the house*.'

'And it was Miss Politt who telephoned to Spenlow?'

'Yes. From the post office at two-thirty—just when the bus comes and the post office would be empty.'

Colonel Melchett said, 'But my dear Miss Marple, why? In heaven's name, why? You can't have a murder without a motive.'

'Well, I think, you know, Colonel Melchett, from all I've heard, that the crime dates from a long time back. It reminds me, you know, of my two cousins, Antony and Gordon. Whatever Antony did always went right for him, and with poor Gordon it was just the other way about. Race horses went lame, and stocks went down, and property depreciated. As I see it, the two women were in it together.'

'In what?'

'The robbery. Long ago. Very valuable emeralds, so I've heard. The lady's maid and the tweeny. Because one thing hasn't been explained—how, when the tweeny married the gardener, did they have enough money to set up a flower shop?

'The answer is, it was her share of the—the swag, I think is the right expression. Everything she did turned out well. Money made money. But the other one, the lady's maid, must have been unlucky. She came down to being just a village dressmaker. Then they met again. Quite all right at frrst, I expect, until Mr Ted Gerard came on the scene.

'Mrs Spenlow, you see, was already suffering from conscience, and was inclined to be emotionally religious. This young man no doubt urged her to "face up" and to "come clean" and I dare say she was strung up to do it. But Miss Politt didn't see it that way. All she saw was that she might go to prison for a robbery she had committed years ago. So she made up her mind to put a stop to it all. I'm afraid, you know, that she was always rather a wicked woman. I don't believe she'd have turned a hair if that nice, stupid Mr Spenlow had been hanged.'

Colonel Melchert said slowly, 'We can—er—verify your theory—up to a point. The identity of the Politt woman with the lady's maid at the Abercrombies', but—'

Miss Marple reassured him. 'It will be all quite easy. She's the kind of woman who will break down at once when she's taxed with the truth. And then, you see, I've got her tape measure. I—er—abstracted it yesterday when I was trying on. When she misses it and thinks the police have got it—well, she's quite an ignorant woman and she'll think it will prove the case against her in some way.'

She smiled at him encouragingly. 'You'll have no trouble, I can assure you.' It was the tone in which his favourite aunt had once assured him that he could not fail to pass his entrance examination into Sandhurst.

And he had passed.

The Voice in the Dark

'I am a little worried about Margery,' said Lady Stranleigh.

'My girl, you know,' she added.

She sighed pensively.

'It makes one feel terribly old to have a grown-up daughter.'

Mr Satterthwaite, who was the recipient of these confidences, rose to the occasion gallantly.

'No one could believe it possible,' he declared with a little bow.

'Flatterer,' said Lady Stranleigh, but she said it vaguely and it was clear that her mind was elsewhere.

Mr Satterthwaite looked at the slender white-clad figure in some admiration. The Cannes sunshine was searching, but Lady Stranleigh came through the test very well. At a distance the youthful effect was really extraordinary. One almost wondered if she were grown-up or not. Mr Satterthwaite, who knew everything, knew that it was perfectly possible for Lady Stranleigh to have grown-up grandchildren. She represented the extreme triumph of art over nature. Her figure was marvellous, her complexion was marvellous. She had enriched many beauty parlours and certainly the results were astounding.

Lady Stranleigh lit a cigarette, crossed her beautiful legs encased in the finest of nude silk stockings and murmured: 'Yes, I really am rather worried about Margery.'

'Dear me,' said Mr Satterthwaite, 'what is the trouble?'

Lady Stranleigh turned her beautiful blue eyes upon him.

'You have never met her, have you? She is Charles' daughter,' she added helpfully.

If entries in 'Who's Who' were strictly truthful, the entries concerning Lady Stranleigh might have ended as follows: *hobbies: getting married.* She had floated through life shedding husbands as she went. She had lost three by divorce and one by death.

'If she had been Rudolph's child I could have understood it,' mused Lady Stranleigh. 'You remember Rudolf? He was always temperamental. Six months after we married I had to apply for those queer things—what do they call them? Conjugal what nots, you know what I mean. Thank goodness it is all much simpler nowadays. I remember I had to write him the silliest kind of letter—my lawyer practically dictated it to me. Asking him to come back, you know, and that I would do all I could, etc., etc., but you never could count on Rudolf, he was so temperamental. He came rushing home at once, which was quite the wrong thing to do, and not at all what the lawyers meant.'

She sighed.

'About Margery?' suggested Mr Satterthwaite, tactfully leading her back to the subject under discussion.

'Of course. I was just going to tell you, wasn't I? Margery has been seeing things, or hearing them. Ghosts, you know, and all that. I should never have thought that Margery could be so imaginative. She is a dear good girl, always has been, but just a shade—dull.'

'Impossible,' murmured Mr Satterthwaite with a confused idea of being complimentary.

'In fact, very dull,' said Lady Stranleigh. 'Doesn't care for dancing, or cocktails or any of the things a young girl ought to care about. She much prefers staying at home to hunt instead of coming out here with me.'

'Dear, dear,' said Mr Satterthwaite, 'she wouldn't come out with you, you say?'

'Well, I didn't exactly press her. Daughters have a depressing effect upon one, I find.'

Mr Satterthwaite tried to think of Lady Stranleigh accompanied by a serious-minded daughter and failed.

'I can't help wondering if Margery is going off her head,' continued Margery's mother in a cheerful voice. 'Hearing voices is a very bad sign, so they tell me. It is not as though Abbot's Mede were haunted. The old building was burnt to the ground in 1836, and they put up a kind of early Victorian château which simply cannot be haunted. It is much too ugly and common-place.'

Mr Satterthwaite coughed. He was wondering why he was being told all this.

'I thought perhaps,' said Lady Stranleigh, smiling brilliantly upon him, 'that *you* might be able to help me.'

'I?'

'Yes. You are going back to England tomorrow, aren't you?'

'I am. Yes, that is so,' admitted Mr Satterthwaite cautiously.

'And you know all these psychical research people. Of course you do, you know everybody.'

Mr Satterthwaite smiled a little. It was one of his weaknesses to know everybody.

'So what can be simpler?' continued Lady Stranleigh. 'I never get on with that sort of person. You know—earnest men with beards and usually spectacles. They bore me terribly and I am quite at my worst with them.'

Mr Satterthwaite was rather taken aback. Lady Stranleigh continued to smile at him brilliantly.

'So that is all settled, isn't it?' she said brightly. 'You will go down to Abbot's Mede and see Margery, and make all the arrangements. I shall be terribly grateful to you. Of course if Margery is *really* going off her head, I will come home. Ah! here is Bimbo.'

Her smile from being brilliant became dazzling.

A young man in white tennis flannels was approaching them. He was about twenty-five years of age and extremely good-looking.

The young man said simply:

'I have been looking for you everywhere, Babs.'

'What has the tennis been like?'

'Septic.'

Lady Stranleigh rose. She turned her head over her shoulder and murmured in dulcet tones to Mr Satterthwaite: 'It is simply marvellous of you to help me. I shall never forget it.'

Mr Satterthwaite looked after the retreating couple.

'I wonder,' he mused to himself, 'If Bimbo is going to be No. 5.'

The conductor of the Train de Luxe was pointing out to Mr Satterthwaite where an accident on the line had occurred a few years previously. As he finished his spirited narrative, the other looked up and saw a well-known face smiling at him over the conductor's shoulder.

'My dear Mr Quin,' said Mr Satterthwaite.

His little withered face broke into smiles.

'What a coincidence! That we should both be returning to England on the same train. You are going there, I suppose.'

'Yes,' said Mr Quin. 'I have business there of rather

an important nature. Are you taking the first service of dinner?'

'I always do so. Of course, it is an absurd time—half-past six, but one runs less risk with the cooking.'

Mr Quin nodded comprehendingly.

'I also,' he said. 'We might perhaps arrange to sit together.'

Half-past six found Mr Quin and Mr Satterthwaite established opposite each other at a small table in the dining-car. Mr Satterthwaite gave due attention to the wine list and then turned to his companion.

'I have not seen you since—ah, yes not since Corsica. You left very suddenly that day.'

Mr Quin shrugged his shoulders.

'Not more so than usual. I come and go, you know. I come and go.'

The words seemed to awake some echo of remembrance in Mr Satterthwaite's mind. A little shiver passed down his spine—not a disagreeable sensation, quite the contrary. He was conscious of a pleasurable sense of anticipation.

Mr Quin was holding up a bottle of red wine, examining the label on it. The bottle was between him and the light but for a minute or two a red glow enveloped his person.

Mr Satterthwaite felt again that sudden stir of excitement.

'I too have a kind of mission in England,' he remarked, smiling broadly at the remembrance. 'You know Lady Stranleigh perhaps?'

Mr Quin shook his head.

'It is an old title,' said Mr Satterthwaite, 'a very old title. One of the few that can descend in the female line. She is a Baroness in her own right. Rather a romantic history really.'

Mr Quin settled himself more comfortably in his chair. A waiter, flying down the swinging car, deposited cups of soup before them as if by a miracle. Mr Quin sipped it cautiously.

'You are about to give me one of those wonderful descriptive portraits of yours,' he murmured, 'that is so, is it not?'

Mr Satterthwaite beamed on him.

'She is really a marvellous woman,' he said. 'Sixty, you know—yes, I should say at least sixty. I knew them as girls, she and her sister. Beatrice, that was the name of the elder one. Beatrice and Barbara. I remember them as the Barron girls. Both good-looking and in those days very hard up. But that was a great many years ago—why, dear me, I was a young man myself then.' Mr Satterthwaite sighed. 'There were several lives then between them and the title. Old Lord Stranleigh was a first cousin once removed, I think. Lady Stranleigh's life has been quite a romantic affair. Three unexpected deaths—two of the old man's brothers and a nephew. Then there was the "Uralia". You remember the wreck of the "Uralia"? She went down off the coast of New Zealand. The Barron girls were on board. Beatrice was drowned. This one, Barbara, was amongst the few survivors. Six months later, old Stranleigh died and she succeeded to the title and came into a considerable fortune. Since then she has lived for one thing only—herself! She has always been the same, beautiful, unscrupulous, completely callous, interested solely in herself. She has had four husbands, and I have no doubt could get a fifth in a minute.'

He went on to describe the mission with which he had been entrusted by Lady Stranleigh.

'I thought of running down to Abbot's Mede to see the young lady,' he explained. 'I—I feel that something ought to be done about the matter. It is impossible to think of Lady Stranleigh as an ordinary mother.' He stopped, looking across the table at Mr Quin.

'I wish you would come with me,' he said wistfully. 'Would it not be possible?'

'I'm afraid not,' said Mr Quin. 'But let me see, Abbot's Mede is in Wiltshire, is it not?'

Mr Satterthwaite nodded.

'I thought as much. As it happens, I shall be staying not far from Abbot's Mede, at a place you and I both know.' He smiled. 'You remember that little inn, the "Bells and Motley"?'

'Of course,' cried Mr Satterthwaite; 'you will be there?'

Mr Quin nodded. 'For a week or ten days. Possibly longer. If you will come and look me up one day, I shall be delighted to see you.'

And somehow or other Mr Satterthwaite felt strangely comforted by the assurance.

'My dear Miss—er—Margery,' said Mr Satterthwaite, 'I assure you that I should not dream of laughing at you.'

Margery Gale frowned a little. They were sitting in the large comfortable hall of Abbot's Mede. Margery Gale was a big squarely built girl. She bore no resemblance to her mother, but took entirely after her father's side of the family, a line of hard-riding country squires. She looked fresh and wholesome and the picture of sanity. Nevertheless, Mr Satterthwaite was reflecting to himself that the Barrons as a family were all inclined to mental instability. Margery might have inherited her physical appearance from her father and at the same time have inherited some mental kink from her mother's side of the family.

'I wish,' said Margery, 'that I could get rid of that Casson woman. I don't believe in spiritualism, and I don't like it. She is one of these silly women that run a craze to death. She is always bothering me to have a medium down here.'

Mr Satterthwaite coughed, fidgeted a little in his chair and then said in a judicial manner:

'Let me be quite sure that I have all the facts. The first of the—er—phenomena occurred two months ago, I understand?'

'About that,' agreed the girl. 'Sometimes it was a whisper and sometimes it was quite a clear voice but it always said much the same thing.'

'Which was?'

'*Give back what is not yours. Give back what you have stolen.* On each occasion I switched on the light, but the room was quite empty and there was no one there. In the end I got so nervous that I got Clayton, mother's maid, to sleep on the sofa in my room.'

'And the voice came just the same?'

'Yes—and this is what frightens me—Clayton did not hear it.'

Mr Satterthwaite reflected for a minute or two.

'Did it come loudly or softly that evening?'

'It was almost a whisper,' admitted Margery. 'If Clayton was sound asleep I suppose she would not really have heard it. She wanted me to see a doctor.' The girl laughed bitterly.

'But since last night even Clayton believes,' she continued.

'What happened last night?'

'I am just going to tell you. I have told no one as yet. I had been out hunting yesterday and we had had a long run. I was dead tired, and slept very heavily. I dreamt—a horrible dream—that I had fallen over some iron railings and that one of the spikes was entering slowly into my throat. I woke to find that it was true—there was some sharp point pressing into the side of my neck, and at the same time a voice was murmuring softly: "*You have stolen what is mine. This is death.*"

'I screamed,' continued Margery, 'and clutched at the air, but there was nothing there. Clayton heard me scream from the room next door where she was sleeping. She came rushing in, and she distinctly felt something brushing past her in the darkness, but she says that whatever that something was, it was not anything human.'

Mr Satterthwaite stared at her. The girl was obviously very shaken and upset. He noticed on the left side of her throat a small square of sticking plaster. She caught the direction of his gaze and nodded.

'Yes,' she said, 'it was not imagination, you see.'

Mr Satterthwaite put a question almost apologetically, it sounded so melodramatic.

'You don't know of anyone—er—who has a grudge against you?' he asked.

'Of course not,' said Margery. 'What an idea!'

Mr Satterthwaite started on another line of attack.

'What visitors have you had during the last two months?'

'You don't mean just people for weekends, I suppose? Marcia Keane has been with me all along. She is my best friend, and just as keen on horses as I am. Then my cousin Roley Vavasour has been here a good deal.'

Mr Satterthwaite nodded. He suggested that he should see Clayton, the maid.

'She has been with you a long time, I suppose?' he asked.

'Donkey's years,' said Margery. 'She was Mother's and Aunt Beatrice's maid when they were girls. That is why Mother has kept her on, I suppose, although she has got a French maid for herself. Clayton does sewing and pottering little odd jobs.'

She took him upstairs and presently Clayton came to them. She was a tall, thin, old woman, with grey hair neatly parted, and she looked the acme of respectability.

'No, sir,' she said in answer to Mr Satterthwaite's inquiries. 'I have never heard anything of the house being haunted. To tell you the truth, sir, I thought it was all Miss Margery's imagination until last night. But I actually felt something—brushing by me in the darkness. And I can tell you this, sir, *it was not anything human*. And then there is that wound in Miss Margery's neck. She didn't do that herself, poor lamb.'

But her words were suggestive to Mr Satterthwaite. Was it possible that Margery could have inflicted that wound herself? He had heard of strange cases where girls apparently just as sane and well-balanced as Margery had done the most amazing things.

'It will soon heal up,' said Clayton. 'It's not like this scar of mine.'

She pointed to a mark on her own forehead.

'That was done forty years ago, sir; I still bear the mark of it.'

'It was the time the "Uralia" went down,' put in Margery. 'Clayton was hit on the head by a spar, weren't you, Clayton?'

'Yes, Miss.'

'What do you think yourself, Clayton,' asked Mr Satterthwaite, 'what do you think was the meaning of this attack on Miss Margery?'

'I really should not like to say, sir.'

Mr Satterthwaite read this correctly as the reserve of the well-trained servant.

'What do you really think, Clayton?' he said persuasively.

'I think, sir, that something very wicked must have

been done in this house, and that until that is wiped out there won't be any peace.'

The woman spoke gravely, and her faded blue eyes met his steadily.

Mr Satterthwaite went downstairs rather disappointed. Clayton evidently held the orthodox view, a deliberate 'haunting' as a consequence of some evil deed in the past. Mr Satterthwaite himself was not so easily satisfied. The phenomena had only taken place in the last two months. Had only taken place since Marcia Keane and Roley Vavasour had been there. He must find out something about these two. It was possible that the whole thing was a practical joke. But he shook his head, dissatisfied with that solution. The thing was more sinister than that. The post had just come in and Margery was opening and reading her letters. Suddenly she gave an exclamation.

'Mother is too absurd,' she said. 'Do read this.' She handed the letter to Mr Satterthwaite.

It was an epistle typical of Lady Stranleigh.

Darling Margery (she wrote),

I am so glad you have that nice little Mr Satterthwaite there. He is awfully clever and knows all the big-wig spook people. You must have them all down and investigate things thoroughly. I am sure you will have a perfectly marvellous time, and I only wish I could be there, but I have really been quite ill the last few days. The hotels are so careless about the food they give one. The doctor says it is some kind of food poisoning. I was really very *ill.*

Sweet of you to send me the chocolates, darling, but surely just a wee bit silly, wasn't it? I mean, there's such wonderful confectionery out here.

Bye-bye, darling, and have a lovely time laying the family ghosts.

Bimbo says my tennis is coming on marvellously. Oceans of love.

Yours,

Barbara.

'Mother always wants me to call her Barbara,' said Margery. 'Simply silly, I think.'

Mr Satterthwaite smiled a little. He realized that the stolid conservatism of her daughter must on occasions be very trying to Lady Stranleigh. The contents of her letter struck him in a way in which obviously they did not strike Margery.

'Did you send your mother a box of chocolates?' he asked.

Margery shook her head. 'No, I didn't, it must have been someone else.'

Mr Satterthwaite looked grave. Two things struck him as of significance. Lady Stranleigh had received a gift of a box of chocolates and she was suffering from a severe attack of poisoning. Apparently she had not connected these two things. Was there a connection? He himself was inclined to think there was.

A tall dark girl lounged out of the morning-room and joined them.

She was introduced to Mr Satterthwaite as Marcia Keane. She smiled on the little man in an easy good-humoured fashion.

'Have you come down to hunt Margery's pet ghost?' she asked in a drawling voice. 'We all rot her about that ghost. Hello, here's Roley.'

A car had just drawn up at the front door. Out of it tumbled a tall young man with fair hair and an eager boyish manner.

'Hello, Margery,' he cried. 'Hello, Marcia! I have brought down reinforcements.' He turned to the two women who were just entering the hall. Mr Satterthwaite recognized in the first one of the two the Mrs Casson of whom Margery had spoken just now.

'You must forgive me, Margery, dear,' she drawled, smiling broadly. 'Mr Vavasour told us that it would be quite all right. It was really his idea that I should bring down Mrs Lloyd with me.'

She indicated her companion with a slight gesture of the hand.

'This is Mrs Lloyd,' she said in a tone of triumph. 'Simply the most wonderful medium that ever existed.'

Mrs Lloyd uttered no modest protest, she bowed and remained with her hands crossed in front of her. She was a highly-coloured young woman of commonplace appearance. Her clothes were unfashionable but rather ornate. She wore a chain of moonstones and several rings.

Margery Gale, as Mr Satterthwaite could see, was not too pleased at this intrusion. She threw an angry look at Roley Vavasour, who seemed quite unconscious of the offence he had caused.

'Lunch is ready, I think,' said Margery.

'Good,' said Mrs Casson. 'We will hold a *séance* immediately afterwards. Have you got some fruit for Mrs Lloyd? She never eats a solid meal before a *séance*.'

They all went into the dining-room. The medium ate two bananas and an apple, and replied cautiously and briefly to the various polite remarks which Margery addressed to her from time to time. Just before they rose from the table, she flung back her head suddenly and sniffed the air.

'There is something very wrong in this house. I feel it.'

'Isn't she wonderful?' said Mrs Casson in a low delighted voice.

'Oh! undoubtedly,' said Mr Satterthwaite dryly.

The *séance* was held in the library. The hostess was, as Mr Satterthwaite could see, very unwilling, only the obvious delight of her guests in the proceedings reconciled her to the ordeal.

The arrangements were made with a good deal of care by Mrs Casson, who was evidently well up in those matters, the chairs were set round in a circle, the curtains were drawn, and presently the medium announced herself ready to begin.

'Six people,' she said, looking round the room. 'That is bad. We must have an uneven number, Seven is ideal. I get my best results out of a circle of seven.'

'One of the servants,' suggested Roley. He rose. 'I will rout out the butler.'

'Let's have Clayton,' said Margery.

Mr Satterthwaite saw a look of annoyance pass over Roley Vavasour's good-looking face.

'But why Clayton?' he demanded.

'You don't like Clayton,' said Margery slowly.

Roley shrugged his shoulders. 'Clayton doesn't like me,' he said whimsically. 'In fact she hates me like poison.' He waited a minute or two, but Margery did not give way. 'All right,' he said, 'have her down.'

The circle was formed.

There was a period of silence broken by the usual coughs and fidgetings. Presently a succession of raps were heard and then the voice of the medium's control, a man called Cherokee.

'Cherokee says you Good evening ladies and gentlemen. Someone here very anxious speak. Someone here very anxious give message to young lady. I go now. The spirit say what she come to say.'

A pause and then a new voice, that of a woman, said softly:

'Is Margery here?'

Roley Vavasour took it upon himself to answer.

'Yes,' he said, 'she is. Who is that speaking?'

'I am Beatrice.'

'Beatrice? Who is Beatrice?'

To everyone's annoyance the voice of Cherokee was heard once more.

'I have message for all of you people. Life here very bright and beautiful. We all work very hard. Help those who have not yet passed over.'

Again a silence and then the woman's voice was heard once more.

'This is Beatrice speaking.'

'Beatrice who?'

'Beatrice Barron.'

Mr Sattherwaite leaned forward. He was very excited.

'Beatrice Barron who was drowned in the "Uralia"?'

'Yes, that is right. I remember the "Uralia". I have a message—for this house—*Give back what is not yours.*'

'I don't understand,' said Margery helplessly. 'I—oh, are you really Aunt Beatrice?'

'Yes, I am your aunt.'

'Of course she is,' said Mrs Casson reproachfully. 'How can you be so suspicious? The spirits don't like it.'

And suddenly Mr Satterthwaite thought of a very simple test. His voice quivered as he spoke.

'Do you remember Mr Bottacetti?' he asked.

Immediately there came a ripple of laughter.

'Poor old Boatsupsetty. Of course.'

Mr Sattherwaite was dumbfounded. The test had succeeded. It was an incident of over forty years ago which had happened when he and the Barron girls had found themselves at the same seaside resort. A young Italian acquaintance of theirs had gone out in a boat and capsized, and Beatrice Barron had jestingly named him Boatsupsetty. It seemed impossible that anyone in the room could know of this incident except himself.

The medium stirred and groaned.

'She is coming out,' said Mrs Casson. 'That is all we will get out of her today, I am afraid.'

The daylight shone once more on the room full of people, two of whom at least were badly scared.

Mr Satterthwaite saw by Margery's white face that she was deeply perturbed. When they had got rid of Mrs Casson and the medium, he sought a private interview with his hostess.

'I want to ask you one or two questions, Miss Margery. If you and your mother were to die who succeeds to the title and estates?'

'Roley Vavasour, I suppose. His mother was Mother's first cousin.'

Mr Satterthwaite nodded.

'He seems to have been here a lot this winter,' he said gently. 'You will forgive me asking—but is he—fond of you?'

'He asked me to marry him three weeks ago,' said Margery quietly. 'I said No.'

'Please forgive me, but are you engaged to anyone else?'

He saw the colour sweep over her face.

'I am,' she said emphatically. 'I am going to marry Noel Barton. Mother laughs and says it is absurd. She seems to think it is ridiculous to be engaged to a curate. Why, I should like to know! There are curates and curates! You should see Noel on a horse.'

'Oh, quite so,' said Mr Satterthwaite. 'Oh, undoubtedly.'

A footman entered with a telegram on a salver. Margery tore it open. 'Mother is arriving home tomorrow,' she said. 'Bother. I wish to goodness she would stay away.'

Mr Satterthwaite made no comment on this filial sentiment. Perhaps he thought it justified. 'In that case,' he murmured, 'I think I am returning to London.'

Mr Satterthwaite was not quite pleased with himself. He felt that he had left this particular problem in an unfinished state. True that, on Lady Stranleigh's return, his responsibility was ended, yet he felt assured that he had not heard the last of the Abbot's Mede mystery.

But the next development when it came was so serious in its character that it found him totally unprepared. He learnt of it in the pages of his morning paper. 'Baroness Dies in her Bath,' as the *Daily Megaphone* had it. The other papers were more restrained and delicate in their language, but the fact was the same. Lady Stranleigh had been found dead in her bath and her death was due to drowning. She had, it was assumed, lost consciousness, and whilst in that state her head had slipped below the water.

But Mr Satterthwaite was not satisfied with that explanation. Calling for his valet he made his toilet with less than his usual care, and ten minutes later his big Rolls-Royce was carrying him out of London as fast as it could travel.

But strangely enough it was not for Abbot's Mede he was bound, but for a small inn some fifteen miles distant which bore the rather unusual name of the 'Bells and Motley'. It was with great relief that he heard that Mr Harley Quin was still staying there. In another minute he was face to face with his friend.

Mr Satterthwaite clasped him by the hand and began to speak at once in an agitated manner.

'I am terribly upset. You must help me. Already I have a dreadful feeling that it may be too late—that that nice girl may be the next to go, for she is a nice girl, nice through and through.'

'If you will tell me,' said Mr Quin, smiling, 'what it is all about?'

Mr Satterthwaite looked at him reproachfully.

'You know. I am perfectly certain that you know. But I will tell you.'

He poured out the story of his stay at Abbot's Mede and, as always with Mr Quin, he found himself taking pleasure in his narrative. He was eloquent and subtle and meticulous as to detail.

'So you see,' he ended, 'there must be an explanation.'

He looked hopefully at Mr Quin as a dog looks at his master.

'But it is you who must solve the problem, not I,' said Mr Quin. 'I do not know these people. You do.'

'I knew the Barron girls forty years ago,' said Mr Satterthwaite with pride.

Mr Quin nodded and looked sympathetic, so much so that the other went on dreamily.

'That time at Brighton now, Bottacetti-Boatsupsetty, quite a silly joke but how we laughed. Dear, dear, I was young then. Did a lot of foolish things. I remember the maid they had with them. Alice, her name was, a little bit of a thing—very ingenuous. I kissed her in the passage of the hotel, I remember, and one of the girls nearly caught me doing it. Dear, dear, how long ago that all was.'

He shook his head again and sighed. Then he looked at Mr Quin.

'So you can't help me?' he said wistfully. 'On other occasions—'

'On other occasions you have proved successful owing entirely to your own efforts,' said Mr Quin gravely.

'I think it will be the same this time. If I were you, I should go to Abbot's Mede now.'

'Quite so, quite so,' said Mr Satterthwaite, 'as a matter of fact that is what I thought of doing. I can't persuade you to come with me?'

Mr Quin shook his head.

'No,' he said, 'my work here is done. I am leaving almost immediately.'

At Abbot's Mede, Mr Satterthwaite was taken at once to Margery Gale. She was sitting dry-eyed at a desk in the morning-room on which were strewn various papers. Something in her greeting touched him. She seemed so very pleased to see him.

'Roley and Maria have just left. Mr Satterthwaite, it is not as the doctors think. I am convinced, absolutely convinced, that Mother was pushed under the water and held there. She was murdered, and whoever murdered her wants to murder me too. I am sure of that. That is why—' she indicated the document in front of her.

'I have been making my will,' she explained. 'A lot of the money and some of the property does not go with the title, and there is my father's money as well. I am leaving everything I can to Noel. I know he will make a good use of it and I do not trust Roley, he has always been out for what he can get. Will you sign it as a witness?'

'My dear young lady,' said Mr Satterthwaite, 'you should sign a will in the presence of two witnesses and they should then sign themselves at the same time.'

Margery brushed aside this legal pronouncement.

'I don't see that it matters in the least,' she declared. 'Clayton saw me sign and then she signed her name. I was going to ring for the butler, but you will do instead.'

Mr Satterthwaite uttered no fresh protest, he unscrewed his fountain pen and then, as he was about to append his signature, he paused suddenly. The name, written just above his own, recalled a flow of memories. Alice Clayton.

Something seemed to be struggling very hard to get through to him. Alice Clayton, there was some significance about that. Something to do with Mr Quin was mixed up with it. Something he had said to Mr Quin only a very short time ago.

Ah, he had it now. Alice Clayton, that was her name. *The little bit of a thing.* People changed—yes, *but not like that.* And the Alice Clayton he knew had had brown eyes. The room seemed whirling round him. He felt for a chair and presently, as though from a great distance, he heard Margery's voice speaking to him anxiously. 'Are you ill? Oh, what is it? I am sure you are ill.'

He was himself again. He took her hand.

'My dear, I see it all now. You must prepare yourself for a great shock. The woman upstairs whom you call Clayton is not Clayton at all. The real Alice Clayton was drowned on the "Uralia".'

Margery was staring at him. 'Who—who is she then?'

'I am not mistaken, I cannot be mistaken. The woman you call Clayton is your mother's sister, Beatrice Barron. You remember telling me that she was struck on the head by a spar? I should imagine that that blow destroyed her memory, and that being the case, your mother saw the chance—'

'Of pinching the title, you mean?' asked Margery bitterly. 'Yes, she would do that. It seems dreadful to say that now she is dead, but she was like that.'

'Beatrice was the elder sister,' said Mr Satterthwaite. 'By your uncle's death she would inherit everything and your mother would get nothing. Your mother claimed the wounded girl as her *maid*, not as her *sister.* The girl recovered from the blow and believed, of course, what was told her, that she was Alice Clayton, your mother's maid. I should imagine that just lately her memory had begun to return, but that the blow on the head, given all these years ago, has at last caused mischief on the brain.'

Margery was looking at him with eyes of horror.

'She killed Mother and she wanted to kill me,' she breathed.

'It seems so,' said Mr Satterthwaite. 'In her brain there was just one muddled idea—that her inheritance had been stolen and was being kept from her by you and your mother.'

'But—but Clayton is so old.'

Mr Satterthwaite was silent for a minute as a vision rose up before him—the faded old woman with grey hair, and the radiant golden-haired creature sitting in the sunshine at Cannes. Sisters! Could it really be so? He remembered the Barron girls and their likeness to each other. Just because two lives had developed on different tracks—

He shook his head sharply, obsessed by the wonder and pity of life . . .

He turned to Margery and said gently: 'We had better go upstairs and see her.'

They found Clayton sitting in the little workroom where she sewed. She did not turn her head as they came in for a reason that Mr Satterthwaite soon found out.

'Heart failure,' he murmured, as he touched the cold rigid shoulder. 'Perhaps it is best that way.'

Four-and-Twenty Blackbirds

Hercule Poirot was dining with his friend, Henry Bonnington at the Gallant Endeavour in the King's Road, Chelsea.

Mr Bonnington was fond of the Gallant Endeavour. He liked the leisurely atmosphere, he liked the food which was 'plain' and 'English' and 'not a lot of made up messes.' He liked to tell people who dined with him there just exactly where Augustus John had been wont to sit and draw their attention to the famous artists' names in the visitors' book. Mr Bonnington was himself the least artistic of men—but he took a certain pride in the artistic activities of others.

Molly, the sympathetic waitress, greeted Mr Bonnington as an old friend. She prided herself on remembering her customers' likes and dislikes in the way of food.

'Good evening, sir,' she said, as the two men took their seats at a corner table. 'You're in luck today—turkey stuffed with chestnuts—that's your favourite, isn't it? And ever such a nice Stilton we've got! Will you have soup first or fish?'

Mr Bonnington deliberated the point. He said to Poirot warningly as the latter studied the menu:

'None of your French kickshaws now. Good well-cooked English food.'

'My friend,' Hercule Poirot waved his hand, 'I ask no better! I put myself in your hands unreservedly.'

'Ah—hruup—er—hm,' replied Mr Bonnington and gave careful attention to the matter.

These weighty matters, and the question of wine, settled, Mr Bonnington leaned back with a sigh and unfolded his napkin as Molly sped away.

'Good girl, that,' he said approvingly. 'Was quite a beauty once—artists used to paint her. She knows about food, too—and that's a great deal more important. Women are very unsound on food as a rule. There's many a woman if she goes out with a fellow she fancies—won't even notice what she eats. She'll just order the first thing she sees.'

Hercule Poirot shook his head.

'*C'est terrible.*'

'Men aren't like that, thank God!' said Mr Bonnington complacently.

'Never?' There was a twinkle in Hercule Poirot's eye.

'Well, perhaps when they're very young,' conceded Mr Bonnington. 'Young puppies! Young fellows nowadays are all the same—no guts—no stamina. I've no use for the young—and they,' he added with strict impartiality, 'have no use for me. Perhaps they're right! But to hear some of these young fellows talk you'd think no man had a right to be *alive* after sixty! From the way they go on, you'd wonder more of them didn't help their elderly relations out of the world.'

'It is possible,' said Hercule Poirot, 'that they do.'

'Nice mind you've got, Poirot, I must say. All this police work saps your ideals.'

Hercule Poirot smiled.

'*Tout de même,*' he said. 'It would be interesting to make a table of accidental deaths over the age of sixty.

I assure you it would raise some curious speculations in your mind.'

'The trouble with you is that you've started going to look for crime—instead of waiting for crime to come to you.'

'I apologize,' said Poirot. 'I talk what you call "the shop". Tell me, my friend, of your own affairs. How does the world go with you?'

'Mess!' said Mr Bonnington. 'That's what's the matter with the world nowadays. Too much mess. And too much fine language. The fine language helps to conceal the mess. Like a highly-flavoured sauce concealing the fact that the fish underneath it is none of the best! Give me an honest fillet of sole and no messy sauce over it.'

It was given him at that moment by Molly and he grunted approval.

'You know just what I like, my girl,' he said.

'Well, you come here pretty regular, don't you, sir? I ought to know what you like.'

Hercule Poirot said:

'Do people then always like the same things? Do not they like a change sometimes?'

'Not gentlemen, sir. Ladies like variety—gentlemen always like the same thing.'

'What did I tell you?' grunted Bonnington. 'Women are fundamentally unsound where food is concerned!'

He looked round the restaurant.

'The world's a funny place. See that odd-looking old fellow with a beard in the corner? Molly'll tell you he's always here Tuesdays and Thursday nights. He has come here for close on ten years now—he's a kind of landmark in the place. Yet nobody here knows his name or where he lives or what his business is. It's odd when you come to think of it.'

When the waitress brought the portions of turkey he said:

'I see you've still got Old Father Time over there?'

'That's right, sir. Tuesdays and Thursdays, his days are. Not but what he came in here on a *Monday* last week! It quite upset me! I felt I'd got my dates wrong and that it must be Tuesday without my knowing it! But he came in the next night as well—so the Monday was just a kind of extra, so to speak.'

'An interesting deviation from habit,' murmured Poirot. 'I wonder what the reason was?'

'Well, sir, if you ask me, I think he'd had some kind of upset or worry.'

'Why did you think that? His manner?'

'No, sir—not his manner exactly. He was very quiet as he always is. Never says much except good evening when he comes and goes. No, it was his *order*.'

'His order?'

'I dare say you gentlemen will laugh at me,' Molly flushed up, 'but when a gentleman has been here for ten years, you get to know his likes and dislikes. He never could bear suet pudding or blackberries and I've never known him take thick soup—but on that Monday night he ordered thick tomato soup, beefsteak and kidney pudding and blackberry tart! Seemed as though he just didn't notice *what* he ordered!'

'Do you know,' said Hercule Poirot, 'I find that extraordinarily interesting.'

Molly looked gratified and departed.

'Well, Poirot,' said Henry Bonnington with a chuckle. 'Let's have a few deductions from you. All in your best manner.'

'I would prefer to hear yours first.'

'Want me to be Watson, eh? Well, old fellow went to a doctor and the doctor changed his diet.'

'To thick tomato soup, steak and kidney pudding and blackberry tart? I cannot imagine any doctor doing that.'

'Don't believe it, old boy. Doctors will put you on to anything.'

'That is the only solution that occurs to you?'

Henry Bonnington said:

'Well, seriously, I suppose there's only one explanation possible. Our unknown friend was in the grip of some powerful mental emotion. He was so perturbed by it that he literally did not notice what he was ordering or eating.'

He paused a minute and then said:

'You'll be telling me next that you know just *what* was on his mind. You'll say perhaps that he was making up his mind to commit a murder.'

He laughed at his own suggestion.

Hercule Poirot did not laugh.

He has admitted that at that moment he was seriously worried. He claims that he ought then to have had some inkling of what was likely to occur.

His friends assure him that such an idea is quite fantastic.

It was some three weeks later that Hercule Poirot and Bonnington met again—this time their meeting was in the Tube.

They nodded to each other, swaying about, hanging on to adjacent straps. Then at Piccadilly Circus there was a general exodus and they found seats right at the forward end of the car—a peaceful spot since nobody passed in or out that way.

'That's better,' said Mr Bonnington. 'Selfish lot, the human race, they won't pass up the car however much you ask 'em to!'

Hercule Poirot shrugged his shoulders.

'What will you?' he said. 'Life is too uncertain.'

'That's it. Here today, gone tomorrow,' said Mr Bonnington with a kind of gloomy relish. 'And talking of that, d'you remember that old boy we noticed at the Gallant Endeavour? I shouldn't wonder if *he'd* hopped it to a better world. He's not been there for a whole week. Molly's quite upset about it.'

Hercule Poirot sat up. His green eyes flashed.

'Indeed?' he said. 'Indeed?'

Bonnington said:

'D'you remember I suggested he'd been to a doctor and been put on a diet? Diet's nonsense of course—but I shouldn't wonder if he had consulted a doctor about his health and what the doctor said gave him a bit of a jolt. That would account for him ordering things off the menu without noticing what he was doing. Quite likely the jolt he got hurried him out of the world sooner than he would have gone otherwise. Doctors ought to be careful what they tell a chap.'

'They usually are,' said Hercule Poirot.

'This is my station,' said Mr Bonnington. 'Bye, bye. Don't suppose we shall ever know now who the old boy was—not even his name. Funny world!'

He hurried out of the carriage.

Hercule Poirot, sitting frowning, looked as though he did not think it was such a funny world.

He went home and gave certain instructions to his faithful valet, George.

Hercule Poirot ran his finger down a list of names. It was a record of deaths within a certain area.

Poirot's finger stopped.

'Henry Gascoigne. Sixty-nine. I might try him first.'

Later in the day, Hercule Poirot was sitting in Dr MacAndrew's surgery just off the King's Road. MacAndrew was a tall red-haired Scotsman with an intelligent face.

'Gascoigne?' he said. 'Yes, that's right. Eccentric old bird. Lived alone in one of those derelict old houses that are being cleared away in order to build a block of modern flats. I hadn't attended him before, but I'd seen him about and I knew who he was. It was the dairy people got the wind up first. The milk bottles began to pile up outside. In the end the people next door sent word to the police and they broke the door in and found him. He'd pitched down the stairs and broken his neck. Had on an old dressing-gown with a ragged cord—might easily have tripped himself up with it.'

'I see,' said Hercule Poirot. 'It was quite simple—an accident.'

'That's right.'

'Had he any relations?'

'There's a nephew. Used to come along and see his uncle about once a month. Lorrimer, his name is, George Lorrimer. He's a medico himself. Lives at Wimbledon.'

'Was he upset at the old man's death?'

'I don't know that I'd say he was upset. I mean, he had an affection for the old man, but he didn't really know him very well.'

'How long had Mr Gascoigne been dead when you saw him?'

'Ah!' said Dr MacAndrew. 'This is where we get official. Not less than forty-eight hours and not more than seventy-two hours. He was found on the morning of the sixth. Actually, we got closer than that. He'd got a letter in the pocket of his dressing-gown—written on the third—posted in Wimbledon that afternoon—would have been delivered somewhere around nine-twenty p.m. That puts the time of death at after nine-twenty on the evening of the third. That agrees with the contents of the stomach and the processes of digestion. He had had a meal about two hours before death. I examined him on the morning of the sixth and his condition was quite consistent with death having occurred about sixty hours previously—round about ten p.m. on the third.'

'It all seems very consistent. Tell me, when was he last seen alive?'

'He was seen in the King's Road about seven o'clock that same evening, Thursday the third, and he dined at the Gallant Endeavour restaurant at seven-thirty. It seems he always dined there on Thursdays. He was by way of being an artist, you know. An extremely bad one.'

'He had no other relations? Only this nephew?'

'There was a twin brother. The whole story is rather curious. They hadn't seen each other for years. It seems the other brother, Anthony Gascoigne, married a very rich woman and gave up art—and the brothers quarrelled over it. Hadn't seen each other since, I believe. But oddly enough, *they died on the same day.* The elder twin passed away at three o'clock on the afternoon of the third. Once before I've known a case of twins dying on the same day—in different parts of the world! Probably just a coincidence—but there it is.'

'Is the other brother's wife alive?'

'No, she died some years ago.'

'Where did Anthony Gascoigne live?'

'He had a house on Kingston Hill. He was, I believe, from what Dr Lorrimer tells me, very much of a recluse.'

Hercule Poirot nodded thoughtfully.

The Scotsman looked at him keenly.

'What exactly have you got in your mind, M. Poirot?' he asked bluntly. 'I've answered your questions—as was my duty seeing the credentials you brought. But I'm in the dark as to what it's all about.'

Poirot said slowly:

'A simple case of accidental death, that's what you said. What I have in mind is equally simple—a simple push.'

Dr MacAndrew looked startled.

'In other words, murder! Have you any grounds for that belief?'

'No,' said Poirot. 'It is a mere supposition.'

'There must be something—' persisted the other.

Poirot did not speak. MacAndrew said:

'If it's the nephew, Lorrimer, you suspect, I don't mind telling you here and now that you are barking up the wrong tree. Lorrimer was playing bridge in Wimbledon from eight-thirty till midnight. That came out at the inquest.'

Poirot murmured:

'And presumably it was verified. The police are careful.'

The doctor said:

'Perhaps you know something against him?'

'I didn't know that there was such a person until you mentioned him.'

'Then you suspect somebody else?'

'No, no. It is not that at all. It's a case of the routine habits of the human animal. That is very important. And the dead M. Gascoigne does not fit in. It is all wrong, you see.'

'I really don't understand.'

Hercule Poirot murmured:

'The trouble is, there is too much sauce over the bad fish.'

'My dear sir?'

Hercule Poirot smiled.

'You will be having me locked up as a lunatic soon, *Monsieur le Docteur.* But I am not really a mental case—

just a man who has a liking for order and method and who is worried when he comes across a fact *that does not fit in.* I must ask you to forgive me for having given you so much trouble.'

He rose and the doctor rose also.

'You know,' said MacAndrew, 'honestly I can't see anything the least bit suspicious about the death of Henry Gascoigne. I say he fell—you say somebody pushed him. It's all—well—in the air.'

Hercule Poirot sighed.

'Yes,' he said. 'It is workmanlike. Somebody has made the good job of it!'

'You still think—'

The little man spread out his hands.

'I'm an obstinate man—a man with a little idea—and nothing to support it! By the way, did Henry Gascoigne have false teeth?'

'No, his own teeth were in excellent preservation. Very creditable indeed at his age.'

'He looked after them well—they were white and well brushed?'

'Yes, I noticed them particularly. Teeth tend to grow a little yellow as one grows older, but they were in good condition.'

'Not discoloured in any way?'

'No. I don't think he was a smoker if that is what you mean.'

'I did not mean that precisely—it was just a long shot—which probably will not come off! Goodbye, Dr MacAndrew, and thank you for your kindness.'

He shook the doctor's hand and departed.

'And now,' he said, 'for the long shot.'

At the Gallant Endeavour, he sat down at the same table which he had shared with Bonnington. The girl who served him was not Molly. Molly, the girl told him, was away on a holiday.

It was only just seven and Hercule Poirot found no difficulty in entering into conversation with the girl on the subject of old Mr Gascoigne.

'Yes,' she said. 'He'd been here for years and years. But none of us girls ever knew his name. We saw about the inquest in the paper, and there was a picture of him. "There," I said to Molly. "If that isn't our 'Old Father Time'" as we used to call him.'

'He dined here on the evening of his death, did he not?'

'That's right, Thursday, the third. He was always here on a Thursday. Tuesdays and Thursdays—punctual as a clock.'

'You don't remember, I suppose, what he had for dinner?'

'Now let me see, it was mulligatawny soup, that's right, and beefsteak pudding or was it the mutton?—no pudding, that's right, and blackberry and apple pie and cheese. And then to think of him going home and falling down those stairs that very same evening. A frayed dressing-gown cord they said it was as caused it. Of course, his clothes were always something awful—old-fashioned and put on anyhow, and all tattered, and yet he *had* a kind of air, all the same, as though he was *somebody*! Oh, we get all sorts of interesting customers here.'

She moved off.

Hercule Poirot ate his filleted sole. His eyes showed a green light.

'It is odd,' he said to himself, 'how the cleverest people slip over details. Bonnington will be interested.'

But the time had not yet come for leisurely discussion with Bonnington.

⋆ ⋆ ⋆

Armed with introductions from a certain influential quarter, Hercule Poirot found no difficulty at all in dealing with the coroner for the district.

'A curious figure, the deceased man Gascoigne,' he observed. 'A lonely, eccentric old fellow. But his decease seems to arouse an unusual amount of attention?'

He looked with some curiosity at his visitor as he spoke.

Hercule Poirot chose his words carefully.

'There are circumstances connected with it, Monsieur, which make investigation desirable.'

'Well, how can I help you?'

'It is, I believe, within your province to order documents produced in your court to be destroyed, or to be impounded—as you think fit. A certain letter was found in the pocket of Henry Gascoigne's dressing-gown, was it not?'

'That is so.'

'A letter from his nephew, Dr George Lorrimer?'

'Quite correct. The letter was produced at the inquest as helping to fix the time of death.'

'Which was corroborated by the medical evidence?'

'Exactly.'

'Is that letter still available?'

Hercule Poirot waited rather anxiously for the reply.

When he heard that the letter was still available for examination he drew a sigh of relief.

When it was finally produced he studied it with some care. It was written in a slightly cramped handwriting with a stylographic pen.

It ran as follows:

Dear Uncle Henry,

I am sorry to tell you that I have had no success as regards Uncle Anthony. He showed no enthusiasm for a visit from you and would give me no reply to your request that he would let bygones be bygones. He is, of course, extremely ill, and his mind is inclined to wander. I should fancy that the end is very near. He seemed hardly to remember who you were.

I am sorry to have failed you, but I can assure you that I did my best.

Your affectionate nephew,

George Lorrimer

The letter itself was dated 3rd November. Poirot glanced at the envelope's postmark—4.30 p.m. 3 Nov.

He murmured:

'It is beautifully in order, is it not?'

Kingston Hill was his next objective. After a little trouble, with the exercise of good-humoured pertinacity, he obtained an interview with Amelia Hill, cook-housekeeper to the late Anthony Gascoigne.

Mrs Hill was inclined to be stiff and suspicious at first, but the charming geniality of this strange-looking foreigner would have had its effect on a stone. Mrs Amelia Hill began to unbend.

She found herself, as had so many other women before her, pouring out her troubles to a really sympathetic listener.

For fourteen years she had had charge of Mr Gascoigne's household—*not* an easy job! No, indeed! Many a woman would have quailed under the burdens *she* had had to bear! Eccentric the poor gentleman was and no denying it. Remarkably close with his money—a kind of mania with him it was—and he as rich a gentleman as might be! But Mrs Hill had served him faithfully, and put up with his ways, and naturally she'd expected at any rate a *remembrance*. But no—nothing at all! Just an old will that left all his money to his wife and if she predeceased him then everything to his brother, Henry. A will made years ago. It didn't seem fair!

Gradually Hercule Poirot detached her from her main theme of unsatisfied cupidity. It was indeed a heartless injustice! Mrs Hill could not be blamed for feeling hurt and surprised. It was well known that Mr Gascoigne was tight-fisted about money. It had even been said that the dead man had refused his only brother assistance. Mrs Hill probably knew all about that.

'Was it that that Dr Lorrimer came to see him about?' asked Mrs Hill. 'I knew it was something about his brother, but I thought it was just that his brother wanted to be reconciled. They'd quarrelled years ago.'

'I understand,' said Poirot, 'that Mr Gascoigne refused absolutely?'

'That's right enough,' said Mrs Hill with a nod. '"Henry?" he says, rather weak like. "*What's this about Henry? Haven't seen him for years and don't want to. Quarrelsome fellow, Henry.*" Just that.'

The conversation then reverted to Mrs Hill's own special grievances, and the unfeeling attitude of the late Mr Gascoigne's solicitor.

With some difficulty Hercule Poirot took his leave without breaking off the conversation too abruptly.

And so, just after the dinner hour, he came to Elmcrest, Dorset Road, Wimbledon, the residence of Dr George Lorrimer.

The doctor was in. Hercule Poirot was shown into the surgery and there presently Dr George Lorrimer came to him, obviously just risen from the dinner table.

'I'm not a patient, Doctor,' said Hercule Poirot. 'And my coming here is, perhaps, somewhat of an impertinence—but I'm an old man and I believe in plain and direct dealing. I do not care for lawyers and their long-winded roundabout methods.'

He had certainly aroused Lorrimer's interest. The doctor was a clean-shaven man of middle height. His hair was brown but his eyelashes were almost white which gave his eyes a pale, boiled appearance. His manner was brisk and not without humour.

'Lawyers?' he said, raising his eyebrows. 'Hate the fellows! You rouse my curiosity, my dear sir. Pray sit down.'

Poirot did so and then produced one of his professional cards which he handed to the doctor.

George Lorrimer's white eyelashes blinked.

Poirot leaned forward confidentially. 'A good many of my clients are women,' he said.

'Naturally,' said Dr George Lorrimer, with a slight twinkle.

'As you say, naturally,' agreed Poirot. 'Women distrust the official police. They prefer private investigations. They do not want to have their troubles made public. An elderly woman came to consult me a few days ago. She was unhappy about a husband she'd quarrelled with many years before. This husband of hers was your uncle, the late Mr Gascoigne.' George Lorrimer's face went purple.

'My uncle? Nonsense! His wife died many years ago.'

'Not your uncle, Mr *Anthony* Gascoigne. Your uncle, Mr *Henry* Gascoigne.'

'Uncle Henry? But *he* wasn't married!'

'Oh yes, he was,' said Hercule Poirot, lying unblushingly. 'Not a doubt of it. The lady even brought along her marriage certificate.'

'It's a lie!' cried George Lorrimer. His face was now as purple as a plum. 'I don't believe it. You're an impudent liar.'

'It is too bad, is it not?' said Poirot. 'You have committed murder for nothing.'

'Murder?' Lorrimer's voice quavered. His pale eyes bulged with terror.

'By the way,' said Poirot, 'I see you have been eating blackberry tart again. An unwise habit. Blackberries are said to be full of vitamins, but they may be deadly in other ways. On this occasion I rather fancy they have helped to put a rope round a man's neck—your neck, Dr Lorrimer.'

'You see, *mon ami*, where you went wrong was over your fundamental assumption.' Hercule Poirot, beaming placidly across the table at his friend, waved an expository hand. 'A man under severe mental stress doesn't choose that time to do something that he's never done before. His reflexes just follow the track of least resistance. A man who is upset about something *might* conceivably come down to dinner dressed in his pyjamas—but they will be his *own* pyjamas—not somebody else's.

'A man who dislikes thick soup, suet pudding and blackberries suddenly orders all three one evening. *You* say, because he is thinking of something else. But *I* say *that a man who has got something on his mind will order automatically the dish he has ordered most often before.*

'*Eh bien*, then, what other explanation could there be? I simply could not think of a reasonable explanation. And I was worried! The incident was all wrong. It did not fit! I have an orderly mind and I like things to fit. Mr Gascoigne's dinner order worried me.

'Then you told me that the man had disappeared. He had missed a Tuesday and a Thursday the first time for years. I liked that even less. A queer hypothesis sprang up in my mind. If I were right about it *the man was dead.* I made inquiries. The man *was* dead. And he was very neatly and tidily dead. In other words the bad fish was covered up with the sauce!

'He had been seen in the King's Road at seven o'clock. He had had dinner here at seven-thirty—two hours before he died. It all fitted in—the evidence of the stomach contents, the evidence of the letter. Much too much sauce! You couldn't see the fish at all!

'Devoted nephew wrote the letter, devoted nephew had beautiful alibi for time of death. Death very simple—a fall down the stairs. Simple accident? Simple murder? Everyone says the former.

'Devoted nephew only surviving relative. Devoted nephew will inherit—but is there anything *to* inherit? Uncle notoriously poor.

'But there is a brother. And brother in his time had married a rich wife. And brother lives in a big rich house on Kingston Hill, so it would seem that rich wife must have left him all her money. You see the sequence—rich wife leaves money to Anthony, Anthony leaves money to Henry, Henry's money goes to George—a complete chain.'

'All very pretty in theory,' said Bonnington. 'But what did you do?'

'Once you *know*—you can usually get hold of what you want. Henry had died two hours after a *meal*—that is all the inquest really bothered about. But supposing the meal was not dinner, but *lunch*. Put yourself in George's place. George wants money—badly. Anthony Gascoigne is dying—but his death is no good to George. His money goes to Henry, and Henry Gascoigne may live for years. So Henry must die too—and the sooner the better—but his death must take place *after* Anthony's, and at the same time George must have an alibi. Henry's habit of dining regularly at a restaurant on two evenings of the week suggest an alibi to George. Being a cautious fellow, he tries his plan out first. *He impersonates his uncle on Monday evening at the restaurant in question.* It goes without a hitch. Everyone there accepts him as his uncle. He is satisfied. He has only to wait till Uncle Anthony shows definite signs of pegging out. The time comes. He writes a letter to his uncle on the afternoon of the second November but dates it the third. He comes up to town on the afternoon of the third, calls on his uncle, and carries his scheme into action. A sharp shove and down the stairs goes Uncle Henry. George hunts about for the letter he has written, and shoves it in the pocket of his uncle's dressing-gown. At seven-thirty he is at the Gallant Endeavour, beard, bushy eyebrows all complete. Undoubtedly Mr Henry Gascoigne is alive at seven-thirty. Then a rapid metamorphosis in a lavatory and back full speed in his car to Wimbledon and an evening of bridge. The perfect alibi.'

Mr Bonnington looked at him.

'But the postmark on the letter?'

'Oh, that was very simple. The postmark was smudgy. Why? It had been altered with lamp black from second November to third November. You would not notice it *unless you were looking for it.* And finally there were the blackbirds.'

'Blackbirds?'

'Four-and-twenty blackbirds baked in a pie! Or blackberries if you prefer to be literal! George, you comprehend, was after all not quite a good enough actor. Do you remember the fellow who blacked himself all over to play Othello? That is the kind of actor you have got to be in crime. George *looked* like his uncle and *walked* like his uncle and *spoke* like his uncle and had his uncle's beard and eyebrows, but he forgot to *eat* like his uncle. He ordered the dishes that he himself liked. Blackberries discolour the teeth—the corpse's teeth were not discoloured, and yet Henry Gascoigne ate blackberries at the Gallant Endeavour that night. But there were no blackberries in the stomach. I asked this morning. And George had been fool enough to keep the beard and the rest of the make-up. Oh! plenty of evidence once you look for it. I called on George and rattled him. That finished it! He had been eating blackberries again, by the way. A greedy fellow—cared a lot about his food. *Eh bien*, greed will hang him all right unless I am very much mistaken.'

A waitress brought them two portions of blackberry and apple tart.

'Take it away,' said Mr Bonnington. 'One can't be too careful. Bring me a small helping of sago pudding.'

The Witness for the Prosecution

Mr Mayherne adjusted his pince-nez and cleared his throat with a little dry-as-dust cough that was wholly typical of him. Then he looked again at the man opposite him, the man charged with wilful murder.

Mr Mayherne was a small man precise in manner, neatly, not to say foppishly dressed, with a pair of very shrewd and piercing grey eyes. By no means a fool. Indeed, as a solicitor, Mr Mayherne's reputation stood very high. His voice, when he spoke to his client, was dry but not unsympathetic.

'I must impress upon you again that you are in very grave danger, and that the utmost frankness is necessary.'

Leonard Vole, who had been staring in a dazed fashion at the blank wall in front of him, transferred his glance to the solicitor.

'I know,' he said hopelessly. 'You keep telling me so. But I can't seem to realize yet that I'm charged with murder—*murder.* And such a dastardly crime too.'

Mr Mayherne was practical, not emotional. He coughed again, took off his pince-nez, polished them carefully, and replaced them on his nose. Then he said:

'Yes, yes, yes. Now, my dear Mr Vole, we're going to make a determined effort to get you off—and we shall succeed—we shall succeed. But I must have all the facts.

I must know just how damaging the case against you is likely to be. Then we can fix upon the best line of defence.'

Still the young man looked at him in the same dazed, hopeless fashion. To Mr Mayherne the case had seemed black enough, and the guilt of the prisoner assured. Now, for the first time, he felt a doubt.

'You think I'm guilty,' said Leonard Vole, in a low voice. 'But, by God, I swear I'm not! It looks pretty black against me, I know that. I'm like a man caught in a net—the meshes of it all round me, entangling me whichever way I turn. But I didn't do it, Mr Mayherne, I didn't do it!'

In such a position a man was bound to protest his innocence. Mr Mayherne knew that. Yet, in spite of himself, he was impressed. It might be, after all, that Leonard Vole was innocent.

'You are right, Mr Vole,' he said gravely. 'The case does look very black against you. Nevertheless, I accept your assurance. Now, let us get to facts. I want you to tell me in your own words exactly how you came to make the acquaintance of Miss Emily French.'

'It was one day in Oxford Street. I saw an elderly lady crossing the road. She was carrying a lot of parcels. In the middle of the street she dropped them, tried to recover them, found a bus was almost on top of her and just managed to reach the kerb safely, dazed and bewildered by people having shouted at her. I recovered the parcels, wiped the mud off them as best I could, retied the string of one, and returned them to her.'

'There was no question of your having saved her life?'

'Oh! dear me, no. All I did was to perform a common act of courtesy. She was extremely grateful, thanked me warmly, and said something about my manners not being those of most of the younger generation—I can't remember the exact words. Then I lifted my hat and went on. I never expected to see her again. But life is full of coincidences. That very evening I came across her at a party at a friend's house. She recognized me at once and asked that I should be introduced to her. I then found out that she was a Miss Emily French and that she lived at Cricklewood. I talked to her for some time. She was, I imagine, an old lady who took sudden violent fancies to people. She took one to me on the strength of a perfectly simple action which anyone might have performed. On leaving, she shook me warmly by the hand, and asked me to come and see her. I replied, of course, that I should be very pleased to do so, and she then urged me to name a day. I did not want particularly to go, but it would have seemed churlish to refuse, so I fixed on the following Saturday. After she had gone, I learned something about her from my friends. That she was rich, eccentric, lived alone with one maid and owned no less than eight cats.'

'I see,' said Mr Mayherne. 'The question of her being well off came up as early as that?'

'If you mean that I inquired—' began Leonard Vole hotly, but Mr Mayherne stilled him with a gesture.

'I have to look at the case as it will be presented by the other side. An ordinary observer would not have supposed Miss French to be a lady of means. She lived poorly, almost humbly. Unless you had been told the contrary, you would in all probability have considered her to be in poor circumstances—at any rate to begin with. Who was it exactly who told you that she was well off?'

'My friend, George Harvey, at whose house the party took place.'

'Is he likely to remember having done so?'

'I really don't know. Of course it is some time ago now.'

'Quite so, Mr Vole. You see, the first aim of the prosecution will be to establish that you were in low water financially—that is true, is it not?'

Leonard Vole flushed.

'Yes,' he said, in a low voice. 'I'd been having a run of infernal bad luck just then.'

'Quite so,' said Mr Mayherne again. 'That being, as I say, in low water financially, you met this rich old lady and cultivated her acquaintance assiduously. Now if we are in a position to say that you had no idea she was well off, and that you visited her out of pure kindness of heart—'

'Which is the case.'

'I dare say. I am not disputing the point. I am looking at it from the outside point of view. A great deal depends on the memory of Mr Harvey. Is he likely to remember that conversation or is he not? Could he be confused by counsel into believing that it took place later?'

Leonard Vole reflected for some minutes. Then he said steadily enough, but with a rather paler face:

'I do not think that that line would be successful, Mr Mayherne. Several of those present heard his remark, and one or two of them chaffed me about my conquest of a rich old lady.'

The solicitor endeavoured to hide his disappointment with a wave of the hand.

'Unfortunately,' he said. 'But I congratulate you upon your plain speaking, Mr Vole. It is to you I look to guide me. Your judgement is quite right. To persist in the line I spoke of would have been disastrous. We must leave that point. You made the acquaintance of Miss French, you called upon her, the acquaintanceship progressed. We want a clear reason for all this. Why did you, a young man of thirty-three, good-looking, fond of sport, popular with your friends, devote so much time to an elderly woman with whom you could hardly have anything in common?'

Leonard Vole flung out his hands in a nervous gesture.

'I can't tell you—I really can't tell you. After the first visit, she pressed me to come again, spoke of being lonely and unhappy. She made it difficult for me to refuse. She showed so plainly her fondness and affection for me that I was placed in an awkward position. You see, Mr Mayherne, I've got a weak nature—I drift—I'm one of those people who can't say "No." And believe me or not, as you like, after the third or fourth visit I paid her I found myself getting genuinely fond of the old thing. My mother died when I was young, an aunt brought me up, and she too died before I was fifteen. If I told you that I genuinely enjoyed being mothered and pampered, I dare say you'd only laugh.'

Mr Mayherne did not laugh. Instead he took off his pince-nez again and polished them, always a sign with him that he was thinking deeply.

'I accept your explanation, Mr Vole,' he said at last. 'I believe it to be psychologically probable. Whether a jury would take that view of it is another matter. Please continue your narrative. When was it that Miss French first asked you to look into her business affairs?'

'After my third or fourth visit to her. She understood very little of money matters, and was worried about some investments.'

Mr Mayherne looked up sharply.

'Be careful, Mr Vole. The maid, Janet Mackenzie, declares that her mistress was a good woman of business and transacted all her own affairs, and this is borne out by the testimony of her bankers.'

'I can't help that,' said Vole earnestly. 'That's what she said to me.'

Mr Mayherne looked at him for a moment or two in silence. Though he had no intention of saying so, his belief in Leonard Vole's innocence was at that moment strengthened. He knew something of the mentality of elderly ladies. He saw Miss French, infatuated with the good-looking young man, hunting about for pretexts that should bring him to the house. What more likely than that she should plead ignorance of business, and beg him to help her with her money affairs? She was enough of a woman of the world to realize that any man is slightly flattered by such an admission of his superiority. Leonard Vole had been flattered. Perhaps, too, she had not been averse to letting this young man know that she was wealthy. Emily French had been a strong-willed old woman, willing to pay her price for what she wanted. All this passed rapidly through Mr Mayherne's mind, but he gave no indication of it, and asked instead a further question.

'And you did handle her affairs for her at her request?'

'I did.'

'Mr Vole,' said the solicitor, 'I am going to ask you a very serious question, and one to which it is vital I should have a truthful answer. You were in low water financially. You had the handling of an old lady's affairs—an old lady who, according to her own statement, knew little or nothing of business. Did you at any time, or in any manner, convert to your own use the securities which you handled? Did you engage in any transaction for your own pecuniary advantage which will not bear the light of day?' He quelled the other's response. 'Wait a minute before you answer. There are two courses open to us. Either we can make a feature of your probity and honesty in conducting her affairs whilst pointing out how unlikely it is that you would commit murder to obtain money which you might have obtained by such infinitely easier means. If, on the other hand, there is anything in your dealings which the prosecution will get hold of—if, to put it baldly, it can be proved that you swindled the old lady in any way, we must take the line that you had no motive for the murder, since she was already a profitable source of income to you. You perceive the distinction. Now, I beg of you, take your time before you reply.'

But Leonard Vole took no time at all.

'My dealings with Miss French's affairs are all perfectly fair and above board. I acted for her interests to the very best of my ability, as anyone will find who looks into the matter.'

'Thank you,' said Mr Mayherne. 'You relieve my mind very much. I pay you the compliment of believing that you are far too clever to lie to me over such an important matter.'

'Surely,' said Vole eagerly, 'the strongest point in my favour is the lack of motive. Granted that I cultivated the acquaintanceship of a rich old lady in the hope of getting money out of her—that, I gather, is the substance of what you have been saying—surely her death frustrates all my hopes?'

The solicitor looked at him steadily. Then, very deliberately, he repeated his unconscious trick with his pince-nez. It was not until they were firmly replaced on his nose that he spoke.

'Are you not aware, Mr Vole, Miss French left a will under which you are the principal beneficiary?'

'What?' The prisoner sprang to his feet. His dismay was obvious and unforced. 'My God! What are you saying? She left her money to me?'

Mr Mayherne nodded slowly. Vole sank down again, his head in his hands.

'You pretend you know nothing of this will?'

'Pretend? There's no pretence about it. I knew nothing about it.'

'What would you say if I told you that the maid, Janet Mackenzie, swears that you *did* know? That her mistress told her distinctly that she had consulted you in the matter, and told you of her intentions?'

'Say? That she's lying! No, I go too fast. Janet is an elderly woman. She was a faithful watchdog to her mistress, and she didn't like me. She was jealous and suspicious. I should say that Miss French confided her intentions to Janet, and that Janet either mistook something she said, or else was convinced in her own mind that I had persuaded the old lady into doing it. I dare say that she believes herself now that Miss French actually told her so.'

'You don't think she dislikes you enough to lie deliberately about the matter?'

Leonard Vole looked shocked and startled.

'No, indeed! Why should she?'

'I don't know,' said Mr Mayherne thoughtfully. 'But she's very bitter against you.'

The wretched young man groaned again.

'I'm beginning to see,' he muttered. 'It's frightful. I made up to her, that's what they'll say, I got her to make a will leaving her money to me, and then I go there that night, and there's nobody in the house—they find her the next day—oh! my God, it's awful!'

'You are wrong about there being nobody in the house,' said Mr Mayherne. 'Janet, as you remember, was to go out for the evening. She went, but about half past nine she returned to fetch the pattern of a blouse sleeve which she had promised to a friend. She let herself in by the back door, went upstairs and fetched it, and went out again. She heard voices in the sitting-room, though she could not distinguish what they said, but she will swear that one of them was Miss French's and one was a man's.'

'At half past nine,' said Leonard Vole. 'At half past nine . . .' He sprang to his feet. 'But then I'm saved—saved—'

'What do you mean, saved?' cried Mr Mayherne, astonished.

'*By half past nine I was at home again!* My wife can prove that. I left Miss French about five minutes to nine. I arrived home about twenty past nine. My wife was there waiting for me. Oh! thank God—thank God! And bless Janet Mackenzie's sleeve pattern.'

In his exuberance, he hardly noticed that the grave expression of the solicitor's face had not altered. But the latter's words brought him down to earth with a bump.

'Who, then, in your opinion, murdered Miss French?'

'Why, a burglar, of course, as was thought at first. The window was forced, you remember. She was killed with a heavy blow from a crowbar, and the crowbar was found lying on the floor beside the body. And several articles were missing. But for Janet's absurd suspicions and dislike of me, the police would never have swerved from the right track.'

'That will hardly do, Mr Vole,' said the solicitor. 'The things that were missing were mere trifles of no value, taken as a blind. And the marks on the window were not all conclusive. Besides, think for yourself. You say you were no longer in the house by half past nine. Who, then, was the man Janet heard talking to Miss French in the sitting-room? She would hardly be having an amicable conversation with a burglar?'

'No,' said Vole. 'No—' He looked puzzled and discouraged. 'But anyway,' he added with reviving spirit, 'it lets me out. I've got an *alibi.* You must see Romaine—my wife—at once.'

'Certainly,' acquiesced the lawyer. 'I should already have seen Mrs Vole but for her being absent when you were arrested. I wired to Scotland at once, and I understand that she arrives back tonight. I am going to call upon her immediately I leave here.'

Vole nodded, a great expression of satisfaction settling down over his face.

'Yes, Romaine will tell you. My God! it's a lucky chance that.'

'Excuse me, Mr Vole, but you are very fond of your wife?'

'Of course.'

'And she of you?'

'Romaine is devoted to me. She'd do anything in the world for me.'

He spoke enthusiastically, but the solicitor's heart sank a little lower. The testimony of a devoted wife—would it gain credence?

'Was there anyone else who saw you return at nine-twenty? A maid, for instance?'

'We have no maid.'

'Did you meet anyone in the street on the way back?'

'Nobody I knew. I rode part of the way in a bus. The conductor might remember.'

Mr Mayherne shook his head doubtfully.

'There is no one, then, who can confirm your wife's testimony?'

'No. But it isn't necessary, surely?'

'I dare say not. I dare say not,' said Mr Mayherne hastily. 'Now there's just one thing more. Did Miss French know that you were a married man?'

'Oh, yes.'

'Yet you never took your wife to see her. Why was that?'

For the first time, Leonard Vole's answer came halting and uncertain.

'Well—I don't know.'

'Are you aware that Janet Mackenzie says her mistress believed you to be single, and contemplated marrying you in the future?'

Vole laughed.

'Absurd! There was forty years difference in age between us.'

'It has been done,' said the solicitor drily. 'The fact remains. Your wife never met Miss French?'

'No—' Again the constraint.

'You will permit me to say,' said the lawyer, 'that I hardly understand your attitude in the matter.'

Vole flushed, hesitated, and then spoke.

'I'll make a clean breast of it. I was hard up, as you know. I hoped that Miss French might lend me some money. She was fond of me, but she wasn't at all interested in the struggles of a young couple. Early on, I found that she had taken it for granted that my wife and I didn't get on—were living apart. Mr Mayherne—I wanted the money—for Romaine's sake. I said nothing, and allowed the old lady to think what she chose. She spoke of my being an adopted son for her. There was never any question of marriage—that must be just Janet's imagination.'

'And that is all?'

'Yes—that is all.'

Was there just a shade of hesitation in the words? The lawyer fancied so. He rose and held out his hand.

'Goodbye, Mr Vole.' He looked into the haggard young face and spoke with an unusual impulse. 'I believe in your innocence in spite of the multitude of facts arrayed against you. I hope to prove it and vindicate you completely.'

Vole smiled back at him.

'You'll find the alibi is all right,' he said cheerfully.

Again he hardly noticed that the other did not respond.

'The whole thing hinges a good deal on the testimony of Janet Mackenzie,' said Mr Mayherne. 'She hates you. That much is clear.'

'She can hardly hate me,' protested the young man.

The solicitor shook his head as he went out.

'Now for Mrs Vole,' he said to himself.

He was seriously disturbed by the way the thing was shaping.

The Voles lived in a small shabby house near Paddington Green. It was to this house that Mr Mayherne went.

In answer to his ring, a big slatternly woman, obviously a charwoman, answered the door.

'Mrs Vole? Has she returned yet?'

'Got back an hour ago. But I dunno if you can see her.'

'If you will take my card to her,' said Mr Mayherne quietly, 'I am quite sure that she will do so.'

The woman looked at him doubtfully, wiped her hand on her apron and took the card. Then she closed the door in his face and left him on the step outside.

In a few minutes, however, she returned with a slightly altered manner.

'Come inside, please.'

She ushered him into a tiny drawing-room. Mr Mayherne, examining a drawing on the wall, stared up suddenly to face a tall pale woman who had entered so quietly that he had not heard her.

'Mr Mayherne? You are my husband's solicitor, are you not? You have come from him? Will you please sit down?'

Until she spoke he had not realized that she was not English. Now, observing her more closely, he noticed the high cheekbones, the dense blue-black of the hair, and an occasional very slight movement of the hands that was distinctly foreign. A strange woman, very quiet. So quiet as to make one uneasy. From the very first Mr Mayherne was conscious that he was up against something that he did not understand.

'Now, my dear Mrs Vole,' he began, 'you must not give way—'

He stopped. It was so very obvious that Romaine Vole had not the slightest intention of giving way. She was perfectly calm and composed.

'Will you please tell me all about it?' she said. 'I must know everything. Do not think to spare me. I want to know the worst.' She hesitated, then repeated in a lower tone, with a curious emphasis which the lawyer did not understand: 'I want to know the worst.'

Mr Mayherne went over his interview with Leonard Vole. She listened attentively, nodding her head now and then.

'I see,' she said, when he had finished. 'He wants me to say that he came in at twenty minutes past nine that night?'

'He did come in at that time?' said Mr Mayherne sharply.

'That is not the point,' she said coldly. 'Will my saying so acquit him? Will they believe me?'

Mr Mayherne was taken aback. She had gone so quickly to the core of the matter.

'That is what I want to know,' she said. 'Will it be enough? Is there anyone else who can support my evidence?'

There was a suppressed eagerness in her manner that made him vaguely uneasy.

'So far there is no one else,' he said reluctantly.

'I see,' said Romaine Vole.

She sat for a minute or two perfectly still. A little smile played over her lips.

The lawyer's feeling of alarm grew stronger and stronger.

'Mrs Vole—' he began. 'I know what you must feel—'

'Do you?' she said. 'I wonder.'

'In the circumstances—'

'In the circumstances—I intend to play a lone hand.'

He looked at her in dismay.

'But, my dear Mrs Vole—you are overwrought. Being so devoted to your husband—'

'I beg your pardon?'

The sharpness of her voice made him start. He repeated in a hesitating manner:

'Being so devoted to your husband—'

Romaine Vole nodded slowly, the same strange smile on her lips.

'Did he tell you that I was devoted to him?' she asked softly. 'Ah! yes, I can see he did. How stupid men are! Stupid—stupid—stupid—'

She rose suddenly to her feet. All the intense emotion that the lawyer had been conscious of in the atmosphere was now concentrated in her tone.

'I hate him, I tell you! I hate him. I hate him, I hate him! I would like to see him hanged by the neck till he is dead.'

The lawyer recoiled before her and the smouldering passion in her eyes.

She advanced a step nearer, and continued vehemently:

'Perhaps I *shall* see it. Supposing I tell you that he did not come in that night at twenty past nine, but at twenty past *ten?* You say that he tells you he knew nothing about the money coming to him. Supposing I tell you he knew all about it, and counted on it, and committed murder to get it? Supposing I tell you that he admitted to me that night when he came in what he had done? That there was blood on his coat? What then? Supposing that I stand up in court and say all these things?'

Her eyes seemed to challenge him. With an effort, he concealed his growing dismay, and endeavoured to speak in a rational tone.

'You cannot be asked to give evidence against your own husband—'

'He is not my husband!'

The words came out so quickly that he fancied he had misunderstood her.

'I beg your pardon? I—'

'He is not my husband.'

The silence was so intense that you could have heard a pin drop.

'I was an actress in Vienna. My husband is alive but in a madhouse. So we could not marry. I am glad now.'

She nodded defiantly.

'I should like you to tell me one thing,' said Mr Mayherne. He contrived to appear as cool and unemotional as ever. 'Why are you so bitter against Leonard Vole?'

She shook her head, smiling a little.

'Yes, you would like to know. But I shall not tell you. I will keep my secret . . .'

Mr Mayherne gave his dry little cough and rose.

'There seems no point in prolonging this interview,' he remarked. 'You will hear from me again after I have communicated with my client.'

She came closer to him, looking into his eyes with her own wonderful dark ones.

'Tell me,' she said, 'did you believe—honestly—that he was innocent when you came here today?'

'I did,' said Mr Mayherne.

'You poor little man,' she laughed.

'And I believe so still,' finished the lawyer. 'Good evening, madam.'

He went out of the room, taking with him the memory of her startled face.

'This is going to be the devil of a business,' said Mr Mayherne to himself as he strode along the street.

Extraordinary, the whole thing. An extraordinary woman. A very dangerous woman. Women were the devil when they got their knife into you.

What was to be done? That wretched young man hadn't a leg to stand upon. Of course, possibly he did commit the crime . . .

'No,' said Mr Mayherne to himself. 'No—there's almost too much evidence against him. I don't believe this woman. She was trumping up the whole story. But she'll never bring it into court.'

He wished he felt more conviction on the point.

The police court proceedings were brief and dramatic. The principal witnesses for the prosecution were Janet Mackenzie, maid to the dead woman, and Romaine Heilger, Austrian subject, the mistress of the prisoner.

Mr Mayherne sat in the court and listened to the damning story that the latter told. It was on the lines she had indicated to him in their interview.

The prisoner reserved his defence and was committed for trial.

Mr Mayherne was at his wits' end. The case against Leonard Vole was black beyond words. Even the famous KC who was engaged for the defence held out little hope.

'If we can shake that Austrian woman's testimony, we might do something,' he said dubiously. 'But it's a bad business.'

Mr Mayherne had concentrated his energies on one single point. Assuming Leonard Vole to be speaking the truth, and to have left the murdered woman's house at nine o'clock, who was the man whom Janet heard talking to Miss French at half past nine?

The only ray of light was in the shape of a scapegrace nephew who had in bygone days cajoled and threatened his aunt out of various sums of money. Janet Mackenzie, the solicitor learned, had always been attached to this young man, and had never ceased urging his claims upon her mistress. It certainly seemed possible that it was this nephew who had been with Miss French after Leonard Vole left, especially as he was not to be found in any of his old haunts.

In all other directions, the lawyer's researches had been negative in their result. No one had seen Leonard Vole entering his own house, or leaving that of Miss French. No one had seen any other man enter or leave the house in Cricklewood. All inquiries drew blank.

It was the eve of the trial when Mr Mayherne received the letter which was to lead his thoughts in an entirely new direction.

It came by the six o'clock post. An illiterate scrawl, written on common paper and enclosed in a dirty envelope with the stamp stuck on crooked.

Mr Mayherne read it through once or twice before he grasped its meaning.

Dear Mister

Youre the lawyer chap wot acks for the young feller. if you want that painted foreign hussy showd up for wot she is an her pack of lies you come to 16 Shaw's Rents Stepney tonight. It ul cawst you 2 hundred quid Arsk for Missis Mogson.

The solicitor read and re-read this strange epistle. It might, of course, be a hoax, but when he thought it over, he became increasingly convinced that it was genuine, and also convinced that it was the one hope for the prisoner. The evidence of Romaine Heilger damned him completely, and the line the defence meant to pursue, the line that the evidence of a woman who had admittedly lived an immoral life was not to be trusted, was at best a weak one.

Mr Mayherne's mind was made up. It was his duty to save his client at all costs. He must go to Shaw's Rents.

He had some difficulty in finding the place, a ramshackle building in an evil-smelling slum, but at last he did so, and on inquiry for Mrs Mogson was sent up to a room on the third floor. On this door he knocked and getting no answer, knocked again.

At this second knock, he heard a shuffling sound inside, and presently the door was opened cautiously half an inch and a bent figure peered out.

Suddenly the woman, for it was a woman, gave a chuckle and opened the door wider.

'So it's you, dearie,' she said, in a wheezy voice. 'Nobody with you, is there? No playing tricks? That's right. You can come in—you can come in.'

With some reluctance the lawyer stepped across the threshold into the small dirty room, with its flickering gas jet. There was an untidy unmade bed in a corner, a plain deal table and two rickety chairs. For the first time Mr Mayherne had a full view of the tenant of this unsavoury apartment. She was a woman of middle age, bent in figure, with a mass of untidy grey hair and a scarf wound tightly round her face. She saw him looking at this and laughed again, the same curious toneless chuckle.

'Wondering why I hide my beauty, dear? He, he, he. Afraid it may tempt you, eh? But you shall see—you shall see.'

She drew aside the scarf and the lawyer recoiled involuntarily before the almost formless blur of scarlet. She replaced the scarf again.

'So you're not wanting to kiss me, dearie? He, he, I don't wonder. And yet I was a pretty girl once—not so long ago as you'd think, either. Vitriol, dearie, vitriol—that's what did that. Ah! but I'll be even with em—'

She burst into a hideous torrent of profanity which Mr Mayherne tried vainly to quell. She fell silent at last, her hands clenching and unclenching themselves nervously.

'Enough of that,' said the lawyer sternly. 'I've come here because I have reason to believe you can give me information which will clear my client, Leonard Vole. Is that the case?'

Her eye leered at him cunningly.

'What about the money, dearie?' she wheezed. 'Two hundred quid, you remember.'

'It is your duty to give evidence, and you can be called upon to do so.'

'That won't do, dearie. I'm an old woman, and I know nothing. But you give me two hundred quid, and perhaps I can give you a hint or two. See?'

'What kind of hint?'

'What should you say to a letter? A letter from *her*. Never mind now how I got hold of it. That's my business. It'll do the trick. But I want my two hundred quid.'

Mr Mayherne looked at her coldly, and made up his mind.

'I'll give you ten pounds, nothing more. And only that if this letter is what you say it is.'

'Ten pounds?' She screamed and raved at him.

'Twenty,' said Mr Mayherne, 'and that's my last word.'

He rose as if to go. Then, watching her closely, he drew out a pocket book, and counted out twenty one-pound notes.

'You see,' he said. 'That is all I have with me. You can take it or leave it.'

But already he knew that the sight of the money was too much for her. She cursed and raved impotently, but at last she gave in. Going over to the bed, she drew something out from beneath the tattered mattress.

'Here you are, damn you!' she snarled. 'It's the top one you want.'

It was a bundle of letters that she threw to him, and Mr Mayherne untied them and scanned them in his usual cool, methodical manner. The woman, watching him eagerly, could gain no clue from his impassive face.

He read each letter through, then returned again to the top one and read it a second time. Then he tied the whole bundle up again carefully.

They were love letters, written by Romaine Heilger, and the man they were written to was not Leonard Vole. The top letter was dated the day of the latter's arrest.

'I spoke true, dearie, didn't I?' whined the woman. 'It'll do for her, that letter?'

Mr Mayherne put the letters in his pocket, then he asked a question.

'How did you get hold of this correspondence?'

'That's telling,' she said with a leer. 'But I know something more. I heard in court what that hussy said. Find out where *she* was at twenty past ten, the time she says she was at home. Ask at the Lion Road Cinema. They'll remember—a fine upstanding girl like that—curse her!'

'Who is the man?' asked Mr Mayherne. 'There's only a Christian name here.'

The other's voice grew thick and hoarse, her hands clenched and unclenched. Finally she lifted one to her face.

'He's the man that did this to me. Many years ago now. She took him away from me—a chit of a girl she was then. And when I went after him—and went for him too—he threw the cursed stuff at me! And she laughed—damn her! I've had it in for her for years. Followed her, I have, spied upon her. And now I've got her! She'll suffer for this, won't she, Mr Lawyer? She'll suffer?'

'She will probably be sentenced to a term of imprisonment for perjury,' said Mr Mayherne quietly.

'Shut away—that's what I want. You're going, are you? Where's my money? Where's that good money?'

Without a word, Mr Mayherne put down the notes on the table. Then, drawing a deep breath, he turned and left the squalid room. Looking back, he saw the old woman crooning over the money.

He wasted no time. He found the cinema in Lion Road easily enough, and, shown a photograph of Romaine Heilger, the commissionaire recognized her at once. She had arrived at the cinema with a man some time after ten o'clock on the evening in question. He had not noticed her escort particularly, but he remembered the lady who had spoken to him about the picture that was showing. They stayed until the end, about an hour later.

Mr Mayherne was satisfied. Romaine Heilger's evidence was a tissue of lies from beginning to end. She had evolved it out of her passionate hatred. The lawyer wondered whether he would ever know what lay behind that hatred. What had Leonard Vole done to her? He had seemed dumbfounded when the solicitor had reported her attitude to him. He had declared earnestly that such a thing was incredible—yet it had seemed to Mr Mayherne that after the first astonishment his protests had lacked sincerity.

He *did* know. Mr Mayherne was convinced of it. He knew, but had no intention of revealing the fact. The secret between those two remained a secret. Mr Mayherne wondered if some day he should come to learn what it was.

The solicitor glanced at his watch. It was late, but time was everything. He hailed a taxi and gave an address.

'Sir Charles must know of this at once,' he murmured to himself as he got in. The trial of Leonard Vole for the murder of Emily French aroused widespread interest. In the first place the prisoner was young and good-looking, then he was accused of a particularly dastardly crime, and there was the further interest of Romaine Heilger, the principal witness for the prosecution. There had been pictures of her in many papers, and several fictitious stories as to her origin and history.

The proceedings opened quietly enough. Various technical evidence came first. Then Janet Mackenzie was called. She told substantially the same story as before. In cross-examination counsel for the defence succeeded in getting her to contradict herself once or twice over her account of Vole's association with Miss French, he emphasized the fact that though she had heard a man's voice in the sitting-room that night, there was nothing to show that it was Vole who was there, and he managed to drive home a feeling that jealousy and dislike of the prisoner were at the bottom of a good deal of her evidence.

Then the next witness was called.

'Your name is Romaine Heilger?'

'Yes.'

'You are an Austrian subject?'

'Yes.'

'For the last three years you have lived with the prisoner and passed yourself off as his wife?'

Just for a moment Romaine Heilger's eye met those of the man in the dock. Her expression held something curious and unfathomable.

'Yes.'

The questions went on. Word by word the damning facts came out. On the night in question the prisoner had taken out a crowbar with him. He had returned at twenty minutes past ten, and had confessed to having killed the old lady. His cuffs had been stained with blood, and he had burned them in the kitchen stove. He had terrorized her into silence by means of threats.

As the story proceeded, the feeling of the court which had, to begin with, been slightly favourable to the prisoner, now set dead against him. He himself sat with downcast head and moody air, as though he knew he were doomed.

Yet it might have been noted that her own counsel sought to restrain Romaine's animosity. He would have preferred her to be a more unbiased witness.

Formidable and ponderous, counsel for the defence arose.

He put it to her that her story was a malicious fabrication from start to finish, that she had not even been in her own house at the time in question, that she was in love with another man and was deliberately seeking to send Vole to his death for a crime he did not commit.

Romaine denied these allegations with superb insolence.

Then came the surprising denouement, the production of the letter. It was read aloud in court in the midst of a breathless stillness.

Max, beloved, the Fates have delivered him into our hands! He has been arrested for murder—but, yes, the murder of an old lady! Leonard who would not hurt a fly! At last I shall have my revenge. The poor chicken! I shall say that he came in that night with blood upon him—that he confessed to me. I shall hang him, Max—and when he hangs he will know and realize that it was Romaine who sent him to his death. And then—happiness, Beloved! Happiness at last!

There were experts present ready to swear that the handwriting was that of Romaine Heitger, but they were not needed. Confronted with the letter, Romaine broke down utterly and confessed everything. Leonard Vole had returned to the house at the time he said, twenty past nine. She had invented the whole story to ruin him.

With the collapse of Romaine Heitger, the case for the Crown collapsed also. Sir Charles called his few witnesses, the prisoner himself went into the box and told his story in a manly straightforward manner, unshaken by cross-examination.

The prosecution endeavoured to rally, but without great success. The judge's summing up was not wholly favourable to the prisoner, but a reaction had set in and the jury needed little time to consider their verdict.

'We find the prisoner not guilty.'

Leonard Vole was free!

Little Mr Mayherne hurried from his seat. He must congratulate his client.

He found himself polishing his pince-nez vigorously, and checked himself. His wife had told him only the night before that he was getting a habit of it. Curious things habits. People themselves never knew they had them.

An interesting case—a very interesting case. That woman, now, Romaine Heilger.

The case was dominated for him still by the exotic figure of Romaine Heilger. She had seemed a pale quiet woman in the house at Paddington, but in court she had flamed out against the sober background. She had flaunted herself like a tropical flower.

If he closed his eyes he could see her now, tall and vehement, her exquisite body bent forward a little, her right hand clenching and unclenching itself unconsciously all the time. Curious things, habits. That gesture of hers with the hand was her habit, he supposed. Yet he had seen someone else do it quite lately. Who was it now? Quite lately—

He drew in his breath with a gasp as it came back to him. *The woman in Shaw's Rents ...*

He stood still, his head whirling. It was impossible—impossible—Yet, Romaine Heilger was an actress.

The KC came up behind him and clapped him on the shoulder.

'Congratulated our man yet? He's had a narrow shave, you know. Come along and see him.'

But the little lawyer shook off the other's hand.

He wanted one thing only—to see Romaine Heilger face to face.

He did not see her until some time later, and the place of their meeting is not relevant.

'So you guessed,' she said, when he had told her all that was in his mind. 'The face? Oh! that was easy enough, and the light of that gas jet was too bad for you to see the makeup.'

'But why—why—'

'Why did I play a lone hand?' She smiled a little, remembering the last time she had used the words.

'Such an elaborate comedy!'

'My friend—I had to save him. The evidence of a woman devoted to him would not have been enough—you hinted as much yourself. But I know something of the psychology of crowds. Let my evidence be wrung from me, as an admission, damning me in the eyes of the law, and a reaction in favour of the prisoner would immediately set in.'

'And the bundle of letters?'

'One alone, the vital one, might have seemed like a—what do you call it?—put-up job.'

'Then the man called Max?'

'Never existed, my friend.'

'I still think,' said little Mr Mayherne, in an aggrieved manner, 'that we could have got him off by the—er—normal procedure.'

'I dared not risk it. You see, you *thought* he was innocent—'

'And you *knew* it? I see,' said little Mr Mayherne.

'My dear Mr Mayherne,' said Romaine, 'you do not see at all. I knew—he was guilty!'

BIBLIOGRAPHY

Agatha Christie's short stories typically appeared first in magazines and then in her short story books, which tended to be different collections in the UK and the US. This list attempts to catalogue the first publication of each, and gives alternative story titles when used.

Down in the Wood

Excerpted from *An Autobiography* (1977).

Murder in the Mews

First published in the US in *Redbook Magazine*, Vol. 67, Nos. 5-6, September/October 1936, and in the UK as 'Mystery of the Dressing Case' in *Woman's Journal*, December 1936. Reprinted in *Murder in the Mews* (UK, 1937) and *Dead Man's Mirror* (US, 1937).

The Case of the Rich Woman

First published in the US as 'The Rich Woman Who Wanted Only to be Happy' in *Cosmopolitan*, August 1932. Reprinted in *Parker Pyne Investigates* (UK, 1934) and *Mr Parker Pyne, Detective* (US, 1946).

While the Light Lasts

First published in the UK in *Novel Magazine,* No. 229, April 1924. Reprinted in *While the Light Lasts* (UK, 1997) aka *The Harlequin Tea Set* (US, 1997).

Triangle at Rhodes

First published in the US in *This Week*, 2 February 1936, and in the UK as 'Poirot and the Triangle at Rhodes' in *The Strand*, No. 545, May 1936. Reprinted in *Murder in the Mews* (UK, 1937) and *Dead Man's Mirror* (US, 1937).

Death by Drowning

First published in the UK in *Nash's Pall Mall,* Vol. 88, No. 462, November 1931. Reprinted in *The Thirteen Problems* (UK, 1932) aka *The Tuesday Night Club* (US, 1933).

The Bird with the Broken Wing

First published in the UK in *The Mysterious Mr Quin* (1930).

The Lemesurier Inheritance

First published as 'The Le Mesurier Inheritance' in the UK in *The Magpie*, Christmas 1923, and in the US in *Blue Book Magazine*, Vol. 42, No. 1, November 1925. Reprinted in *Poirot's Early Cases* (UK, 1974) and *The Under Dog* (US, 1951).

The House of Lurking Death

First published in the UK in *The Sketch*, No. 1658, 5 November 1924. Reprinted in *Partners in Crime* (1929).

Tape-Measure Murder

First published in the US in *This Week*, 16 November 1941, and in the UK as 'The Case of the Retired Jeweller' in *The Strand*, No. 614, February 1942. Reprinted in *Miss Marple's Final Cases* (UK, 1979) and *Three Blind Mice* (US, 1950).

The Voice in the Dark

First published in the US in *Flynn's Weekly*, Vol. 20, No. 2, 4 December 1926, and in the UK as 'The Magic of Mr Quin No. 4' in *Storyteller*, No. 239, March 1927. Reprinted in *The Mysterious Mr Quin* (1930).

Four-and-Twenty Blackbirds

First published in the US in *Collier's*, Vol. 106, No. 19, 9 November 1940, and in the UK as 'Poirot and the Regular Customer' in *The Strand*, No. 603, March 1941. Reprinted in *The Adventure of the Christmas Pudding* (UK, 1960) and *Three Blind Mice* (US, 1950).

The Witness for the Prosecution

First published in the US as 'Traitor Hands' in *Flynn's Weekly*, 31 January 1925. Reprinted in *The Hound of Death* (UK, 1933) and *The Witness for the Prosecution* (US, 1961).

ALSO AVAILABLE

Summertime – as the temperature rises, so does the potential for evil. From Cornwall to the French Riviera, whether against a background of Delphic temples or English country houses, Agatha Christie's most famous characters solve even the most devilish of conundrums as the summer sun beats down. Pull up a deckchair and enjoy plot twists and red herrings galore from the bestselling fiction writer of all time.

'Agatha Christie is the gateway drug to crime fiction both for readers and for writers'

VAL McDERMID